The Truth About Love and Dogs

LILLY BARTLETT

Copyright © 2019 Michele Gorman

Cover images © GoodStudio

All characters and events in this publication, other than those clearly in the public domain, are fictitious and any resemblance to real persons, living or dead, is purely coincidental.

All rights reserved. No part of this publication may be reproduced, stored in a retrieval system, or transmitted, in any form or by any means, without the prior permission of the publisher.

ISBN: 978-1700450579

Also by Lilly Bartlett

The Happy Home for Ladies
The Wedding Bluff (The Big Little Wedding in Carlton Square)
The Reinvention Café (The Second Chance Café in Carlton Square)
The Big Dreams Beach Hotel
Christmas at the Falling-Down Guesthouse

Writing as Michele Gorman

The Boyfriend Tune-Up
The Curvy Girls Club
The Curvy Girls Baby Club
Perfect Girl
Christmas Carol
Life Change
Single in the City (Single in the City I)
Misfortune Cookie (Single in the City II)
Twelve Days to Christmas (Single in the City III)

A NOTE

In writing this book I worked with Penaran Higgs, a qualified counsellor in pet behaviour problems and the owner of Pet Shrink (www.petshrink.co.uk). Pen holds a Postgraduate Diploma in Companion Animal Behaviour Counselling from Southampton University and is a full member of the APBC (Association of Pet Behaviour Counsellors), a member of ASAB (The Association for the Study of Animal Behaviour) and a member of the CABTSG (Companion Animal Behaviour Therapy Study Group). Pen helped me with the behavioural techniques throughout the book and hopefully I haven't misrepresented them. Any errors in this area are mine alone.

Chapter 1

Scarlett barely had time to register the furry flash of red before it rugby-tackled her in the park. One second she was talking to the dog owners and the next she was staring up at the grey March sky through the bare branches of the horse chestnuts.

'Oh, bugger, I'm so sorry!' A man was running towards them. 'Murphy, no! Bad dog! Bad dog, Murphy.'

But the Irish setter humping Scarlett's shin was too intent on lovemaking to be put off by his owner's shouts.

Struggling to her feet, Scarlett managed to pry the dog gently off her jeans. She couldn't help feeling sorry about the profoundly desperate look on his face.

None of this was what she'd pictured when she'd first found out that being a dog behaviourist was an actual thing people got paid to do. In her head, she was the love child of Doctor Dolittle and Sigmund Freud, a fairy dogmother who transformed pet owners' lives across Greater London. In reality, she spent a lot of time being drooled over in the mud.

She bet Sigmund hadn't had problems like that with his clients.

'He slipped his collar.' The man circled Murphy's solid neck with his even more solid arm. 'Are you okay?'

'Oh, yeah, don't worry about me,' she said. 'Occupational hazard. I'm flattered that Murphy wants to make me his girlfriend.'

That raised a nervous giggle from a few of the dog owners gathered around. Nobody seemed quite sure how to react to the dog-on-girl action they'd just seen.

Scarlett's face flamed. How was she supposed to exude canine expertise with Murphy giving her those come-to-bed eyes? People didn't take her seriously as it was. She could tell them till she was blue in the face about her Masters in Companion Animal Behaviour Counselling or her undergraduate degree in psychology. They still suspected she was a dog walker with aspirations above her station.

She gathered her flyaway blonde curls back into a ponytail. Ponytails meant business. 'Hiya!' she said to the dozen people before her. 'Thanks loads for coming! Today's an introduction, where we'll check that group training is right for your dog. A few might be better off with one-on-one sessions, but no one should feel embarrassed or worried that their dog is a hopeless case.'

She glanced at Murphy, who'd slipped into a post-coital glow.

'Seeing as we've sort of met Murphy,' she said to the man scratching his red setter's ears, 'maybe you can tell us a little bit about you both?'

Murphy's owner gave everyone a friendly wave and gathered them all in with his huge smile. Despite the early spring chill in the air he was wearing just a T-shirt with his jeans. Scarlett didn't see any gooseflesh on his tanned biceps, and she was definitely looking.

She twisted her wedding ring. It was nearly five years since she had married Rufus, and they weren't so much in the honeymoon phase as the honey-shall-we phase. Unfortunately, lately the answer was no.

The other women were staring too, and no wonder. Murphy's owner was about three steps to the right side of gorgeous. Mid-thirties, with a full head of wavy brown hair and one of those dimply boy-next-door faces that made one think about knocking on his door for more than a cup of sugar.

Judging by his cocky smile, he knew it. 'Alright, I'm Max.' His voice was surprisingly squeaky, given those arms. 'And this is Murphy. He's three, and he's very fond of the ladies.'

'That's why you've brought Murphy today?' Scarlett asked over everyone's laughter.

'I had to do it,' he said. 'He hates the lead so I've got to be able to walk him without one, but he jumps on anyone who moves, dogs or people. Even males. He's open-minded like that.'

'Have you thought about having him neutered?'

Max winced. 'Not if I don't absolutely have to.' He shielded his own crotch in solidarity. 'I won't have to, will I?'

'Well, we'll see what we can do.' Scarlett already knew Murphy would need individual sessions. Humpers were too disruptive in a group class.

Just as she was about to ask a raven-haired young woman to introduce herself, she noticed the paunchy middle-aged man standing uncomfortably close to her. If he stared at the woman's chest any harder, he'd strain his eyes.

'Excuse me, can we help you?' Scarlett snapped.

The guy practically had his nose in the poor woman's cleavage.

'I'm here for Ruff Love.' His face bloomed red.

'I'm sorry, sir, but you have to have a dog to join us.'

For a second he looked confused. 'Oh! I get it. You mean role play, like collars and leashes and the like? I'm usually less S and more M, but I can do submissive. Someone can be my owner.'

He went back to staring at the young woman, who pulled her jacket more tightly around herself.

Scarlett sighed. If only people would read the advert properly. That *Fifty Shades* had a lot to answer for. 'Can I ask where you heard about Ruff Love?'

'My mates told me.' He looked like the penny was beginning to drop. At least he'd stopped ogling the pretty girl. 'This isn't a sex club, then?'

'No, I'm really sorry. It's a dog-training course. Ruff Love. As in ruff, ruff,' she barked.

That proposition got Murphy's attention.

'I did wonder about meeting in the park,' the man murmured, backing away. 'Sorry.'

A few seconds later everyone heard him shout into his phone. 'You *wanker*!'

Scarlett clamped her hand over her mouth, but a snort squeezed out anyway.

The pretty girl relaxed once the sex pest had left, but she wouldn't make eye contact with Scarlett. Some people needed a bit of time to get comfortable, so she smiled at one of the other men in the group instead.

'Oh, me? Okay, well, I'm Charlie. Hi everyone! Meet Barkley. He's a five-year-old yellow lab.' He lowered his voice and turned away from the dog, who was sitting on his ample haunches. 'Barkley has an eating issue.

Don't stare at him, though – it makes him self-conscious.'

When Barkley lifted his head to gaze with gentle brown eyes at Charlie's back, furry rolls appeared at the back of his neck.

'I inherited him last year from my mum when she died.'

The dog's ears perked up at hearing Charlie say 'mum'.

'Is it just a matter of feeding him less?' Scarlett wondered.

When Charlie shook his head a thatch of blond hair flopped into his eyes. 'If only. He hoovers up everything he can find. Honestly, he's a nightmare to walk. He's been to the vet twice already because of it. He ate my iPhone plug. Not the cable. The plug. That was three nights at the vet's. I suppose his problem is that Mum spoiled him?'

Oh, good – mother issues! Barkley would be an interesting case. But then most dogs were interesting. That was why she loved her job.

Their owners were usually interesting too. Scarlett stole a glance at a blonde woman as she hovered at the edge of the group. She was tense, and sort of folded in on herself like one of those origami fortune tellers with the four little pyramids that you'd put your fingers in to decide if someone liked you.

When Scarlett walked towards her, the Jack Russell at her feet started madly barking. 'Are you with us?' Scarlett shouted over the din.

'No, I'm just waiting for Charlie.' She leaned down to stroke the dog. 'It's okay, Hiccup, nobody's going to hurt you.'

'Actually, if you don't mind a little advice… Patting Hiccup when she's being aggressive like that rewards her for her behaviour. If you want to walk her away a bit, she'll feel less stressed. I don't want to back up because that'll make her think she's scared me off.'

'I'm sorry,' the woman said. 'I didn't mean to disturb you. I can come back.'

Charlie's eyes followed the woman as she left, before Scarlett continued her usual spiel about meeting in the community centre for the evening classes and in the park on weekends.

As everyone wrote down their details in the signing-in book, Scarlett noticed a middle-aged woman pleading with her cocker spaniel from the end of a long retractable lead. The spaniel was trying her best to weave everyone in the park together with her leash.

'Oh, please won't you come here, Biscuit?' the woman begged. The strap of her handbag kept sliding off her shoulder and her duffle coat had flapped open. Scarlett recognised the coat – her mum had the same one from Boden. However, judging by the woman's pearl earrings and chunky gold necklace, she probably didn't get hers at the charity shop like her mum had.

'There's a good girl.'

Biscuit was having none of it. She wove another figure of eight, neatly tying together two more people and a dog.

'Biscuit?' Tentatively the woman tugged the dog's lead. 'Please come?'

Biscuit stopped her weaving long enough to unleash a tirade on her owner.

'Hiya,' Scarlett said, approaching carefully. 'Are you with us?'

'I am! I'm sorry, I'm so bloomin' hopeless! Come *here*, Biscuit, please!'

Biscuit ignored the request.

'Be sure to add your details so I can send you a questionnaire, okay Mrs...?'

'Margaret. I'm just Margaret.' Her auburn hair was cut into a chin-length bob with stylishly flippy-outy bits around her ears, while the deep laugh lines surrounding her mouth gave her face a friendly look.

She started hurrying towards Scarlett but got tangled up in Biscuit's lead. 'Oh, what am I like?!' Hopping on one leg, she managed to reel her dog in a few feet. 'I'll get her under control eventually. Sorry everybody!'

They waved away her apology. Everyone there was in the same doghouse, after all.

'We're home!' Rufus called over Fred and Ginger's melody of jingly collars and tapping toenails on the front hall floor tiles.

Just hearing their chaotic entrance made Scarlett smile. It was her favourite part of the day.

'How were my dogs?' she shouted from the kitchen. She heard the hollow plop of rubber hitting floor tiles as Rufus used his toe to pry his trainers off. Those shoes, with their squashed-down heels, would sit in the middle of the hall until she shoved them under the bench.

Two furry streaks of white hurled themselves at Scarlett's socked feet. Rufus ambled in behind them. '*My* dogs were very well-behaved, thank you.' Neither of them claimed Fred and Ginger when they barfed up shredded loo roll. 'Fred's got a new trick.'

Scarlett heaved a sigh, a contented spectator now that Rufus was back. The kitchen was his domain. As she hopped up on one of the stools at the granite island, she whacked her knee on the cabinet underneath. 'Always the same frickin' spot!' The previous owners hadn't left enough room for legs under the worktop.

Rufus smirked. 'You do have to ask yourself: if the cabinet never moves, then why do you keep throwing your knee against it?'

She rubbed away some of the sting. 'It's a sign of insanity to do the same thing over and over and expect a different outcome. Please promise me we can redecorate when we win the lottery.'

'First thing on the list after our matching Ferraris,' he said as he started pulling veg and meat from the fridge for their usual weekend stew.

'I've told you, we can't get Ferraris. No room for the dogs.'

'I'm sorry you bashed your knee. Again.' His blond stubble buffed her chin when she puckered for a kiss.

'Thanks, I'll live. What's Fred's trick?'

Abandoning their dinner ingredients, he called Fred over. 'Watch this. Watch. Are you ready? Sit, Fred.'

When he showed Fred his palm, Fred raised his paw.

'Did you see that? High five! Good boy!'

'I hate to break it to you, but he already shakes paws. I like your enthusiasm, though.'

'Scarlett, darlin', this is so much better than paw shaking. Didn't you see the extension there? It was definitely a high five. We should hire him out to film crews.'

'I'm not sure there's as much demand for high-fiving dogs as you'd think.'

Rufus considered Fred, who looked quite pleased with himself. But then, West Highland terriers usually did. 'Maybe not. I guess it still needs some work. Shannon must be teaching him.'

Saint Shannon: their dog walker, best friend and Scarlett's business partner. Which reminded her to check her text from earlier. 'Does Ginger do it too?' she asked, scrolling through her phone.

'Nope, just Fred. Maybe ask her on Monday to show Ginger too.'

'You can ask her yourself,' Scarlett said. 'I've got evening training, remember? I should be home by eight or so.'

Strictly speaking, they didn't need a dog walker during the day when they were at work – the dog flap into the garden worked perfectly well. But it was nuts not to use Scarlett's own company's services. Besides, they'd learned a long time ago that it wasn't a good idea to leave West Highland terriers alone to make their own fun.

She sidled up to Rufus, looping her arms around his torso from behind. She loved the solid feel of his chest. He had muscles and contours that fit her perfectly. His skin wasn't as tanned as when they'd first met, but then neither was hers.

It was a complete holiday cliché to start a romance on a dive boat in Australia, but it was one with a happy ending.

He'd already been in the outback for three months when they met. The unrelenting sun had turned his stubble to the palest blond, though still a few shades darker than his hair. Between the tan and his nearly white wavy mop he looked a bit like a photo negative. An extremely sexy photo negative.

She couldn't have been more attracted to him if he'd had his own gravitational pull. The feeling was definitely mutual, and that was the first time *that* had ever happened to Scarlett.

They only ever admitted it to each other, but not

even the Great Barrier Reef could compete with the excitement of being together.

Yet they didn't make it into bed until the last night of their trip. Looking back, Scarlett wasn't sure how she'd survived the sexual tension. They'd flirted. They'd kissed. They'd shared secrets deep into the early morning hours as they lounged together under a blanket of stars on deck. Those hours and days were amongst the most sensual of Scarlett's life. Even almost five years later, just thinking about the delicious anticipation of everything ahead of them was enough to make her feel a bit dizzy.

It didn't seem possible that sleeping together could be as mind-blowing as they'd imagined. It was. They'd both cried that night.

He was still sex on legs to her, which had made things doubly hard lately. And the back of his smooth neck, just below his hairline, never failed to drive her mad. Her lips were inches from reaching it. She stood on tiptoes to kiss her favourite spot. 'I've got to send out the Ruff Love questionnaires and then I'm all yours for the rest of the night,' she murmured. 'Do with me what you will.'

As he turned from the sink, he stared deeply into her eyes. 'I know exactly what we should do.'

The excitement in his expression made Scarlett's nether parts start to wibble. Finally, they were on the same page… or at least in the same book. She didn't mind skim-reading ahead to get to the good bits if she had to.

'Let's start a new box set! Just let me finish up here. We can get at least three hours in by the time the stew's ready.'

He pecked her on the nose and turned back to the sink.

For god's sake. What did a woman have to do to sleep with her husband? 'Or you could take me to bed,' she said to his broad back. There was a time when he wouldn't have needed that kind of instruction.

He smiled at her over his shoulder. 'The box set will last longer.' He made this sound playful, but Scarlett wasn't laughing.

'Sex is more...' She just stopped herself from saying important. 'Satisfying.'

'But there's less pressure to watch the box set,' he said. He was still smiling, but he wasn't moving to the bedroom.

Her sigh caught Ginger's attention. At least someone noticed. She poured herself a glass of wine and went into the living room to text Shannon back.

LILLY BARTLETT

Chapter 2

'Seriously, Sampson?' Shannon mumbled, pulling the bulldog away from the wheel. But it was too late. 'I'm so sorry!' she said to the woman giving her evils.

Sampson didn't know what to make of this change in plan. His leg stayed cocked as he hopped away from the pram. It was one of those old-fashioned ones that cost more than Shannon's first car, the show-offy kind that only people with an enormous front hall could fit in their house.

'Your dog *weed* on my baby!' the pram's owner said.

'Well, technically, he weed on your pram wheel. I am sorry. Here.' Shannon rummaged around in her giant shoulder bag. 'I have a bottle of water. You can wash it off. It's here somewhere.' As she sank to her knobbly knees to dump her bag on the pavement, she looked like a crane toppling over.

A sketch pad got caught in the lining and several coloured pencils rolled off the kerb. 'Oh, here, it was stuck in my jumper.'

'I don't want your *water*,' the woman snapped. 'I'll

have to disinfect it now to get the wee off.'

'You've probably wheeled through worse stuff, you know,' Shannon pointed out as the woman stomped off down the park path. 'Just saying.'

Shannon glared at the dog. 'You are so not worth your fee.'

Sampson wheezed up at her, tongue sticking out through his underbite.

His companions, Fifi and Clive, had disdainfully watched the whole exchange. Now they looked down their black poodle noses at the bulldog. *What a philistine.*

Not that you two are a piece of cake, either, Shannon thought.

If you'd told her five years ago that one day she'd be a professional dog walker, she'd have laughed in your face. Actually, since she didn't know you very well, she probably would have blushed terribly, mumbled something and run away.

It wasn't because she disliked dogs. She loved them. It was because she was in art school and dog poo wasn't a medium she'd planned to work with full-time. But then she hadn't planned to lose her café job either, right after she started her course. Right after she signed a one-year lease on her bedsit.

Rufus and Scarlett took pity on her, even though they still denied it. Scarlett claimed she'd been desperate to start up the dog-walking side of her business anyway. Perfect timing, et cetera, et cetera.

What had been perfect timing, Shannon thought, was Rufus and Scarlett meeting in the first place. She'd probably be flipping burgers at McDonald's to pay her rent if they hadn't.

'You've got to meet this woman,' Rufus had told

her soon after returning from Australia.

Yeah, right, Shannon thought, steeling herself for the usual routine. *That'll be fun.*

She'd gazed at that familiar look on his still-jet-lagged face – thunderstruck and full of passion. It always made her excited and sorry for him at the same time.

The problem wasn't that she disliked Rufus's girlfriends. It was that she liked them. He always went out with nice, cool women – dozens of them over the years. He wasn't so much a player as a serial monogamist. Each time he threw himself into his latest romance, Shannon had let herself get close to his girlfriend. It always ended in tears (the girlfriend's) when Rufus figured out that she was not, in fact, The One. That was usually the last that Shannon saw of the girl too. Over the years she'd learned not to bother.

But it was different when Rufus found Scarlett. From the start they both knew that they'd found someone special. Finally, Shannon got to keep one of Rufus's girlfriends. And she'd never admit it to him, but in some ways, she was closer to Scarlett than she was to Rufus. He might have known her since primary school, but she and Scarlett were in the sisterhood, they loved each other *and* they ran their business together. Besticles before testicles! Though she'd never say that to Rufus, either.

Gathering up the dogs' leads again, and the contents of her handbag, Shannon steered them towards the big grassy area where Fifi and Clive liked to run.

That was the fib she told herself every day: she was going where the poodles liked to run. Nothing to do with the possibility that Mr Darcy might be there. That would be a bonus. After the welfare of her clients.

She fluffed her hair and scanned the field. Dogs liked routine, so you could generally set your watch by a dog's daily circuit. She spotted a fuzzy form in the distance. It might be him. Or it might be a bald OAP leaning on a Zimmer frame.

Sneaking her thick-framed black glasses from her bag, she hunched into her biker jacket and held them to her eyes. It *was* him! She kept her gaze trained on the figure as she slid the specs off again.

She was still cross with Scarlett for talking her into getting them. Only cool people got away with NHS frames, not people like her. And they weren't cheap, either, so she couldn't justify replacing them.

'Fifi, go play with that greyhound!' She unclipped Fifi's lead. 'Go on, girl. You too, Clive. Doesn't he look like fun?'

The dogs sneered. *We know what you're trying to do. Those are* his *dogs, aren't they? Pretty pathetic.* They trotted off, away from the greyhound, wafting judgment as they went.

'Thanks a lot,' Shannon murmured after them. 'What about you?' She scratched Sampson's ear, sending him into paroxysms of bliss and drool. 'I don't suppose you're up for running with greyhounds?'

Sampson sat heavily on her foot. 'Didn't think so.'

She wasn't so much Sampson's dog walker as his mode of transport. She might coax him to the other side of the field, but then it would be a long walk home, especially if she had to carry him. Which she often did. There was no shifting him once he decided he was tired.

People usually figured she was fit when they heard she was a dog walker, but she didn't walk nearly as much as they thought she did. Especially not with bowlegged asthmatic bulldogs like Sampson.

Still watching the blurry form across the field, she rang Scarlett. 'What's wrong?' she asked when Scarlett picked up. 'You sounded funny last night.'

'We didn't talk last night.'

'Your texts. There was a tone.'

'You're interpreting my texts now?' Scarlett laughed. 'Nothing's wrong. What are you doing?'

'I'm in the park with Sampson and the poodles. They really are judgmental toffs, you know.'

'Mm-hmm, just like their owners,' Scarlett said. 'The husband refers to himself in the third person, like the Queen.'

Shannon was grateful that Scarlett handled all of the admin with clients. Play to your strengths, her father had always said. Shannon's strengths didn't stretch to people. Nearly every week when they had their staff meeting – which was what they called the walk in the park when they talked about their business – Scarlett reminded Shannon that she was welcome to take on some client management, of the two-legged sort, whenever she wanted. Nearly every week Shannon cringed, thanked her and declined.

'Sampson pissed on a lady's pram,' Shannon said.

'That must've gone over well. Did the lady see?'

'Of course. It happened right in front of her. With the baby in the pram. I offered my water to clean it off.'

'That doesn't really make up for pissing on her child, though, does it?'

'That's what she said.' Shannon squinted across the grass at the figure who, she hoped, wasn't really a bald OAP with a Zimmer frame. 'I think Mr Darcy's here.'

She didn't need to explain who she meant. Mr Darcy was a permanent, if abstract, character in her life.

'Do you have a good dress on?'

'Yes, *Mum*, and clean knickers too.'

She wore her usual cool weather uniform – a floral dress with clashing cardigan, biker jacket, boots and a deep purple hand-knitted scarf that she wound round her neck till she nearly suffocated. In winter she added woolly tights that clashed with her cardigan *and* her dress, or men's long johns. In summer she ditched the scarf and tights and traded her boots in for Converse high-tops. Otherwise her look was the same every day.

'Have you talked to him?'

Shannon glanced again to where Mr Darcy stood, unaware that he was about to become the object of her hopeless fantasy.

'Of course. He ran straight over with three dozen long-stem roses. That man worships me,' she said, staring at the man who didn't know she existed. She wasn't sure if it was possible to be in love with someone she'd never met, even though superfans of popstars seemed to do it all the time. Mr Darcy wasn't a popstar – as far as she could tell – but she was definitely a superfan. 'It's hard to get a word in with him constantly telling me how much he loves me,' she told Scarlett. 'I had to drag him behind the holly hedge and promise all kinds of things just to shut him up. We've been at it like bonobos since lunchtime. He's an absolute animal.'

'In other words, you still haven't talked to him. Come on, Shannon, it's so easy! You both walk dogs in the park at the same time. Maybe today's the day? Do it when you get off the phone.'

'I don't think so,' Shannon said. 'Not today, no.'

Not today, not yesterday, or the day, or the week or the month before that. The poodles were right. She was pathetic. How many thirty-two-year-olds couldn't manage to say hello to someone, even with such an obvious conversation starter sniffing around their feet? It should be easy.

It would be, if she wasn't a total coward.

If nothing else, she should at least find out his real name. But her pale, thin face bloomed with puce blotches just thinking about speaking to him. If she got too close, poor Mr Darcy would probably fear catching scarlet fever off her.

For someone so hopelessly infatuated with a stranger, she was pragmatic. Lots of people, she reasoned, never met the object of their desire. That didn't mean he couldn't still be the highlight of her day. Sometimes they walked their dogs past each other, and Shannon would snatch a glimpse, adding another tiny detail to her fantasy, before looking away. The incredible green eyes with dark rings around the irises. Always the stubble on his razor-sharp jaw that flashed bits of blond if the sun caught it just right. Dark pink kissable lips and just-long-enough auburn hair. Even when they didn't pass, sneaking a glance through her glasses at his fit, jeans-clad form in the distance made her happy.

She'd secretly stared at him so often through her dorky glasses that she'd sketched him from memory. On the psycho scale, that was probably up there. She was too embarrassed to ask Scarlett.

LILLY BARTLETT

Chapter 3

'But I'm not unhappy,' Scarlett objected as Gemma poured her more green tea. Her sister couldn't resist being righteous about drinks when they went for dim sum together. As if that made up for being a total glutton when she ate most of the dumplings.

She shouldn't have told Gemma about Rufus. Now she would push, and Scarlett wasn't ready to admit out loud the thing she most feared. Even to her sister. The frustration about the other night had just sort of slipped out.

It was par for the course, really – a course they'd been playing for months and months. What was wrong with her, that meant she barely ever enticed the man she'd married into bed anymore?

Having thoughts like that tucked inside her head was bad enough, but clanging around out there for everyone to see? No, thank you. She didn't even want to admit them to Rufus. What if he had a confession of his own? People did go off each other. Even in madly-in-love relationships as *theirs* was. Hopefully not as theirs *was*.

'Things are okay, Gem.' If she said it enough, maybe it would be true.

'But you would tell me if something was really wrong, right?' Gemma asked. 'I don't want you to be unhappy. I love you like a sister.'

'Good thing, since you are my sister.'

'All the more reason,' Gemma said, absently sticking her fingers into her springy blonde-tipped curls. Gemma had inherited her kinky hair, gorgeous caramel complexion and mile-long legs from her Scottish-Caribbean mum rather than their shared dad. Scarlett's own mum couldn't be more Caucasian, so her own paper-pale skin, blonde hair and blue eyes shouldn't have surprised anyone. The only feature Scarlett shared with her half-sister, and you had to look really closely to notice it, was their father's freckles across both their noses.

'Maybe you've got the seven-year-itch early,' Gemma continued, making a grab for the last prawn dumpling. 'Do you feel itchy?' She scratched her armpit with a chopstick to demonstrate.

'Charming.'

Gemma grinned. 'Relax, it's not the end I'm eating with.'

'Still. No, I'm not itchy. Everything is fine. We're both just busy with work. And we have been together for almost five years. Of course there'll be things that get on our nerves by now. Probably the same things that bug you about Jacob. Dirty pants on the floor, not saying when we're low on milk. Just the usual domestics. It's unrealistic to expect mad passion all the time.'

Gemma looked up sharply. 'What do you mean by that?'

'Nothing, nothing! But when the rose-tinted glasses

come off, we see each other's natural human flaws. That's all I mean. And don't play dumb. I know for a fact that Jacob drives you nuts sometimes.'

'What?! You mean my husband, the light o' my life? I wanted to push his face into the bin the other day when the bag broke from overfilling, again. I'm not proud of that.'

'Understandable, though.'

'Right, as long as you're still making time for each other, Scarlett. You know, romantically. How long did you say it's been?'

'I didn't, Gem.'

'So?'

'A month,' Scarlett said. 'Let's get the bill. You know I hate missing the trailers.'

Gemma let the discussion go, but Scarlett knew she'd be on the alert now.

When she got back to the house, slightly sick from all the sweets Gemma had bought, Scarlett could tell that Rufus was still up. The TV projected a luminous blue through the front room curtains. It wasn't just the pick 'n' mix upsetting her tummy, though.

How sad. She shouldn't be nervous to see her own husband.

He had his feet on the coffee table and a dog's chin on each thigh. Their eyes opened when she came in, but they didn't move from the sofa. Traitors.

'They're not supposed to be on there.' But she returned his smile. This was Rufus. *Rufus*. 'It doesn't look good, you know, when a trainer's dogs misbehave.'

'Good thing the police haven't come around to check up on us yet.' He shifted his legs. 'Fred, Ginger, you heard Scarlett. Off the sofa.'

If they were teenagers, they'd have rolled their eyes. They were in no rush to get down, but eventually they trotted towards Scarlett to beg some more attention.

'Come join me, darlin'.' Rufus opened his arms. 'There's a terrible film on. The guy with the hat is an alien. So is his talking cat.'

As she threw herself on top of him, his arms pulled her close, the way they always had: one across her shoulders and the other low down on the small of her back. His hands radiated heat even through the weave of her thick jumper. It was almost too hot, but she didn't want to lose the moment by moving. Instead she exhaled, sinking closer into his chest, where she could smell the minty citrus scent at the hollow of his throat. How she loved that sharp smell. It was only cheap shower gel but to her it was the finest perfume. It was her husband.

'I've been thinking,' he whispered into her hair. His breath sent a shiver up her neck. 'Let's go out tomorrow night in London. On a proper date. We haven't done that in too long.'

That was exactly what they needed. The niggling feeling skulked a bit further into the corner. A candlelit dinner, maybe, or the theatre or a gig where they'd dance into the wee hours like they used to do. Her mind raced to her wardrobe. She had a nearly-new dress that she could wear with her highest heels. Did she have time for a haircut? Maybe she could squeeze one in between her afternoon puppy classes.

She glanced down at her old skinny jeans and slightly pilled jumper.

Working with the dogs was a double-edged sword. They only cared that she had treats somewhere about her person. It didn't make sense to wear nice clothes when she spent so much of her time on the ground. She saved a fortune but usually looked like a slob.

'Let me plan it,' Rufus said. 'You'll be busy with your classes. I can look something up while I'm at the office. I'll squeeze it in between shopping on eBay and my phone Scrabble tournament.'

They both knew that was bollocks. Rufus had worked his arse off for the same ethical PR firm since leaving university. The only break he'd had was when he went on his Australian sabbatical and even then, he spent all but the last two weeks volunteering for a literacy charity. Scarlett was pretty sure she wouldn't be so noble if she'd had that kind of time off from work.

With those credentials, Rufus could have been an insufferably worthy do-gooder. But if anything, his grin let everyone know that he was an impossibly cheeky do-badder. 'I suppose you'll need something to fill your time while you bunk off,' she teased. 'At least one of us works for a living.'

'You? You play with dogs all day.'

But he gently took her chin between his thumb and the crook of his forefinger, tipping her face up for a soft kiss. She always found it such a tender gesture, and just the sight of those lips made her smile. They were nearly too pink for a man's face, but she knew from the first time she saw them that they'd be excellent at kissing.

Rufus might joke, but he was incredibly proud of the business she'd built up from scratch. She was too.

She gazed at the TV, where the alien talking cat seemed to be arguing with a crowd of children. Rufus was right. It was a terrible film. She dozed off on his chest with his arms draped around her, swayed by the slow rise and fall of his breath beneath his soft cotton shirt.

Anticipation bubbled in her tummy the next day, and her classes passed in a blur. They were mostly puppy training courses, but she managed to avoid their slobbery kisses so she wouldn't turn up to the restaurant smelling too much of dog.

By the time she left the salon, she'd admired herself in the mirror more than most teenage girls. Her usually flyaway pale blonde hair fell to her shoulders in soft waves and she'd even gone for the blackest mascara she could find.

Two hours at the salon and results pretty good, she texted Shannon.

Photo please! xo S

She scanned the narrow Soho street. Flicking the selfie button on her phone, she pretended to snap something interesting in the brickwork of the building beside her. The lens caught her blush nicely.

The things I do for you, she texted with the photo.

GORgeous! In contrast, this is my day, responded Shannon.

It was a photo of Sampson's behind.

You glamourpuss. xo Scarlett

She was a few minutes early to the restaurant Rufus had booked for them. 'Yes, madam,' the slender young waiter said when she gave him her name. 'The gentleman is already here.'

When Rufus spotted her coming across the restaurant, his face split into the kind of smile that made her tummy churn. It wasn't just his smile, though, tonight. With the contrast of his black jumper against his golden complexion and the way his pale blond hair curled around his ears, he brought to mind a strapping Swedish man. Maybe one sailing a burnished teak boat or chopping down trees in the crisp sunshine.

In other words, one whom you definitely *would*.

Rufus stood when she got to the table. His hand found her cheek, his fingers gently using the curve of her jaw to guide her lips to his. One kiss. Two. Then three, lingering.

When Scarlett opened her eyes, she saw a few women watching them. She would have gloated if she hadn't remembered that this definitely hadn't been the norm lately. She hoped it would be from now on, though.

'Plus points for the decor!' She sank into the apple green brocade reading chair that was pulled up to the table. Wide pillars stood sentinel around the room. Some were ringed with rich wooden book-lined shelves, others hung with dozens of framed photos. Together with the mismatched chairs, it made a convincing eccentric aunt's Victorian living room.

'This is so trendy!' she said. They used to go to new restaurants and bars a lot when she lived in London. 'Why have we never been here before?'

'Because we're not trendy. Face it, darlin', we get excited when the Häagen-Dazs goes on sale in Morrisons.' He shrugged. 'Who needs to be trendy? Then people just go off you when the next thing comes along. We're classical, timeless, like the *Mona Lisa*.'

'Only happier,' Scarlett said, hoping that was true as

she opened her menu. 'My god, have you seen these prices?'

'I've been googling while I waited for you, to see where I can sell my plasma for quick cash.' He reached for her hand across the table. 'We can afford this every once in a while.'

'I know, but wow. Sixteen pounds for a mango salad? It's only a fiver at Chiang Mai and we get free prawn crackers.' Her finger slid down the menu. 'Eighty-five quid for pork?! What are they serving, Miss Piggy?' She tried not to see the entrees as a percentage of their mortgage. 'Now I know why we've never done this before.' She was fine with their local takeaway. 'And I guess this is why we don't live in London.'

'Yeah, I remember it was the price of pork that put us off, not the million-pound price tag on houses,' Rufus joked.

They'd both had rented flats when they first got together, though Rufus was based in Reading and Scarlett had a one bedroom in North London that even estate agents were embarrassed to spin as 'cosy'. She could flick on her kettle in the kitchen from the end of her sofa.

With their savings and the cash their parents gave them for their wedding, they just managed to scrape together a down payment for their house.

They hardly ever went out in London anymore, even though they both commuted there for work. Their routine had definitely become routine.

'As you're selling your plasma anyway, want to splurge and get champagne?' she asked. Maybe they needed some shaking up.

'Careful, in my depleted state you'll get me drunk.'

She laughed like it hadn't occurred to her. She knew she shouldn't be thinking about getting him pissed to have sex, but how else was she supposed to get pregnant? Last time she checked she wasn't called Mary, with the Holy Spirit on speed dial, and Rufus didn't even seem to remember that they were supposed to be trying.

'Waiter? A bottle of Moët, please.'

Some of the champagne had worn off by the time they'd waited in chilly Paddington for a late train home, but Scarlett was as resolved as ever not to let a perfectly tipsy night go to waste.

'H'lo, dogs!' Rufus shouted as he opened their front door near midnight.

Silence.

'We've got to apologise,' said Scarlett. 'Otherwise they'll take it out on the loo roll.'

'We live ridiculous lives,' Rufus said. But he went into the lounge anyway. 'H'lo, Ginger! H'lo, Fred!'

Fred, at least, lifted his head from the sofa cushion. Ginger kept hers stubbornly between her paws, staring balefully at Rufus. They weren't even bothering to hide the fact that they'd been rolling around on the furniture all evening. *Oh, you're finally back?* their looks said. *Good for you.*

They only managed to put aside their resentment when they saw Rufus with their leads. 'I'll take them out,' he said.

Scarlett bit down her frustration at the delay. This would quickly turn into the same-old-same-old if she wasn't careful.

As soon as he'd closed the front door, Scarlett flew upstairs to the bedroom. Rummaging in the bedside table drawer, she found some matches to light the dusty candles on the dressing table. That way Rufus wouldn't be tempted to turn on the overhead light. It was like doing foreplay on an operating table in that light.

Mild panic rose as she rushed into the bathroom to brush her teeth, then stripped off for the world's fastest shower without washing out her hair and make-up in the process.

Just as she turned off the water, she heard Rufus pass the bathroom door on his way to the bedroom.

Dammit.

Her sexy underwear was still in the drawer, and her high-heeled shoes were under the bed where she'd kicked them off.

Which was more erotic? Strutting naked into the room, or throwing herself on Rufus with her dress on and letting him peel it off?

She scrutinised herself in the mirror. Even under the harsh bathroom bulb she looked all right. Gravity hadn't yet taken hold and working with the dogs every day meant her legs and arms were toned.

Still, it was a bit obvious, maybe, to turn up starkers when she usually wore at least a T-shirt to bed. But then the whole point was to be obvious, wasn't it? She wanted to have sex with the man, not do his taxes.

Fred and Ginger launched themselves at her ankles as soon as she opened the bathroom door. 'Not now,' she hissed. 'Go downstairs!'

They ignored her. They weren't about to let her out of their sight. What if she snuck off again to London, to eat steak and play with squeaky toys that were miles better than the ones they had at home? She might even be paying attention to other dogs, for all they knew. *City* dogs.

They stayed inches from Scarlett's feet as she made her way to the bedroom door. 'Dogs, no, you're not coming in.'

Ginger cocked her head. Fred pretended he didn't hear her.

She had to use her hands to fend them off, otherwise they'd scoot under the bed as soon as the door was opened. That meant bending over to hold them at bay and reaching behind her to open the door.

'That's quite an entrance,' Rufus said as Scarlett backed through the door naked arse first.

As she whipped around, the dogs shot under the bed. 'No, Fred, Ginger!'

By the time Rufus had lured them out with the second round of dog treats, the passion had gone as flat as the champagne in Scarlett's tummy.

They climbed into bed, Scarlett now in her T-shirt and Rufus in his boxers, and went to sleep.

Chapter 4

Scarlett's new clients, Margaret and Biscuit, lived in a terraced cottage in leafy Hampstead Village, on a steep road just off the high street. Thick wisteria vines twisted over the front door and up the yellow brick to the windows on the first floor. The cherry trees against the garden wall were heavy with pink blooms and an enormous lavender bush at the edge of the well-tended lawn would be glorious come summer.

She'd been there less than thirty seconds and already she was building up a picture of Margaret's life. Everything about it so far screamed *Good Housekeeping* family of the year.

She used to be intimidated by the kind of wealth that Margaret seemed to have. She'd look at a big house with its fancy car in the drive and practically pull her forelock and curtsy when she met the owner.

It must have been age or inexperience that had made her feel like that because she hardly ever did now. Besides, there were always cracks once she got to know a client. It might be the new bottles of whisky that she'd noticed every week on the sideboard in the living room or the red-top bills stuck to the fridge. Nobody's life was perfect.

'Oh, it's you! Hello, Dr Deering,' Margaret said as she answered Scarlett's knock while trying to pull Biscuit back by the collar.

The cocker spaniel's mad barking nearly drowned out Margaret's greeting.

'Oh, Biscuit, will you please stop?' she said.

But Biscuit wasn't about to be told what to do. Her jowls were firmly downturned, in that way spaniels can get when they're agitated, like she was about to tell everyone off.

'Come in, come in, please.' Holding Biscuit's collar, Margaret backed into the wide white hallway. 'I'm sorry I'm not quite ready for you. I was just – you were due at two, right?'

'One-thirty,' Scarlett said.

'Cor, I'm so sorry!'

'And please call me Scarlett. I'm not a doctor.'

'Oh no... I'm afraid I can't do that!' When Margaret laughed, the lines at the corners of her eyes crinkled merrily. She was as stylish as she'd been in the park, in jeans again and a soft-looking lilac jumper. 'Mrs Deering, then. I suppose I'm a little formal that way. I hope you don't mind!' She scooted backwards with the dog, snatching some shopping bags from the floor as she went. 'I was just going to put these away, but I can do it after. I'll just put them in the kitchen. Come through, please.'

Scarlett followed Margaret and Biscuit through the hall and into the roomy kitchen extension at the back. She could see a big garden through the bifold doors.

The kitchen, like the rest of what she'd seen so far, was pristine. A black Aga hulked against one wall and rustic cream cabinets lined the others. Bunches of fat pink, white and yellow ranunculus sat in enamel pitchers on the enormous waxed oak farm table. Scarlett didn't see so much as a fork or a piece of post on any of the worktops.

Nobody actually lived in photo-ready houses like this, did they? Scarlett and Rufus's kitchen was dotted with piles of paperwork, clothes that they meant to fold and the usual tannin-stained teacups in the sink. There were definitely little puffs of dog hair under their sofa. Normal, in other words.

Scarlett tugged at her jumper, aware that it was a little short from a too-hot wash.

Margaret absently wiped the oak worktop with her hand, maybe checking for crumbs that weren't there. 'Would you like a cup of tea?'

They both jumped when Margaret's phone rang. 'Oh, excuse me, it's my husband. Hello? Hello, darling. Slow-roasted lamb shanks with red wine. It took me forever to get the rosemary stuffed inside. They're in the Aga now. I'll do them with mash, baby carrots and parsnips. It's that wonderful recipe from that chef who – no, not any special time. All right. See you later, darling!'

'I'm so sorry,' she said to Scarlett, who'd been sniffing the air for the aroma of lamb shanks. 'How about that tea?'

'No, thank you,' Scarlett said. 'Since we only have an hour we should probably get started.'

'Yes, yes… of course, how silly of me,' she said. 'This isn't a social visit.'

Biscuit watched Scarlett from her tartan basket next to the Aga. As Margaret explained the trouble she was having, Scarlett found herself warming to Margaret and cooling towards the dog. As much as she wanted to love all her clients, some were definitely less appealing than others.

'You must get a lot of interesting cases,' Margaret said. 'Is most of your work in homes like this? Or mostly in classes?'

Homes like Margaret's? Hardly, but she knew what Margaret meant. She had back-to-back group classes Monday to Friday, she told her, and a handful of individual clients like her too. Plus the occasional session on a Saturday. 'I can only take on a few individual clients at a time.'

'Well, I'm ever so grateful that you chose us!'

'There's no need to be grateful, Margaret.' She was paying for the course, after all, and they weren't cheap. 'I'm pleased to take Biscuit on and I'm always happy to have new clients.'

Margaret's eyes glistened. 'Thank you. That's very kind.'

Scarlett finished explaining about the business, but she was anxious to get to work, starting with getting to know Margaret. Unfortunately, every time she tried to get her to talk about herself, she talked about her family instead. It seemed that nobody else had a problem getting Biscuit to mind.

'For one thing it sounds like we'll need to work on her view of the pecking order in the family,' Scarlett said. 'We've got to make you top dog.'

'Good luck doing that!' said Margaret. 'I've never really been top anything.'

'We'll see about that.' Scarlett got Margaret to put the lead on Biscuit and walk her round the kitchen. The dog practically strangled herself.

'See? That's what she's always like. It drives my husband crazy.'

Scarlett frowned. 'Your husband? Why would it drive him crazy? It's happening to you, isn't it?'

'Oh, I only mean he wants the bloomin' dog to behave and she won't with me.'

Scarlett let the comment pass. 'What's happening with Biscuit is really common. When she gets her way by pulling on her lead, it tells her that pulling works. But it doesn't always work, so she has to try it all the time to improve her odds of getting what she wants. Does that make sense? We can try an exercise to start changing that association between pulling all the time and getting her way. Got your treats handy? It's all about the treats.'

As Margaret practised rewarding Biscuit every time she walked nicely for even a step, Scarlett murmured encouragement – to Margaret, not Biscuit.

Most of her job was about training owners and showing them how their pet's behaviour reflected their own actions. It wasn't about pointing any fingers of blame, though. It was encouraging, really, because once the owners changed their behaviour, the dogs did too. Her clients just didn't realise how the two things were related.

Why should they? If it came naturally, she'd be out of business.

'Keep practising whenever you can and we'll add more exercises next time,' she said when the hour was up. 'I'd better leave you to your cooking. Same time on Thursday?'

'Hmm? Oh, yes, thanks ever so much. Excuse me,' Margaret said, moving beside Scarlett to slide the shopping bags to the other end of the worktop.

Scarlett caught a glimpse of the boxes inside. She

could have sworn they were frozen slow-roasted lamb shanks.

Chapter 5

Rufus set two lurid green drinks in front of Shannon while business types milled around their table in the crowded bar. The only reason he liked this place was because it reminded him of one of the boozers where they drank as teens. The clientele might be different, but the decor was the same – dark wood, dark drink-soaked carpet and dark thoughts. It was as claustrophobic as being inside a whisky barrel. Exactly the same reason Shannon didn't like it.

'Shots, seriously? What's wrong with you?' Shannon said when he'd perched again on the high stool opposite her. 'There's no way I'm drinking that.'

'Why not?'

'Because it looks vile. And I'm not sixteen.'

'It's not even really a shot, Shann, just something they're giving out at the bar. It's happy hour.'

'If ever there was a better reason not to drink it…'

'Suit yourself.' He downed both drinks with a badly-acted look of satisfaction.

'Gonna have another?' she teased.

'I'd hate to be greedy. Save some for the others.'

'That's very generous of you.'

'You know me.'

She did know him. That was why she knew something was wrong, despite his denying it every time she'd asked him. 'How's work?'

His blue-eyed gaze held hers. 'You never ask about work. Are we finally becoming *those* friends who have nothing left to talk about?'

Of course not. Just the opposite, actually. They had *everything* to talk about, and had done since they were seven. Even the humiliating stuff when they were teenagers was fair game, like the time he feared he'd caught something off a toilet seat when his mother's new washing powder was giving him itchy pants, or when she failed her driving test for the third time.

So why wasn't he playing by their usual rules?

'Since something is obviously bothering you, I'm just trying to narrow down the options. Is it not work, then?'

'Jesus, Shannon! I just want to have a relaxing night out. It doesn't mean there's anything wrong. Don't you ever just want to have fun?'

Ouch. He knew she constantly worried about being a bore. 'Sorry if you're not having fun with me.'

'No. No way,' he said, possibly louder than he meant to, since a few people turned to look. 'Don't you dare pout. You know that's not how it works with us. If I have to be your girlfriend and advise you on guys and nail varnish and shit like that, then you've got to be my mate. That means no emotional blackmail. That's our deal.'

She smiled. That was exactly how it worked with them. They shared everything, honestly and without agenda. That's why it had worked so well for twenty-five years.

'Have you talked to Mr Darcy yet?' he asked.

She let him change the subject. 'Not yet.'

'Is he even real, Shann?' he asked. 'Or are you making him up to keep us from going on at you about dating?'

God, one imaginary boyfriend when you're thirteen and you're never allowed to forget it. 'I promise he's real. And obviously talking about him doesn't work, because you are going on at me. Besides, why would I make up someone that I'm *not* having a relationship with?'

He considered that. 'It would be a pretty crap alibi, that's true. You should find someone that you *will* talk to.' Shannon's heart leaped into her throat when he turned around to scan the bar. 'I can be your wingman.' He looked her up and down. 'You don't look so bad tonight.'

'You flatterer, you.' As much as he and Scarlett tried to boost her confidence, she knew her shortcomings, and not in that faux-modest way from the films. There was no amazing transformation when she took off her glasses, shook out her ginger hair or painted her pale face. She wasn't an ugly duckling waiting to be a swan. Her brother had dubbed her Meccano, and thanks to that lifelong hang-up she wore only dresses and bunchy cardigans. Anything to hide her flat chest and bony arms.

'Pick someone and we'll go talk to him together,' Rufus said.

'He'll think we're after a threesome.'

'Come on. Like we used to do,' he said.

'Like you used to do,' she snapped. She couldn't

really blame him for the fact she'd had exactly one boyfriend since leaving uni, though she definitely blamed him for not telling her the guy was a complete knob. It would have saved her a lot of arseholery.

She knew people met in bars all the time. Just the idea made her want to throw up. Even if she could bring herself to walk up to a stranger, she'd never find anything interesting to say. She'd only slink away after a few minutes.

People seemed to have new theories all the time about what was wrong. Implication: with *her*. It might come from love, but it was still frustrating having to listen to it.

She should try meeting friends of friends, they said. Well, yes, okay. Where were they? Advice was plentiful. Actual flesh-and-blood dates, not so much.

She couldn't include her art degree course friends in her mental rant, since they didn't know many eligible men who weren't interested in other eligible men. 'It was different at uni,' she said. 'It was easier.'

'Everything was easier.'

It might be happy hour all around them, but the mood at their table had turned. 'You okay?' she asked.

His normally playful expression was drawn. 'Do you ever wish… do you ever wish you weren't a grown-up?'

The question implied she was a grown-up in the first place. She didn't feel like it. Maybe because art school was letting her live in a kind of adult limbo. Maybe because she walked dogs for a living and had flatmates who were students too.

'Imagine living without the pressure,' he went on. 'You know, buying the house, getting the mortgage, having the job that actually matters and someone else depending on you.'

'Rufus, it sounds like you're having a midlife crisis.'

'I'm thirty-two.'

'Quarter-life crisis?'

'Quarter-life? How long do you think we're going to live? No, I don't know. Sometimes I miss the old days, that's all. We didn't have anything to worry about. I don't know,' he said again. 'I'm just feeling nostalgic, I guess.' He suddenly looked at her like he'd noticed her for the first time. 'Do me a favour and keep that to yourself, okay? I don't want to worry Scarlett. She's been so sensitive about everything lately. What happens on guys' night, stays on guys' night, right?'

Great, thanks Rufus. Way to put your friend in an impossible position. She couldn't talk to Scarlett now that he'd explicitly asked her not to say anything. But what if there was something wrong and she kept quiet when she could have helped? Having husband-and-wife besties wasn't easy. She was constantly at risk of being the messenger with a bullet in her head.

Chapter 6

The next afternoon, Scarlett heard a key in the front door as she was rummaging through her bag for her Oyster card. 'Rufus?' she called just as the sound of Fred and Ginger's jingly collars reached her ears.

'Nope, it's just me,' Shannon called back as she unhooked the dogs' leads.

She was being daft. He never came home that early. Unless she'd rung him for an 'insemination session'. She flinched at how unsexy even the thought was, let alone actually doing it. At first, they'd tried to make it romantic. With candles and everything. That was when they still believed it would happen. Nearly a year ago now.

She had Rufus on the brain. 'Come here, you dogs,' she said.

They threw themselves at her legs, wriggling their warm bodies against her shins. Shannon kicked off her shoes and followed them into the kitchen.

'Were they good?' Scarlett asked.

Shannon smiled. 'Perfect, as always.' With a deft flick of the wrist she spun her long hair into a bun on top of her head, using a few of the strands to tie up the rest.

'You're so biased,' Scarlett said. 'I know they're not angels.'

Shannon knelt down on the lino to scoop up the dogs. 'I think they're angels, don't I, dogs? Don't I?'

Fred and Ginger were madly in love with Shannon. Of course they were. She got to be the fun auntie who never scolded them.

'This is a nice surprise.' Shannon picked some dog hair off her lip where it had stuck to her Chap Stick. 'I thought you had class.'

For two women who ran a business together, they didn't often see each other during the work day. They walked together for their weekly staff meetings, but couldn't gossip round the kettle or share family-size bags of Maltesers like normal office workers did. Shannon's dogs were all local to Reading, where they lived, and Scarlett travelled in to London, where it was more convenient for her clients to meet.

That was what Scarlett told herself anyway, when people asked her why she didn't just run classes closer to home. It wasn't like London had the monopoly on misbehaving dogs.

'I was with the puppies earlier,' Scarlett told her friend, 'but I forgot the new client questionnaires for tonight. I wanted some of that pasta anyway.' She pointed to the bowl on the worktop. She'd been thinking about it since the first pangs of hunger after breakfast. She'd made a rare foray into the kitchen last night while Rufus and Shannon were out. 'Want some? Are you hung-over? Rufus was slow this morning.'

'That's because he drank the shots they were giving away at the bar. No, thanks, I feel all right, and I've had lunch.'

'Shots? No wonder he was delicate.' Her yawn triggered one in Shannon. Rufus had woken her up when he got in, wanting to tell her about his night. It was sweet, but meant she'd then lain awake listening to him snore. 'Right, I'm off or I'll be late. You're okay to lock up?' Like Shannon didn't do it every day.

'Don't worry about us. I'll feed everyone and take off in a few minutes. Good luck with your new students.'

'You're still coming for supper Friday, right?' Scarlett asked. 'Rufus is making gnocchi and you know how he likes an audience.'

Shannon smirked. 'Wouldn't miss it. Unless I'm out of the country, obviously, with Mr Darcy. He could throw himself down on one knee in the park and beg me to elope with him. It's been moving in that direction, what with all the time we spend together now. I imagine we'd go on honeymoon somewhere hot and exotic straight after the wedding.'

'Right. So does seven o'clock on Friday work?' Scarlett asked.

'Yeah, I'll bring wine.'

Scarlett stuffed the Ruff Love assessments into her courier bag, hugged her batty friend and left Shannon rooting around in their cabinets.

She never minded taking the slow train to London. Even with the extra travel from the station to the community centre, she always gave herself plenty of time before class.

With the park closed after dark, she ran her classes indoors on weeknights at this time of year. She'd used the same park and same community centre since she first started her business. They were just around the corner from her old flat.

She trotted up the stairs leading from the station to the road. Then she caught the first whiff of curry from the Indian takeaway that stood next door. That tangy tingle of familiarity was as delectable as the smell itself.

She might not get to live there anymore, but there was nothing stopping her from pretending for a few minutes. *Just popping around the corner for a pint of milk*, she told herself. When she passed the fruit shop that sold her favourite Medjool dates, the Turkish owner waved. She beamed him back a smile of long-lost friendship.

It wasn't that she didn't love their Reading house. She really did. She just hadn't quite adjusted to the idea of living there instead of London. Wrenching herself from the city where she'd spent almost all of the past fifteen years was the hardest thing she'd ever done. It was worth it, for love, but the stabs of nostalgia still got her whenever she saw students hanging out in great noisy gaggles. Just like she'd done, living in halls just off Great Portland Street. Did those kids realise they were living in golden moments? She hoped they knew how lucky they were.

Her only time away from London had been the year she did her animal behaviour course, and she got back as quickly as she could when she finished.

But Rufus had exactly the same love for Reading, where he and Shannon had studied and lived afterwards, and his feelings were just as strong as hers. If London property hadn't been so eye-wateringly dear, she'd have given him more of a fight about where they should settle.

At least she got to work on her home turf now, even if she no longer slept there.

The evening yoga class was just finishing up when

she reached the community centre. When Krishna, the instructor, spotted Scarlett, she pointed her prayer hands at her. 'Namaste.'

Scarlett mumbled 'nom nom steak' back, minus the prayer hands. If Krishna noticed the mispronunciation, she didn't let on.

Krishna did look the part with her long grey-streaked hair and flowing robes, but she was about as Indian as Scarlett. She'd only had a yogic conversion after holidaying at an ashram. She returned home, changed her name and started spreading the sun salutation across North London.

Max and Murphy turned up as Scarlett was throwing open all the windows.

'Okay to come in? Murphy, you remember Scarlett, the nice lady from the park?'

'Sure, come in. I'm just clearing the room.' Krishna might not mind thirty people farting their way through the downward-facing dog but it wasn't an aura that Scarlett wanted hanging around during her class.

Murphy couldn't be more thrilled with their reunion. As soon as he saw Scarlett he lunged to the end of his lead. There were legs to be had.

But Max kept a tight hold, which left Murphy dangling briefly on his hind legs. 'Easy, boy. Nice place.'

Was it? She looked around, trying to see it through a newcomer's eyes. No, it was a shithole. The sickly yellow paint was peeling from the walls and the furniture pushed to the edges of the large room was a mishmash of cast-offs. The bright blue lino was rubbed colourless near the door and marked with decades of scuffs and gashes. Actually, thinking about it, Krishna did well to get her class into their meditative state in what looked like a bad dream.

'I'm sorry, I got lost on the way here,' Max confessed. 'It's all those little one-ways, it's really confusing.'

'Don't worry, you're still on time. I guess you don't get to London that often?'

His building work could be anywhere, he told her, since the reputation for his dad's firm had travelled across the entire South East. But he was a homebody, and Kent was home.

Scarlett watched him as he shrugged out of his hoodie and got his treats bag ready. He wasn't quite as hot as he'd seemed when she first saw him. Still really good-looking, with another fitted T-shirt, white this time, and jeans. His wavy hair was wet at the ends and he had a five o'clock shadow that was darker than his hair. When he smiled, which was often as he told her about him and Murphy, she noticed dimples.

She knew from his application that he lived alone, but it was nice to build up a more detailed picture. 'Yeah, it's just me and Murphy. It's a lad's pad, isn't it, boy?' His hands rarely left Murphy's sleek coat. 'I wish I didn't have to leave him home while I'm working.'

Murphy's wagging tail shifted up a gear as Scarlett moved closer. By the time she reached down to stroke his silky head, his entire back end was in on it.

'I did try bringing him along when he was a puppy, but he just got in the way. It's hard when you're working. Well, you probably know, you must have dogs?'

They were only a few feet from each other, but Max took a step forward anyway.

She took a step back. 'Two Westies, but we have a walker for them.'

Max moved towards her again. 'We?' He glanced at her hand. 'You're living with your husband, yeah?'

Scarlett started at his question. 'Uh, yes.' Back she stepped, trying to put a stop to this game of space invaders.

But forward went Max. 'He's a lucky guy. I'd love to be married. One day I will be, I'm sure of it.' His head was cocked to one side in a posture so keen that Scarlett's heart bent for him.

Far from being one of those clients who thought dog training was code for singles party, Max sounded like a romantic. She stepped backwards anyway.

They might have danced like that around the room for the whole session if Murphy hadn't decided to cut in. When he launched himself at the back of Max's thigh, Max just rolled his eyes. 'Murphy, get off! Don't mind him.'

But it was Scarlett's job to mind him. 'Has Murphy got a favourite toy?' she asked.

'Oh, yeah,' Max answered as he tried to calm his dog's ardour. 'A few, actually. He loves Bunny Wabbit.'

Murphy's head snapped to attention. Did someone mention Bunny *Wabbit?* His best friend in the entire *world*, Bunny Wabbit?

'Okay. Next time, please bring Bunny Wabbit.' Scarlett bit down her smirk. 'Keeping Murphy occupied should stop him from getting bored. Bored dogs look for ways to entertain themselves that might not be ideal. I'd like you to walk with him around the room and keep his lead long. If he mounts again, try moving your body away. Don't say anything or even look at him. Just walk away. He's getting the attention he wants when you tell him off, so I'd like you to practise diffusing the situation, okay?'

'I love you, mate,' Max grumbled to Murphy, 'but the lady says you're a bloody great show-off.'

Max had looked up Scarlett, he told her as they walked, when the vet suggested neutering. She was Murphy's last chance to hang on to his balls. No pressure or anything.

'We need to be clear about expectations,' she told him. 'We'll try everything we can, but it's really hard to stop some dogs from humping. You'll have to be realistic.'

Max's face drained of colour. 'And if you can't fix him?'

'Well, then he'll probably need the procedure. I know it's not what you want but—'

'I'm pretty sure he doesn't want it, either!'

'I promise we're going to do our best, Max.'

When Max told Scarlett that Murphy was his first dog, she could see that the bond was even more special. When he said that he and his girlfriend picked him out together, she found herself grinning. Between Max's squeaky voice and his sentiment, he was far from the arrogant bloke he'd seemed at first glance. 'That's romantic.'

'Ah, no, sorry, I should have said ex-girlfriend. We broke up. Ages ago, though! We're still great friends. In fact, she's marrying my mate. I'm happy for them.'

Scarlett wouldn't be nearly as big-hearted if one of her exes got together with a friend. Just the thought of Rufus with another woman made her tummy cave in.

But Max was convinced that love trumped all. Really, *really* convinced. Besides, he said, he couldn't hold a grudge against his mate, just as he'd never let a little thing like friendship get in the way of romance. Everyone had potential when one was constantly looking. And Max was, Scarlett knew by the time his first session was finished, a man who was constantly looking.

Chapter 7

Murphy noticed the new arrivals first. He rushed to greet Barkley and Charlie with a deep woof and his trademark full frontal assault. Since Max had been practising with him off the lead, there was nothing to stop him. 'Get back here!' he shouted.

But Murphy had other plans.

Barkley watched eighty pounds of setter barrelling towards him. He didn't sidestep, or even seem to mind Murphy's nose jammed up his backside.

That was one mellow dog.

'Don't worry, he's friendly,' Max said as he jogged to catch up with Murphy.

'That's all right. You're Max, right? Charlie.' He stuck out his hand to shake while the dogs sniffed their hellos. Then Charlie said, 'Actually, I was going to ask Scarlett for your details. I need some updating done in my mum's kitchen. Would you be able to have a look and give me a quote? Honestly, I wouldn't ask normally, but I don't know any other builders. Even, like, friends of friends, and I'm pretty desperate to get it done.'

'Sure, mate, I can have a look,' Max said, reaching for the phone in his pocket. 'Give me your number. It's just the kitchen you want redone?'

As his phone emerged, something flew out of his pocket with it. It arched gracefully away from Max and fell to the lino.

Max saw it.

Barkley saw it too.

The dog's lunge yanked a startled Charlie forward. 'Barkley, no!'

But it was too late. In a single gulp, it disappeared.

'I'm sorry! I hope that wasn't important?'

'It was twenty quid, mate. I was going to the pub with that.'

Barkley's tail wagged as he digested his snack. Paper was one of his very favourite things to eat.

Charlie fished two tens from his wallet. 'So… you'll ring me?'

It wasn't the best start to his training, thought Scarlett, but it did give her a good idea about how much work they had to do.

Charlie seemed like a good guy. He had the kind of goofy, friendly demeanour that made Scarlett feel at ease. 'Have you been for a run?' she asked.

He glanced down at his tracksuit and trainers. Then he shot daggers at Barkley. 'I tried.'

'Mm-hmm, it's not always easy with a dog. My old Labrador was a good jogger, but my dogs now are hopeless. Though they've only got little legs, so I can't be too hard on them.'

'Barkley doesn't have that excuse.'

Barkley sat with a grunt.

'We both need to get into shape,' Charlie went on, patting the belly protruding under his fleece, 'but I can't run with him, can I? I don't know what to do. I can't get rid of him.'

He looked completely desperate. 'Couldn't you jog without Barkley?'

'There's no time to take him out, then run and still get to work by eight-thirty. Same thing in the evening. He's alone all day so he needs a good walk when I get home. Barkley is doing my head in.'

The dog's head shot up at his name. Was it snack time?

She was tempted to ask if he even wanted to keep Barkley, but she got the feeling it wasn't about what Charlie wanted. He and Barkley were tied together by more than the lead between them.

He really was stuck between a rock and a hard dog. Unless they could curb Barkley's snacking, the prospects weren't bright for either of them.

When Charlie sighed, there was resignation in his eyes. 'I had friends over for dinner on Saturday night. I made a gorgeous roast chicken. From Jamie Oliver? Barkley jumped up on the table and ate half of it before I could get to him.'

They both looked at Barkley's chubby yellow backside. Scarlett had to admire his determination, if not his behaviour.

'We had to order Chinese,' Charlie finished glumly. 'No vet visits this week, though. He's just been snacking on the usual Kleenex and fag packets.'

She moved towards Barkley, who was hopefully sniffing the lino for another morsel to eat. 'When a dog eats inappropriate things off the ground it's usually either because he's looking for attention or because it's become a habit. Either way, we want to teach him that there are more rewarding ways to behave.' She handed Charlie her treat bag. 'Please throw a treat on the floor out of Barkley's reach.'

Barkley watched something hit the floor. He looked up. He looked up again. Was that food falling from the ceiling? His relaxed demeanour disappeared as he found the concentration of a bomb disposal expert. But no matter how hard he strained at his lead, he couldn't reach the snack. When he sat down, looking in confusion at Charlie, Scarlett said, 'Now give him a treat.'

Barkley was ecstatic. Treats? Just for *sitting*?

'Now toss another treat out of reach and repeat the process till Barkley sits straightaway and looks at you for at least two seconds.'

Barkley's cycle was stuck on strangle/sit/repeat for quite a while, but eventually he figured out the routine.

'You're teaching him that he has to ask your permission to eat anything off the ground.'

'That is awesome!' Charlie said. 'Good boy, Barkley.'

'Don't get too confident yet. This isn't a real-life situation.' She guessed there were probably still a lot of half-digested fag packets in Barkley's future.

'So you're saying don't get cocky?'

'Exactly.' Although cocky was just about the last word anyone would use to describe Charlie. Love-struck, yes, she realised as she listened to him during the session. Sometimes Scarlett wondered how much of her class was for the dogs and how much for their owners.

That woman who'd hung about at the introductory day, Naomi, was Charlie's girlfriend after all. 'Honestly,

Hiccup is really a problem,' he said as Scarlett scattered a few squeaky toys around the floor.

'Now lead Barkley towards one of the toys, but don't let him reach it. Wait for him to sit and then reward him. We're showing him that the rule applies to anything on the ground. Hiccup is Naomi's Jack Russell, right?'

'I can't get near my own girlfriend with that dog around,' he complained. This was no little grumble for him. He looked absolutely miserable. 'And she doesn't just growl either. She bites.'

Biting was a last resort for dogs. 'Is Naomi getting help for her?'

He shook his head as he threw another treat out of Barkley's reach. Barkley was starting to suspect that Charlie's aim might not be accidental. 'No, but we've got to do something. When I sell Mum's house I really want us to move in together, but I can't even go to her flat now with Hiccup there. We spend all our time at Mum's, but that's not really relaxing since Naomi has to go home to let the dog out. I really hoped she'd sign up with you when she agreed to come to the park. But she thinks she can do everything on her own.'

Scarlett's heart went out to him. 'Let's focus on Barkley's habits for now. I'm always happy to talk to Naomi if that's something she wants.'

He nodded. 'I think Barkley's really getting the hang of it now.'

'It takes a while for dogs to get used to new habits.'

'Even a genius like Barkley?'

They both stared at the dog, who'd started licking the linoleum like it was the finest gelato.

'Better keep practising,' Scarlett said.

'I'll have to.' Charlie's face went serious as he pulled his dog away from the puddle of saliva he was tending. 'I can't keep him the way he is, and I can't get rid of him. He was my mum's. He's all I've got left of her.'

Chapter 8

'Will you be my sous-chef?' Rufus asked Scarlett on Friday night as she came into the kitchen. When he shook the potato flour into a bowl, a lump of it escaped, exploding down the front of his jeans and covering his bare foot. He shrugged. 'You can't make an omelette without breaking a few eggs.'

'But you could at least try keeping the flour off the floor.' She tied a navy blue and white striped apron round her middle. He was wearing the frilly red polka dot one Gemma got him for Christmas. It was meant to be a joke, but he really liked it.

'You can't restrain the creative process of a genius,' he said. He didn't even try to keep a straight face.

'I'm not restraining the genius, just the flour.' She looked again at the footprints Rufus was tracking across their tile floor. 'And sous-chefing is just title inflation,' she pointed out, 'when you mean doing all the chopping and cleaning up.'

He kissed her temple. 'And pouring wine for the kitchen staff. That's us. Remember when we used to do this every weekend?'

Scarlett smiled. Friday nights were party nights when they first got together, but Saturdays and Sundays were theirs alone, and sacrosanct. They always stayed at hers, got up without the alarm and made their way to Borough Market to get the ingredients for a feast. They slipped in tiny delicacies and always a decent bottle of wine. Once they got back to her flat, they turned the double lock and didn't leave until it was time for work on Monday. They might watch films or the latest box set or read on the sofa or crawl back into bed together, until it was time to start cooking. 'I remember.'

'We should start that up again,' he said.

'Mm-hmm.' Those weekends were Scarlett's idea of heaven. Flushed with the memories, she suddenly wished Shannon wasn't due any minute.

Rufus deftly flicked an eggshell into the bin. 'Why don't we do it tomorrow?'

She wondered whether the farmer's market was still going. She smiled, remembering when they used to stroll through it each week when they first moved back to Reading, hand-in-hand, with their reusable bags slung over their shoulders. Had it really been years since they'd done that?

Rufus was nodding. 'We could get everything at Lidl and save loads of money on takeaways.'

The thing about reality wasn't that it was a let-down, exactly, but that when it crashed into your fantasy it made such an awful mess. If Rufus only remembered those weekends as the chance to economise on their weekly shop, things really did need to change.

'That's just charming, Rufus, very romantic. How could I not be swept off my feet with a comment like that?'

'I'm sorry, I didn't realise I was supposed to be sweeping you off your feet.' His tone matched hers. 'I thought I was cooking dinner while we chatted. Maybe you should write me a script so I know what I'm supposed to be doing, or a schedule or something. Oh, wait. That's all you've been doing lately.'

Well, then, maybe you could try following it once in a while, she thought. *And stop acting like you're being forced into a job you don't want.*

How else did he think she was supposed to get pregnant? They weren't twenty-somethings anymore. She was only going by the advice the GP gave them. He shouldn't blame her for being a little more precise about when they had sex. It wasn't like she was limiting them to certain days. Sadly, she realised she didn't need to. Rufus wasn't exactly springing erections on her.

She couldn't stop herself from thinking back to the way they used to be together in bed. Holy mother of all things sexy, they couldn't keep their hands off each other. She never imagined that sex could be that good. Sure, she'd heard about it, but it was like trying to explain a spectacular sunset to someone who'd never seen one. When they started trying for a baby, far from killing their lovemaking, it moved up a gear. She was having spectacular sunsets every time, so much so that she had trouble keeping her mind on her business. God, she loved those sunsets. Even thinking about them now turned her on. Which wasn't going to help matters. The contrast only made her sad.

How had they gone so wrong in so little time?

The doorbell sent the dogs into a meltdown. 'Oh,

relax, hounds of hell, it's only Shannon.' Fred and Ginger were sure that burglars only got into a house after politely ringing the bell.

Scarlett stalked to the door to let their friend in, composing herself as she went. It wasn't Shannon's fault that her husband mistook one of Scarlett's dearest memories as the chance for a two-for-one offer on oven chips.

'You could have used your key,' she told Shannon as she opened the front door.

'Oh, no, I feel like I shouldn't when you're home. I'm not working now.'

Scarlett wondered if she'd offended Shannon, treating her like an employee instead of their best friend. 'No, you're right. You're our dinner guest. Rufus has started on the gnocchi. We've both started on the wine.' Not to mention the sniping. They'd never argued in front of anyone before. Tonight didn't seem like the time to start.

Shannon unwound her giant purple scarf and shrugged out of her leather jacket. Without the layers she looked like she'd been drawn with crayons by a three-year-old. When they first met, Scarlett had worried about an eating disorder, but Shannon ate like a prop forward.

Shannon took off her boots without bothering to ask and kicked them under the bench in the hall. She knew the house as well as Scarlett did.

'Did you see Mr Darcy today?' Goodness, her question sounded so normal, like she and Rufus hadn't just blown up at each other.

Shannon blushed all the way to her ginger roots. 'We passed each other.'

'Did you hide behind your lace fan and make eyes at him?'

'Of course not. I practically ran away when he looked at me.'

'Well, at least he looked at you. So despite what you say, he does know you exist.'

Shannon nodded. 'Yes, he knows me as that weird woman who won't stop staring at him in the park.'

'That's still progress,' Scarlett said as they reached the kitchen.

'What's progress?' Rufus wanted to know, catching Scarlett's eye. 'H'lo, Shannon!' He embraced her warmly, leaving a flour-covered handprint on her loose red cardigan.

'Mr Darcy noticed Shannon in the park today,' said Scarlett, reaching over to wipe Shannon's back.

'How could he not notice you?! Look at you, you're…'

Shannon's look of horror stalled him.

'Rufus,' warned Scarlett, just to be sure. 'Don't make Shannon self-conscious!' He knew how sensitive she was. She might actually melt with shame.

Now Rufus blushed. 'Well, you're not exactly run-of-the-mill, are you? That's all I'm saying. I don't mean that you look like a freak or anything.'

Scarlett crossed her arms. *Let's see you dig your way out of this one.* He was on a roll tonight. Shannon didn't look like a freak at all. She just had an unusual dress sense. And very ginger hair.

'You're striking. That's all I meant.' He gestured to the chopping board where his gnocchi was laid out. 'I'm just going to go back to cooking and shut up.'

'Excellent idea,' Shannon said. 'Besides, I'm really here to see Scarlett.' She picked up the wine Scarlett poured for her. 'Living room? We'll leave you to your cooking,' she told Rufus. 'It won't be too long, right? I can't stay late. I'm setting up for my show in the morning.'

'Yes, miss, I'll be as quick as I can, miss,' he said. 'I feel like the hired help.'

'Oh, but you're not,' replied Shannon, 'since we're not going to pay you.' She swooped in to kiss his cheek, then followed Scarlett to the living room.

'Happy anniversary.' Shannon raised her glass after she'd thrown herself on to the squishy sofa and pulled her teal dress back down over yellow tights.

Scarlett never dared ask her if she was actually colour-blind. The last thing she'd ever do was risk knocking her confidence. But she did suspect that Shannon's eyes worked differently to everyone else's.

'Thanks, but that's not till May.' Scarlett sipped her wine anyway.

'Not you and Rufus. You and me. We met four years ago today. Rufus cooked us dinner.'

Love swelled up for her sentimental friend. That's right, he had cooked. It was Italian too. Puttanesca, that time. He'd been so nervous about them meeting that he was pretty drunk by the time she arrived. That was when she realised how serious he was about her. That had made her nervous. What if she failed the best mate test and Shannon hated her? Would it sour Rufus's feelings?

She never got the chance to find out because her friendship with Shannon took off that night, despite them being opposites in many ways. If they hadn't had Rufus to introduce them, they'd never have chosen each other as friends. Which just went to show how easy it was to miss out on something great by sticking with what was familiar.

Shannon was as artsy-fartsy as Scarlett was practical, and as shy as Scarlett was chatty. At first, she mistook Shannon's bashfulness for unsociability, but they weren't the same thing. Shannon did love being around people. It was talking to strangers that gave her the sweats.

'You remembered the actual date we met?' Scarlett asked.

Shannon blushed. 'The day I met my best friend? Of course. I always remember. What kind of friend would I be otherwise?'

Oh, I don't know, thought Scarlett, *you might be a shite friend like me who definitely hadn't remembered.*

'Though today's also my dad's birthday, so it's hard to forget.' She grinned, obviously pleased about the wind-up.

'Oh, you cow. I actually felt guilty, you know. I was trying to remember if I had a blank card I could pretend I'd had all along. You nearly got a Christmas card with happy anniversary scribbled over the front.'

'I'd give it back to you next year,' she said.

They both laughed at the inside joke. There was a birthday card – tattered and stained now, with a puppy holding a giant red heart – that had been passed back and forth between Shannon and Rufus since they were teens. At each birthday, the previous year's custodian crossed off his or her name and re-signed the card to the other. The messages through the years, in biro, permanent marker and, once, crayon, were always a new excuse for not being able to buy a fresh card. No matter what else Rufus got for his birthday, that card from Shannon was the thing he most looked forward to.

Inside jokes. Sometimes she envied that about Rufus and Shannon's childhood friendship. She'd come late to the party, and she suspected that some of the best songs might have been played already.

Maybe if she'd been there from the beginning, she'd find it easier talking to Rufus now. He and Shannon never seemed to have any tension between them. Perhaps that was the privilege of such a long friendship.

In a million years Scarlett never imagined they'd be one of those couples with a communication problem. Not *them*. They'd always cut through the B.S. with each other. There was nothing they couldn't discuss like proper functioning adults. Yet here they were, hardly talking at all, let alone about anything real. Whenever she thought about how different things were now, she wanted to cry over the loss. All because they couldn't manage to fertilise an egg.

Rufus didn't stay in the kitchen for long. 'Are you two really going to sit here while I do all the cooking?'

'Yes,' they both said, not moving.

'Then you'll need more wine.' He took the bottle from behind his back and refilled their glasses. As he poured for Scarlett, he caught her eye again.

I'm sorry, he mouthed.

Me too.

'What are we talking about?' he asked Shannon.

'It's our anniversary,' she said. 'Scarlett's and mine.'

'I knew that, obviously. That's why I'm making home-made gnocchi.'

'Liar,' Shannon said. 'You had no idea.'

'None whatsoever.' He sat between them, once again the third side in their triangle.

Later, Rufus gathered Scarlett into his arms as they lay together in bed. His thumb stroked the inside of her arm. It tickled, but she loved the feeling of closeness too much to mention it.

They'd had fun with Shannon over dinner. Things were always more carefree with her around. The strain showed when they were alone.

When Rufus's hands started telling her that the fun wasn't finished for the night, Scarlett dared to believe that things might be getting better. Finally, after months, he was the one instigating instead of her.

It felt so *good* to be having sex because they wanted to, instead of having an agenda. She let herself sink into the feeling of being wanted. If only Rufus would let himself be enticed as easily. He just said he wasn't in the mood when she tried. That only made her self-conscious, and frightened. She didn't press him about why his passion had cooled, in case the answer tore them apart for good.

'Thanks for the bonus round,' she said after.

His satisfied smile disappeared. 'Isn't it possible, just for one second, to not think about that?'

'I only meant that I appreciated it. Jesus, don't be so touchy.'

'But it's not the right time or it wouldn't be the bonus round, right?' He shook his head. His voice was filled with sadness.

'It doesn't matter,' she said, but she knew she'd ruined the mood.

Rufus pulled his T-shirt back on. 'Obviously it does matter or you wouldn't have said it. I'm sorry it was fun instead of... useful.'

'It was fun! Very fun, thank you. Let's not fight.' With a deep sigh, she laid her head on his chest and one arm over his stomach. She could feel his heart beating against her cheek, slowing as his breathing did.

'Sorry. That was dickish.' When his arm closed over her, she knew they'd fall asleep like that.

What she really wanted to do was lie on her back with her legs up against the wall. Just in case.

Chapter 9

The last thing Scarlett expected when she turned up at Margaret's house was a full-blown domestic. Her client didn't seem the type who would say boo to a goose, yet there she was shouting at her son.

The skinny, hairy young man was glaring at Margaret from beneath his boyband fringe. 'I can wash my own damn clothes.'

'Yes, but darling, you never do,' Margaret pointed out. 'And then I end up rushing around getting you clean pants. I was just trying to save myself a step.' She waved Scarlett into the hallway. 'I'm awfully sorry about this, Mrs Deering. Please make yourself comfortable in the sitting room. This will only take a minute.'

They moved into the kitchen, leaving Scarlett to perch on the cream silk brocade sofa and eavesdrop.

'Now what am I supposed to do about the shirt?' the teenager demanded as cutlery clattered in the sink.

'Can't you wear another one?' Margaret's voice was

appeasing. Scarlett would have been furious.

'That's the one I want to wear. Unfortunately, I can't. Thanks to you, it's soaking wet.'

'Let me iron it dry,' Margaret said. 'It'll only take a minute. Will that be okay, darling?'

He must have mimed his response – probably rudely – because next Scarlett heard the metallic clack of an ironing board being set up. A few minutes later the teen stormed out the front door.

'I'm so sorry about that,' Margaret said, collecting Scarlett from the living room. 'And the caterer rang earlier saying she needs to stop by too. It's all happening round here today, but hopefully we won't be interrupted too much! Please come through.'

Biscuit's eyebrows twitched as she watched Scarlett from her bed by the Aga, but she didn't lift her chin from her paws. She perked up her spaniel ears, though, when Margaret got the treats down from the kitchen cabinet that sat above a gleaming Italian espresso machine. Everything in Margaret's house looked new and perfect. Scarlett thought about her own splattered and stained coffee maker. One day they'd get around to replacing the carafe with one that didn't need gaffer tape on the handle.

'I'm sorry about Archie,' said Margaret. 'Now where is the new pack? I know I bought them, just like you asked.' She flung open the other cabinets till she found what she was looking for. 'Success!' She shook the treats packet.

Margaret shrugged into her duffel coat to take Biscuit into the garden. 'If it's all right, I'll just keep the doors open so I can listen for the caterer,' she explained as a cool wind blew a pile of papers off the kitchen table. 'I'm sorry she's coming. Hopefully she won't disturb us too much.'

If this was how Margaret's days usually went, then Scarlett could see why she seemed so frazzled. 'I'm sure we can work around the caterer,' Scarlett said when Margaret had snapped the leash to Biscuit's collar. 'Today we're going to make you leader of the pack.'

'Me? Leader?' Margaret laughed. 'I haven't been leader of anything since… well, hardly ever, really. I'm more of a follower. Though I did join the WI last year. Arthur thought it would be a good way for me to make some friends. He wants me to join the committee, but I'd rather not. All that attention.' She made a face.

All Margaret needed, really, was a bit of shoring up so she could stick up for herself. Everyone would probably fall in line pretty quickly if she did.

No, Scarlett, she scolded herself, *you must not get too involved.* She had a terrible habit of doing that with clients. It was an occupational hazard, after spending weeks with someone in their home, helping them change something as fundamental as their relationship with their pet, who was part of the family anyway.

'We want Biscuit to see you as her leader,' she said, 'so that she pays attention to you. She needs to learn that she only gets what she wants after you get what you want. Right now, it's all about her.'

'Story of my bloomin' life!'

She got Margaret to walk Biscuit up and down the length of their long garden. Every time the dog pulled at the end of her lead, she had Margaret stop and wait for her to come back to where she was standing.

That was how it was meant to go.

But Biscuit had her human perfectly trained. She wasn't happy with these new rules. When Margaret stopped, Biscuit stopped. But she stayed stubbornly at the end of the lead, waiting for Margaret to move forward again.

'Stand your ground,' she called down the garden to Margaret, who waved over her shoulder with her free hand. 'You're doing well. She'll give in.'

'If you say so, Mrs Deering!'

Eventually, Biscuit sauntered back to see why Margaret wasn't obeying.

They practised over and over. Each time Margaret was gobsmacked when her dog minded, which just showed how rarely that happened.

Biscuit, and Margaret, were finally getting the hang of the drill when the doorbell rang. The dog's head whipped round towards the house. Then her body whipped round too, and she started tearing back up the garden.

Margaret ran behind her, trying to keep up. 'Oh, that's the caterer. I'll just get it. Won't be a minute.'

'But Margaret, you're supposed to be walking Biscuit, not the other way around…' The dog dragged her human through the bifold doors and back into the kitchen.

By the time Scarlett reached the kitchen – she'd be damned if she'd let Biscuit set the pace – she could hear a woman's slow, measured voice in the hall. '*I'm* sorry, Margaret,' she said, sounding anything but sorry. 'You've got plenty of time to get people in.'

Scarlett crept closer to the doorway between the kitchen and the hall. When she peered around the corner she could see them standing by the front door. Margaret was trying to catch her breath. 'Blimey, I'm unfit,' she wheezed. 'Your decorating will be beautiful, Octavia, but we don't really have the budget to repaint. Couldn't we put up cloth or something in the right colour to make it blend?'

Octavia had a severe black fringe and bob. Her lips were a deep red that contrasted with her pale skin, but she was no delicate beauty. Her broad chin jutted out, making her seem belligerent. Or maybe her words were doing that.

'Margaret, I don't see why you want to bother with the Thousand and One Nights theme in the rest of the house if you're not going to do it in the hall where everyone will get their first impression.'

'But I don't want Thousand and One Nights in the rest of the house,' Margaret murmured. 'That was your idea.'

'Have you not asked me to be your party planner? Do you expect me to just turn up and sling some food? Because if that's the case, then I don't see how we're meant to work together. Maybe I'd better just leave you to do whatever you want. You could get some quiche or something from M&S.'

'No, Octavia! I'm ever so grateful for your help. I didn't mean to give the impression that I wasn't. Of course you have to do the party, and your theme will be wonderful. I guess I can find the money to repaint.'

Then she noticed Scarlett. 'I've just got our dog trainer here, so may I please leave you to get on with things?'

She sounded like a child asking permission to use the loo. Worse, she sounded like she'd rather wee in her pants than cause a fuss if the answer was no.

The sooner she learned to be leader of her pack, the better.

'Blimey, I wish I'd never started this party idea,' Margaret confessed as they went back into the garden with Biscuit. 'It's for my birthday, you see.' She laughed. 'The big five-oh. I can hardly believe it. I didn't want a fuss.'

'Octavia sounds scary,' Scarlett ventured.

'She frightens the pants off me! But she's Arthur's boss. Well, his boss's wife. What would he say if we didn't use her company for the party, especially now that we've agreed? We couldn't use anyone else.'

'I suppose it would be awkward, but, Margaret, if she's suggesting things that you don't want to do?'

'Well, Arthur wants it to be a certain way, with inviting his work contacts and all.'

That didn't sound like much of a party for Margaret. It sounded like a work do for her husband.

Margaret didn't seem to have a bad opinion of herself so much as no opinion at all. She was the neutral beige jumper or the safe option on the menu.

By the end of their session Biscuit was finally sitting quietly by Margaret's side. 'Wonders will never cease,' she said. 'You must be a good influence on her, Mrs Deering.'

Scarlett was just about to point out that technically, Margaret should have told Biscuit where to sit rather than the other way around. As it was, the dog was still in charge. But no, look how pleased Margaret was. Let the poor woman have that.

Margaret snatched her mobile as soon as she heard it ringing. 'Hello, darling. Oh, you'll love it. Beef Wellington with potatoes dauphinoise. I've already started on it so it's ready when you get in.'

Of course she'd washed his jeans, she added, glancing at the pile of denim on the worktop. As she talked about how tricky it was to get the potatoes sliced correctly, she took a bottle of Febreze from the cabinet and squirted the jeans.

Scarlett was willing to bet her freezer was full of ready-made dinners too. Clearly Margaret wasn't holding the lead in any part of her life.

Scarlett knew exactly how it felt not to have control over your own life. She'd always liked the idea that Fate had a hand in the good things that happened to her. But it wasn't such a comfortable feeling when it kept her from getting what she wanted. She was starting to think that, actually, Fate was a pretty mean bugger.

Chapter 10

'Sorry, I shouldn't have said that,' Scarlett told Fate via her bathroom ceiling the next day. 'I'm sure you're not really a mean son of a bitch. You're probably very nice, in fact, in general circumstances. Kind, even. And accommodating, especially to someone who might have treated you a bit unfairly lately.'

At least she hoped that was true.

Taking a deep breath, she peed on the stick.

'If you're listening, I've got a proposition for you.'

Fate didn't answer. The only sound in the house was the knocking of the old cast-iron radiator in the hallway. When they first moved in, they woke in the night to what sounded like a panicked neighbour at their door. The system needed flushing, her mother had told her. But everything in their house had to be coaxed just to work, so they didn't want to risk upsetting the delicate balance. Knocking was better than freezing.

A beardy white muzzle appeared through the inch-wide crack under the bathroom door – wonky doors were another charming feature of the house – as Ginger tried to sniff out what was going on in there. Scarlett knew it was Ginger rather than Fred. He always left the manual labour to his sister. He'd be right beside her, though, awaiting her report.

A minute passed.

'I promise I'll… I'll sort out my overdraft,' she told the ceiling. 'At least half of it. And I really will eat five portions of fruit and veg a day like I've told Gemma I've been doing. And I won't ask for anything else,' she told Fate, 'for at least a year.'

But then she thought again. She'd probably need Fate's help sooner, especially if things went to plan.

She checked her phone. Two minutes.

'Or six months anyway,' she murmured. 'No requests for a solid six months, but I'll clear my whole overdraft.'

She'd lost count of the times she'd had this conversation with her bathroom ceiling. Why had she ever thought that bargaining like this was fun? Probably because she used to have confidence in the test result. It's easy to be glib when you think you know the answer.

Ginger began to whine. The dogs hated a closed door. They were sure that was when their favourite foods landed all over the floor and the unlimited tummy scratches went on offer.

Two minutes and thirty seconds. She was sick of the whole process, to be honest. Sick and scared.

Three minutes.

She picked up the stick.

Not Pregnant.

Thanks for nothing, Fate.

It had been so exciting when they officially went from avoiding babies to trying for one. Finally, she got to wave goodbye to that oh-shite fear that her period would be late. Together they imagined a child with spun-sugar hair and the perfect combination of both their features. Their little golden clone. They couldn't wait.

They chucked away the birth control and shagged with gay abandon. Scarlett could practically *feel* her eggs fertilising in the middle of her cycle. 'Do you think there's a baby in there?' she'd whisper to Rufus as they lay together holding hands in their bed.

'I think so,' he'd say.

Scarlett always knew she wanted children. She and Gemma played two mummies even after it was explained that those probably weren't sisters in the diversity books they read.

Then she'd met Rufus, who loved children, and he was infinitely shaggable too. Win-win.

Except it wasn't win-win, was it?

She shoved the stick deep into the rubbish bin. She didn't tell Rufus about those tests anymore. They were supposed to be in this together, but it was too hard seeing him shift a little further away from her every time she did.

She was just glad they hadn't mentioned that they were trying to anyone else. She couldn't handle disappointing their parents every month too. It had become her dirty little secret.

You've got one thing to do, she berated her uterus. *One thing. Why don't you pull your socks up and do your job?*

But it was no use. Her reproductive system was on strike and she had no idea how to coax it back to work. Maybe her radiator needed flushing too.

The dogs shot through the open bathroom door to step all over her socked feet. 'Did you miss me?' She ran her fingers through their wavy white coats. 'You know it's rude to bother a person through the door when she's in the loo.'

Then you should leave it open, their looks said. *Don't blame us.*

She sat on the floor, burying her face in Fred's furry back. 'Want to come to Max's session with me?'

She didn't usually bring them, but she'd rather not be alone at the moment.

'Come on, I'll drive. You can stick your heads out the window and bark at the cars.'

'Just because it's taking longer than we hoped to get pregnant,' she reasoned to her dogs in the rear-view mirror as she came off the exit into London, 'doesn't mean, absolutely and definitively, that there's a problem, does it?'

Definitely not, Fred and Ginger agreed.

'Besides, I'm not even sure how accurate those ovulation kits are. We're doing it when it says to, but who knows? Sorry to give you that kind of detail about your parents' sex lives.'

The dogs waited for more. They didn't have much choice, being harnessed in by their dog seatbelts.

'Maybe we should be doing it more around the peak time. On other days, I mean. It might increase our chances. Though it's not like I don't try throwing in some random times as it is.' She sighed. 'You've seen him. Just getting him to do it on the peak day is hard enough.' She squirmed with embarrassment thinking about the calls she'd made to Rufus at work: Come home now. At first it was fun – a little afternoon delight – but lately it had been as impersonal as ordering a pizza. And the deliveryman was bored.

'I'm not exactly chomping at the bit, either, but we've got to make the effort if we really want a baby.' Scarlett caught her breath. 'We do. We definitely do.'

She glanced in the rear-view mirror. Ginger lay down with a grunt.

Scarlett had lost her audience. She'd have to wait till she got home to google *How long does it take to get pregnant*. Again.

Like she didn't know the odds by heart. Twenty per cent got pregnant within a month (the lucky sods), seventy per cent were up the duff within six months and eighty-five per cent were pregnant within a year.

We are the eighty-five per cent… hopefully, Scarlett thought. Which sounded like the world's lamest pregnancy slogan.

Tears blurred the view of the road up ahead. What if it never happened? She tried to stop her mind going there, but it had been eleven months already without so much as a late period. They'd failed to make eleven babies, babies who now could never be born. They'd missed those chances.

What would those babies have been like? Would they have had Rufus's eyes or hers, his nose or her freckles? They might have been easy births. Or she might have spent days in labour, worrying she wasn't strong enough to get through it. Maybe they would have slept through the night after the first few weeks, or they might have been colicky little windbags.

She'd never know now, yet those babies were as much a part of her as any child she could imagine. They were once possible children, just like the one they still hoped for. The difference was that what was once possible now could never be. She'd never get to kiss those tiny fingers or pat those backs after a feed or feel those warm little bodies snuggle against hers.

It felt like mourning. Every single day she mourned those impossible babies.

Was she going insane? Surely the lightning-quick and totally overwhelming hatred that overcame her at the sight of pregnant strangers wasn't normal. That wasn't sadness or regret. It was much worse. She wished very bad things to happen to those women. If she couldn't have it, then nobody else should get to either. She'd be happy for them once she had her own baby.

She'd never tell Rufus about those feelings. Just knowing they were trying and failing was sucking the joy out of their relationship. That frightened her. Imagine if Rufus knew he'd married a crazy person who loathed people she'd never met.

Besides, part of her did still flicker with hope that she'd be pregnant soon. She snatched at the flimsiest of anecdotes. The fifty-three-year-old woman who conceived while on the pill? Scarlett had practically memorised the newspaper article. Women getting pregnant just as they got approval for adoption? Those stories were more common than one would think. Surrogate *and* client miraculously pregnant at the same time? Granted, it was a little bit tabloid, but she was too greedy for positive news to be discerning. She still hated the mum-to-be for getting lucky, yet she gorged on the hope it gave her. She was afraid of what would happen if she stopped.

Bucking herself up, she popped on her hands-free headset to ring Shannon.

'Clive, get off your sister!' Shannon shouted as she

picked up. 'Sorry. He's such a bully. What's up?'

'Nothing, really, just feeling a bit meh today.' Understatement. 'Tell me something cheery.'

'Clive! Sampson doesn't want to be your girlfriend either. Honestly, that dog. Are you driving?'

'It's okay. Hands-free headset. I'm going to class.'

'How come you're meh?'

Shannon didn't know about the pregnancy tests and it was too big a conversation for the M4. 'Just an off day.'

'You're not the only one. I threw a full poo bag away a minute ago and missed the bin opening. The bag fell out and emptied on my foot. It's always on my foot. Why is that?'

'Like toast landing buttered side down. It's a mystery. Sorry about your poo foot.'

'Sorry about your meh day. Feel better to know my foot stinks?'

'That definitely helped.'

Chapter 11

Shannon stood back from the huge white wall to study the canvases. The bottom left corner of each one was definitely lower than the right. Yet they were perfectly level on top. She didn't need a maths degree to know her paintings weren't square.

Which would have been useful to notice before she'd painted her entire degree show on them. But no.

That was what she got for buying cut-price canvases from her classmate's dodgy cousin.

Her friend, Julian, sidled up from across the room where he'd hung his own work – collages made from lad's magazines and butterflies. They were quite beautiful at a distance, but disturbing close up. 'Happy?' He bumped her hip with his as he examined her paintings.

'Do you think it's a problem that the canvases aren't square?' she asked.

'Not at all. It makes you avant-garde. How fabulous!' He clapped his manicured hands, making the sparkly blue nail varnish twinkle.

Everything about Julian twinkled, with or without polish. During their first week of class he'd decided he would be Shannon's closest art school friend – and there was never any point arguing with him. Besides, art school was as cliquey as secondary school had been, and even more competitive. It would have been unbearable if not for Julian.

'How many invites did you send out?' he asked. His deep brown, kohl-rimmed eyes sought hers and, as usual, his beauty took her breath away. His Jordanian parents had given him all their best genes. Incredibly perfect skin and a nose that could be the prototype for plastic surgeons. And those huge eyes. He looked like Conchita after electrolysis.

Julian had been slightly more butch when they first started their programme. Slightly. She cringed now to think that she'd actually contemplated him as a potential boyfriend. She'd figured he was gay, but wondered: just how gay? Like, were the chances of his ever seeing a vagina more or less than seeing a unicorn?

Less, as it turned out.

'Eight, I think,' Shannon answered him. 'My family are coming, and a few friends. You?'

'Fifty-two.' He flicked a strand of sleek black hair over his shoulder. 'One can never have too many wallets around when it comes to art, darling.'

Shannon wasn't sure she even knew fifty-two people. Maybe if she included the family who ran the corner shop and every neighbour on her road that she'd ever said hello to. Even if she did know them, though, she'd never impose an invitation. She'd been embarrassed enough inviting Scarlett and Rufus.

No wonder she couldn't talk to Mr Darcy, when she balked at asking her friends to come along to a free event with wine. Banksy had the right idea. Anonymous art sounded like the way to go. She could post her wonky paintings under cover of darkness all over London.

She had to go straight back to Reading from the gallery to pick up the poodles. Their owners wanted them as tired and empty of wee as possible when they got home from work. The park was off limits after dark, but Fifi and Clive preferred the pavement anyway.

'My paintings are crooked,' she told them as they meandered away from their house. 'For the show next week. Not just crooked on the wall. They're not square.'

Fifi sniffed at a signpost. *That's typical.*

'It's not like I have loads of money for canvases. Your parents don't exactly pay me a lot.'

Clive glanced up at her. *That's not our problem, is it? Get another job.*

It's not just a job, though, it's my business, she thought with the same quiet rush of pride she always felt. It might have been easier to have a well-paid office gig with regular hours, treats on casual Fridays and Christmas parties in January, but then she wouldn't have been able to finish school.

She jumped when her phone rang. Scarlett. They'd already talked today. 'What's up?'

'I just wondered what you're doing.'

'I was in London earlier.' But Scarlett knew that. 'Now I'm with the poodles.'

'Oh. You're back already? I was ringing to see if you could sneak off for a drink with me before my next class.'

'Sorry, if I'd known I'd have left the gallery a little earlier. I had to come back for the poodles.' She glanced at Clive. He snubbed her. 'Ring Rufus. He's always good for bunking off.'

'Yeah, I will. Okay. Have fun with the poodles.'

'As if.'

Something felt funny as she hung up. Scarlett didn't usually sound that… what was it? Meh, she'd said the other day. First Rufus's quarter-life crisis (even if he didn't admit it) and now Scarlett. What was going on with those two?

Despite her promise to Rufus, she couldn't sit by if she thought her best friends were unhappy.

Clive deigned to look her way before turning twice and crouching on the small patch of grass under the street lamp.

She pulled a roll of poo bags from her pocket.

'I bet Banksy doesn't have to do this.'

Clive looked pleased with himself.

Chapter 12

Fake it till you make it, Scarlett dared the image that stared back at her from her bathroom mirror. That's what those women's magazines advised, between articles about who broke up, cheated or changed gender and the beach snaps of celebrities and their personal sun-cream application assistants.

Scarlett just couldn't give in to all the *uns* –unsure, unhappy, unpregnant… *unwomanly* – or she'd end up depressed, bumping along the floor like a wrinkled birthday balloon long after the party.

Her world was now divided into twenty-eight-day cycles, and every month had the same punchline. Though these days she stopped herself from feeling the anticipation of those pregnancy tests, so at least she didn't have as far to fall. Maybe she should let herself be optimistic again. Then at least she'd get a few days of excitement before the inevitable.

No matter how much she told herself that pregnancy didn't define womanhood, and it certainly didn't define her, she still ended up feeling awful after she buried the wee stick in the bathroom bin.

She and Rufus were failing to do what millions of others seemed to manage on a reckless night out. And they weren't even having fun trying.

Just try being passionate when you feel about as sexy as a colonic irrigation.

'Dogs, we need a change. Fake it till you make it, right?' She took a deep breath. 'I *am* sexy,' she told the bathroom mirror.

Fred and Ginger looked unconvinced.

'I am sexy and FABulous. Sexy, fabulous and GORgeous!' She made a kissy-face pout. God, if anyone saw her... 'Yeah, right. You're practically Gisele's twin, except for your eyes, nose, mouth, and your skin, and your hair, and...'

She peered at her eyebrows. They'd gone feral and gave her face a permanently frowny expression.

'If I tweeze it, he might come.'

She scrutinised the rest of her face. She looked tired. And where had that long hair under her chin come from? It looked like an inch of thread was stuck to her face. It could have been waving at people for months.

Once upon a time, before her facial hair had gone rogue, she'd kept appointments at John Lewis's brow bar.

But she couldn't let the hair stay on her face now that she knew it was there.

Then she glanced at the razor in the shower (also sorely neglected lately).

Once she started tweezing she couldn't stop herself. She found a few more hairs under her chin. They needed plucking. And she nearly got her brows under control, though the left one was a little stubbier than the right.

Rufus's shave gel was luxuriously thick and soft on her legs. Carefully she shaved past her knees, all the way up her thighs. She hadn't done that in months. Nice and smooth.

She stared at her pubic hair. Her eyebrows had been too bushy, and she had tidied *them* up.

She watched the blondish clumps swirl away down the plug hole.

Definitely trimmer, though now her bikini line looked unkempt in comparison. So she dragged the razor over the sensitive skin.

That just showed up her undercarriage.

She worked with the concentration of a brain surgeon. She really didn't want the razor to slip now.

Staring down at herself, she realised she'd gone too far. Instead of the perfectly normal muff she'd known and loved for most of her life, her pubic area was covered by a weirdly uniform patch that reminded her of the sticky felt pads they'd put on the bottom of the dining chair legs.

Scarlett felt as naked as a mole rat.

Her mum rang just as she and Rufus were getting into the car. 'Can you please give me a ride to your dad's?' Julia asked breathlessly when Scarlett answered.

'Why are you wheezing?' Scarlett wanted to know.

'I ran from down the road,' said Julia.

'*Why* did you run from down the road?'

'I was chasing the tow truck. They have my car.'

'What?!'

Rufus started at Scarlett's outburst. She made an 'eek' face at him.

'It's been towed,' said Julia. 'Now, can you pick me up or do I have to ring a taxi? You know how cross William gets when we're late.'

'I'm sure he wouldn't mind in the circumstances, but, yeah, we're leaving now. See you soon.'

Rufus kept glancing at Scarlett as they drove towards her mum's. She waited for him to say something.

Glance.

Nothing.

Glance, glance.

Silence.

Finally, she couldn't take it anymore. 'Is something wrong, Rufus?'

'No, not at all!' He reached for her hand as usual. 'I've got the feeling something is different about you. New haircut?'

Well, thought Scarlett, *in a manner of speaking*. 'I've got make-up on.'

'Maybe that's it.' He signalled off the motorway.

Scarlett had a wicked thought. 'I've also shaved my pussy.'

What the hell was she thinking? She never said things like that.

He stared at her as they came to at a light. 'You didn't! Let me see.'

She got a rush seeing Rufus's playful grin. But there was something more intent beneath it. That thrilled her more.

'What, here? No way.' Her heart was racing. She did have a dress on. He could see for himself if she got her knickers off.

This was crazy. Her mother was waiting for them just around the corner.

His hand found her thigh. He seemed to have the

same idea. 'Show me,' he said. Her skirt lifted.

'I can't. I'm wearing pants.'

'Take them off and show me.'

She glanced at the bulge growing in his jeans. 'Let's go somewhere.' She wriggled out of her knickers and laid them across his thigh. 'You can't look,' she teased. 'Keep your eyes on the road.'

'Jesus, Scarlett.'

They were nearing the house where she grew up. 'Turn left here. Behind those garages.' She used to smoke back there with her next-door neighbour. In her wildest dreams she never imagined she'd have sex there one day.

'We'd better be quick,' she murmured. 'We've got to pick up Mum.'

'Please don't mention your mum and sex in the same breath.' They both smiled as she climbed into his lap.

'Things never to talk about,' she said. 'Mums, taxes.'

He laughed as she tried to find a comfortable space for her leg. 'The car's MOT,' he added. 'Your damn ovulation schedule.'

She reeled back. 'Way to kill the mood.'

'Well, on the list of unsexy things, you've got to admit it's up there.'

'Why is it *my* ovulation schedule?'

'They are your ovaries.'

'It's *our* schedule, Rufus.' She crawled back into the passenger seat. Suddenly there seemed to be much more than the gearbox coming between them.

His expression clouded over. 'What are you doing?'

'We'll be late picking up Mum.'

'Are we not going to—?'

'Oh, right. You still want to get your end away after

making me feel like crap with a comment like that. You know how I feel about everything we're going through.'

'Oh, yeah, I know it. But what about me, Scarlett? Do you think I want to feel like a performing monkey dancing because the organ grinder tells me to? Believe me, that got old months ago.'

Did he really just call her an organ grinder? 'I'm sorry that it's such a chore to do what I *thought* we both wanted.'

'It's all you seem to think about. I just want us to be normal again. Without all the pressure.'

'What does that mean? Don't you want a baby?'

'I do.' But he didn't sound as sure as he used to. As sure as Scarlett was. 'I just don't want this.' He gestured between them. 'This is too hard.'

Scarlett felt sick. 'What are you saying? That you don't want *us*?'

'I want us the way we were, before this constant stress. Don't you?'

'Of course, Rufus, but I also want a baby. I thought we both did. That doesn't just happen, at least not for us. I'm sorry, but there's got to be some planning or it's never going to work. I can't change biology. I'm sorry, but I can't.'

'I'm sorry too,' he said, starting the car's engine. 'Because this is no fun.'

They drove in silence to her mum's house. What was she supposed to do? Rufus was asking the impossible. They couldn't go back to normal unless they stopped trying for a baby.

She couldn't stop doing that.

'Are you ill?' Gemma scuttled away when Scarlett made

her way into their dad's living room. 'You're flushed.'

Gemma overreacted if she detected so much as a sniffle. She didn't get headaches. She got brain tumours. Her parents had no idea where her hypochondria came from, since neither of them were inclined towards overreacting. But Scarlett knew her sister went through a phase of reading *The Complete Dictionary of Diseases* before bed. Gemma came away with a mortal fear of every lump and bump she'd found since.

Luckily, she'd married a doctor. She and Jacob were in love within weeks, engaged and married in a year. Not only was he a very good husband and in-law, he saved the NHS loads of money by keeping his wife and her imagination away from the GP's surgery. Both the Fothergill family and the health service were very pleased to have him in Gemma's life.

'You're making a rare appearance,' she said to Jacob as he shook hands with Rufus. 'Have you killed off all your patients?'

His deep brown eyes twinkled as he flashed her a smile worthy of a toothpaste advert. 'I couldn't miss Felicia's meal.'

She jostled her brother-in-law fondly. 'You are such a suck-up.'

'Come here,' said Felicia, reaching for Scarlett's forehead. The electric blue metal bangles piled up her wrist jangled as she checked for a fever.

'I'm fine, don't worry.' Scarlett waved away their concern. 'We were in a rush to get here, that's all.' She wasn't about to mention what happened on the way. Her mum had been suspicious enough when she got into the car. The little hatchback was thick with tension.

'What do you want to drink?' Felicia asked. 'Gemma? Jacob?'

'Water is fine, thanks,' Gemma said.

'Are you detoxing again?' Scarlett accused her. 'I've told you that's not healthy. Jacob, you're the doctor, tell her.'

'Actually, in this case water's okay,' he said, glancing at his wife.

'I'm not detoxing. But I won't be drinking for a while.' The smile bloomed over Gemma's face. 'Or eating sushi or blue cheese or about a million other things I love.'

Scarlett stared at her sister. 'ARE YOU?'

'I am!'

Tears sprang to Scarlett's eyes. 'Are you sure you didn't just eat too much pasta? You're not mistaking a carb tummy again?' She couldn't be pregnant when Scarlett was supposed to be the pregnant one.

'Ha ha. I've taken the test. It's official. Eight weeks today. Believe me, it was a surprise to us too!' Gemma noticed her sister's tears. 'Scarlett? Are you okay?'

She absolutely could not say anything about her and Rufus trying. She'd only steal Gemma's thunder and shift attention to herself. And she definitely did not want that. 'I'm just overwhelmed by the news,' she said. 'Though I do feel a bit warm, actually. Maybe I am coming down with something.'

A blanket of jealousy enveloped her so quickly that it was suffocating. She actually hated her sister at that moment. So much that she didn't want her to be pregnant. How could she feel like that? She loved her sister.

No, she hated her.

Rufus moved to her side. 'Are you okay?' he whispered as the family circled Gemma and Jacob.

In those three words, Scarlett heard the old Rufus.

The Rufus she loved more than anything. She'd missed him so much these last months. 'I will be,' she said. ''Scuse me a sec. I just need the loo.' She would *not* cry in front of everyone. It would only ruin everything.

As she made her way towards the stairs, she heard Rufus say, 'Shit, my phone. It's in the car. Be right back.'

He caught up with her halfway up the stairs. 'Scarlett, hold on,' he whispered. 'Come here. Come here.' Gathering her into his chest, his arms tightened. 'I'm sorry. I know,' he murmured into her hair. 'But you've got to keep thinking that this will happen for us too. And then how great will it be? You've got to hold on to that. You *will* get pregnant.'

His words comforted her. They also helped take some of the sting off what he'd said earlier. He wasn't going to give up just yet.

'It's not fair!' she said. 'They weren't even trying.'

She felt him nod. 'I know,' he said. 'Fucking lucky bastards. You're right, it's not fair. Fate is an arsehole.'

'She's a total bitch. Rufus, this sucks. I'm supposed to be happy for my sister.'

Then he tipped her face up until she met his eyes. 'Stop with the supposed-tos, darlin'. You'll only drive yourself mad. You *should* feel whatever you feel. It's okay. I'm just sorry I haven't been able to give you what you want yet. What we want.'

They clung to each other on the stairs while Scarlett's family celebrated what she and Rufus couldn't have.

The next morning, Scarlett couldn't stop shivering. Only her eyes were blisteringly hot. As her nose streamed, one limp hand felt beside the bed for the loo roll she'd staggered to find in the middle of the night.

Being ill did nothing to distract her from Gemma's news, though. It just gave her another reason to feel sorry for herself.

'How are you feeling, darlin'?' Rufus set a steaming mug of coffee beside her and rubbed her back.

'I'b so sick!' she honked. The flu had come on so fast that she didn't even have time to wheedle for sympathy. One minute they were driving back from her dad's and the next she had the plague. 'I can't do the classes today.'

'Definitely not. You've got to stay in bed and rest. I could ring in if you want, and look after you?'

She stared at her husband, her mouth open so she could breathe. When she inhaled through her nose, her nostril whistled. He really did love his feverish, dribbling, slack-jawed wife. 'Would you?'

'Of course.' He kissed her in spite of the dribble. 'I'll ring them now. Stay in bed and drink your coffee. Can I make you some toast?'

'Do thanks, I'b not hungry.'

'I'll go out and get some more food anyway. What might you want for later? Name it, anything you like. I can even get the pasta maker out for some fettuccini action.'

'It's like my last meal on death row,' she said.

'I hope not. I couldn't lose you.' He took her chin in his fingers and kissed her again.

They both heard the dogs whining at the bedroom door. 'We can't keep them out forever,' Rufus said. 'You know they'll make us pay for it.'

Fred and Ginger bounded through the door when Rufus opened it. They were unfazed by their owner's decline. Their little legs were too short to get them onto the mattress, though, and Scarlett dozed off again with one hand over the side of the bed to pet them.

Later, she awoke to find Rufus lying on the floor beside the bed.

'What are you doing?'

'Your dogs found the loo roll,' he said, gingerly scooping up a wet white lump with kitchen roll. 'I think they got most of it out of their systems.'

She drifted back to sleep, thinking of loo roll and babies.

Chapter 13

'Scarlett sends her apologies again,' Rufus told Shannon as he kissed her flushed cheek. 'She couldn't even get out of bed today, she's been so ill. But she promises she'll see the show before it ends. It doesn't look like you're short of admirers anyway.' He scanned the packed room where artists, their friends and families and, Shannon hoped, a few real clients milled around clutching glasses of warm Pinot Grigio.

She didn't need to tell him that the crowd belonged to other students. Rufus knew all the same people she did. Her family and a few of their school friends had already come and gone. Maybe she shouldn't have rushed them out like she did, but it was for their own good. There was only so much polite talk about student artwork one should be expected to make.

'Poor Scarlett!' Shannon said. 'It sounds like she

went down like a ton of bricks. It was kind of you to come, though.'

'A huge art lover like me? I wouldn't miss it.'

'You're a liar,' she said. 'But I appreciate it.'

He scanned the abstract paintings in front of them. 'These are really good. Did you use a brush? The paint looks trowelled on.'

Shannon glared at him.

'I don't mean trowelled on like your make-up!... I mean like *one's* make-up. You don't even wear make-up. I just mean I can't see any paint strokes and it looks too thick for a brush.' He glanced over his shoulder. 'Should I just go now? I can show myself out.'

'It's acrylic and palette knives, you cretin. That's why it looks trowelled on.'

'I do like the colours. They're not garish like those cheesy paintings they put in cheap hotel rooms.'

She followed his gaze as it wandered to her fellow student's neon street scenes. They were definitely garish.

'I suppose that's a friend of yours,' he said.

'My fiancé, actually,' she quipped. 'He painted his way into my heart with those neon acrylics and now we're very much in love. We spend our weekends together touring Holiday Inns to admire the art.'

'Just don't tell Mr Darcy,' said Rufus. 'He'd never get over the heartbreak.'

They laughed over the Mojave Desert that was Shannon's love life.

Then Rufus said, 'Guys should be falling at your feet.'

'Tell that to the world.' It came out more harshly than she'd meant, but hooked-up people were always making those kinds of announcements. What they never considered was that if guys *weren't* falling at her feet, there must be a reason. And it might not feel exactly comfortable to wonder if it was her. 'Unfortunately, the guys I know aren't usually in the market for a girlfriend. If they're not gay, they've already got someone, or they don't know I'm alive.'

'But why not, Shannon? That's what's always bothered me. I mean, look at you. You stand out in a crowd. In a good way. It does make me cross that a woman like you doesn't have someone who worships her. You're so easy to get on with, and I'm not just saying that because we're mates. You're funny and smart and nice and so relaxed. You're great to spend time with.'

He was just being nice, of course.

She spent the rest of the show avoiding eye contact with anyone she didn't know. She nearly fainted every time a stranger approached her paintings. *Please don't talk to me*, she thought. In theory it was fine to create art for other people's enjoyment. But what if they didn't enjoy it? What if they sneered or muttered about a lack of originality, or talent? She'd rather not know, thank you very much.

'Shannon!' Julian sang later, when he finally broke off from holding court on the other side of the gallery. 'You're coming for drinks, yes? It's nine o'clocktail!' He did a double take when he noticed Rufus. 'The delectable Rufus! *Enchanté*.'

Rufus just barely missed being kissed on the mouth. 'Nice to see you again, Julian. Has the night gone well for you?'

'I've sold three! And they were the expensive ones too.' He held his hand over his mouth to speak. Shannon and Rufus leant in to hear him. 'They're the ones I put the price up on. The punters think they're worth more now!' When he threw his head back to laugh, the diamante choker at his neck sparkled. He was channelling Audrey Hepburn, demurely dressed in a vintage black dress with his dark hair in a man bun. 'So… drinks, yes? You too, Rufus, of course.'

'Sure, I'll come along. Let me just ring Scarlett and see how she's feeling.'

Julian put his hands over his heart. 'Such devotion. The good ones are always taken.'

Shannon rolled her eyes.

'Don't feel obliged to come,' Shannon told Rufus after he'd hung up with Scarlett. 'You probably want to get home.'

'No, actually I really want to. And drinks are on me tonight, by the way. You're celebrating.'

'I wouldn't say that too loudly,' she warned. 'The other students will be on you at the bar like a pack of hyenas.'

The bar was one of those places that tried being all things to all people – café, bar, laptop doctor, beard-trimming parlour and dog groomer, that sort of thing.

The huge, bright loft-like space was strewn with Formica tables, stackable wire chairs and millennials. Like ants sent out into the forest, everyone in the group foraged until they'd found enough chairs to spill out into the aisle.

'A normal bar wouldn't let us be fire hazards like this, but I guess as long as we're all drinking. If you're going to the bar, I'd do it quick,' she whispered, 'before the others catch on.'

Too late. Julian was suddenly at her side. He'd changed into frayed boyfriend jeans and a form-fitting blue and white striped T-shirt. 'Catch on to what?'

'Drinks,' said Rufus. 'Can I get you one?'

Shannon noticed a few heads turn their way. *Don't*

make eye contact, she willed him.

'Something fruity, please,' Julian answered. 'Surprise me, as long as it's non-alcoholic.'

Julian watched him weave his way to the bar. 'Exactly how happily is he married, darling? Surely he's too adorable to be off the market. He'd be perfect for you.'

'Yeah, right, except that he's my best friend. As is his wife... that's his *wife*, Julian. Don't be such a homewrecker.'

'I'm just looking out for your needs, darling.'

'I don't have needs.'

'You don't?'

'Nope, not me, none. I'm like a self-cleaning oven. No upkeep required. You don't need to worry about me.'

'Well, just remember. It's not healthy to self-clean for too long.' He looked towards the bar. 'She didn't take long.'

Rufus was chatting with a Marilyn Monroe lookalike. She stood about a foot too close and kept touching him when she laughed.

Roxy the Rocket, their class's very own man-eater. She'd been round the campus more times than the Domino's delivery guy.

'Should we save him?' Julian wondered.

'Save him? We're not twelve.' She looked again. 'He's coming back.'

'So is she.'

Sure enough, Roxy had wriggled her way in front of Rufus to be sure he got a look at her best side.

Shannon looked pointedly at the three chairs they'd gathered as Rufus handed out the drinks. *Count them, Roxy*, she thought. *Three chairs, not four.* 'Hi, Shannon!' Roxy made a big show of kissing her on both cheeks like they were friends.

She seemed to be accepting an invitation that hadn't been made, the trespasser.

'Rufus was just telling me about your paintings,' she said. 'I'm afraid I didn't see them, but I'll be sure to have a look tomorrow.'

Like her own work was so mesmerising that she couldn't tear her eyes away to notice anyone else's. She hovered beside one of the empty chairs, making Shannon feel increasingly awkward.

Finally, Rufus said, 'Sit, everyone. I'll grab another chair.' He set both his pints down – he wasn't joking about cutting loose.

Roxy deftly shifted the woman beside her out of the way to make room for Rufus when he returned. Shannon caught Julian's did-you-see-that face.

'Roxy was just telling me she sold all her paintings tonight,' Rufus said. He gulped down most of the first beer.

'It helps to know people.' She even mimicked Marilyn's breathy voice. Shannon thought she sounded like she needed an inhaler. 'How did you do?'

'Okay,' Shannon murmured, watching Rufus start on the second pint. 'I guess you had a lot of friends there tonight?'

Roxy nodded. 'A few friends, but mostly prospective clients. I'm building up my private client list so that I can sell my works exclusively.'

When she re-crossed her legs and swivelled towards Rufus, the skirt of her electric blue dress rode up her thigh. The sight wasn't lost on him. He took another gulp of his beer.

'If you'd like to be on my list,' she breathed at him, 'I can take your contact details. Or you could have mine.'

'I doubt I know enough about art to be one of your clients.'

'But you do know what you like, don't you?' she purred, looking deep into his eyes.

It was like watching a car about to skid on black ice. Rufus was her friend. Rufus was her friend's husband. Rufus wasn't available as Roxy's next conquest.

What would Scarlett do in the same situation, if she saw a woman making a play for Mr Darcy (assuming Shannon had more than a stalking relationship with the poor man)? Scarlett was fearless. She'd probably knock Roxy off her chair. Shannon bit back a smile imagining that.

'I do know exactly what I like,' Rufus told Roxy, leaving the statement hanging in the air.

Roxy smiled. 'Well, then, you'd better give me your number.'

Shannon cleared her throat. Roxy faltered before pretending she hadn't heard, but Rufus looked her way. 'Scarlett's got good taste, though,' Shannon said to him. 'That's Rufus's wife, Roxy.'

Rufus seemed to snap out of the spell. 'She definitely has good taste,' he finally said. 'And as for what I like, I'd have to go with Shannon's paintings. I love how she uses palette knives.'

Shannon let out the breath she hadn't realised she was holding. What the hell did he think he was playing at?

Roxy lost interest in hanging around Shannon and Julian once she figured out she wasn't going to collect Rufus as an admirer. The tension seemed to ease from them all when she left. But seriously, what was that?

It was after eleven by the time they slumped into a taxi together from Reading station. Shannon felt relaxed for the first time in weeks. She'd survived opening night.

'You'll be okay getting into the house?' she asked.

'Aw, yeah. I've got my keys—' he patted his pocket '—right here. Scarlett'll let me in if I lose them between here and the front door. But I'm not that hopeless.'

He kissed her on both cheeks, then drew back a bit unsteadily to look at her, but he didn't say anything more. He just smiled.

Chapter 14

Even though she still felt like death warmed up, Scarlett couldn't face staying in bed any longer. She'd been mummified in her duvet for most of the week. She needed airing out as much as her bedclothes did. Rufus, bless him, had made sure the fridge was stocked with food, and milk for coffee, till he got home from work. She'd cancelled her training classes so there was no earthly reason to leave the house.

She was just sorry she'd missed the opening for Shannon's degree show. She'd make it up to her after her session tonight with Max and Murphy.

'You guys are going to think it's Christmas,' she told her dogs as she carried them off the train, one under each arm. 'We're having Italian food after this! You just need to help me with Murphy first.' They'd proved to be excellent stooge dogs at his last session. They weren't snappish like many of their breed, so Murphy didn't risk a nip when he got overly friendly.

She rang Rufus as they got into the park. 'Whatcha doing?'

'Just trying to think of another word for green.'

'You know how to live on the edge.'

'Don't I, though? Talk about playing fast and loose with the adjectives. Good thing I like my job.'

'It's the weekend. You promised to give yourself the day off.'

'I'm not working, really. I just got thinking about it and figured if I could find another word…'

'Chartreuse?'

'Nice one, but not in context.'

'Emerald? Lime? Aquamarine, aqua, sage, verdant?'

'Have you got a thesaurus with you or something?'

'Just a bigger vocabulary,' she teased. 'I may be late back after dinner. I've got the dogs with me so don't think they've been kidnapped when you get home.'

'How much do you figure they'd go for, ransom-wise? Ten quid or so?'

'Maybe for the pair.'

She was tempted to tell him not to fall asleep before she got home, wink wink, but it sounded too premeditated. That was the last thing she wanted. As much as it hurt to be called Rufus's organ grinder, she *had* been over-the-top about the whole process. Why wouldn't he think going to bed with her was about as appealing as his dental check-up? They needed more spontaneity in their love life, not less. She'd be sure to plan that in.

'Alright, Scarlett, are you feeling better?' Max called when he saw her coming up the park path.

'Yes, thanks. Taking a few duvet days did me good.' She pulled a Kleenex from her pocket to give her nose a honk.

Murphy was ecstatic to see Fred and Ginger again. He ran in circles around Max with his hind end tucked in. *Chase me, chase me, chase me on the grass, come on, guys, chase me! I'm running, see? I'm running!*

Scarlett's dogs watched this enthusiastic display with their usual detachment. *Run yourself silly if you must, but don't expect us to follow you. We're mostly here for the meal after.*

Max found Bunny Wabbit in his bag. That stopped Murphy in his tracks. His tail wagged madly at the prospect of being reunited with his best friend.

But even with Bunny Wabbit in his mouth, Murphy considered his options, glancing from Fred to Ginger. A Westie sandwich didn't seem out of the question.

Then he got a better idea. With a playful woof, he leapt at Scarlett. Unfortunately, Max didn't have his lead gathered in tightly.

Murphy made his affection clear. 'Max, could you get between Murphy and me so you can guide him away?'

To be fair, Max only did what he was told. Murphy found himself cut out of the coupling, replaced by Max. His hulking frame enveloped Scarlett.

'Erm, Max? I didn't mean for you to hump me instead.'

'What? Oh, fuck, of course.' He jumped away. 'I wasn't, really.' He reached over clumsily to brush off her thigh, which just made things worse.

'I'm sorry, this is a nightmare.' He turned to his dog and whispered, 'This is all your bloody fault.'

Murphy wagged his tail.

She waved away his apology. 'Just remember to distract Murphy.' She wondered how to distract Max, whose face glowed with embarrassment.

She didn't need to worry. As they practised keeping Murphy off the other dogs, he told Scarlett about the latest woman he fancied. The more he talked, the more she got the feeling that he was no stranger to the flush of new romance.

'Her name is Violet. Isn't that a beautiful name?' If he was a teenage girl, he'd have doodled their names together on his hand.

'Those old-fashioned names have made a comeback.' She and Rufus liked the classic names too. They'd tried out a bunch, back when they believed they'd have a reason to use one. Though Scarlett wasn't so sure about Violet. It sounded like a great auntie's name. She could end up in a knitting circle with an Ethel and a Maude.

'She's as beautiful as her name,' Max gushed. 'I can't wait to meet her.'

'But if you haven't met yet, how do you know she's beautiful? And watch Murphy. He looks like he's getting ideas.'

The dog was walking behind Max, eying a bit of calf-porn.

'I've seen her photos. We're perfect for each other. I already know I'm going to love her.'

As Max went on, Scarlett saw that he wasn't exaggerating. He really would love this Violet person if she'd let him. He seemed to be able to overlook flaws the size of the Grand Canyon when it came to romance. 'Just don't get too far ahead of yourself,' she said. 'At least don't fall in love till you meet.'

'Too late!' Max sang happily.

Scarlett didn't have the heart to burst his bubble. Besides, who said level-headedness was better than impulse? She was in no position to dish out advice about relationships.

Barkley and Charlie were a few minutes early for their session. Barkley's chin was inches from the grass. *All the better to eat you, my dear.*

'Don't mind us!' Charlie waved from the edge of the field. Scarlett and Max kept jogging with Murphy. He could just about hold it together when walking, but speed turned him on.

'I think that's enough for today,' Scarlett wheezed, pulling another wad of Kleenex from her pocket as they started towards Charlie. Her cold medicine was wearing off.

Barkley sniffed curiously at Bunny Wabbit, wondering if the fact that he was clenched in Murphy's jaws meant he was edible. Meanwhile, Murphy sized up Barkley's potential for a quickie before they headed off.

'Since I've got you both here,' she said, 'I was wondering how you'd feel about doing your sessions together? Both dogs could use the socialisation and I can't always bring Fred and Ginger.' She squatted down to give her dogs some attention.

'Sure, that'd be great,' Charlie said, stroking Barkley's head. 'Which time is better? I can do yours if you want.'

Max grinned. 'That'd be great! See you both next week, then. And hopefully I'll have good news about Violet!'

He hurried off to dream his Violet dreams so Scarlett and Charlie could begin.

'He's done a great job on the kitchen, you know,' Charlie said, watching Max go. 'The estate agent upped the sales price by five grand. She thinks it'll be a quick sale.' He didn't look very pleased about that. 'I could do with some more time. I think Naomi needs it. Though Hiccup did let me into her flat over the weekend. Then she pissed in my shoe.'

'I'm sorry.' Scarlett made a face. 'If it makes you feel any better, mine have done it when we've left them alone for too long.'

Fred and Ginger looked like butter wouldn't melt.

'Hiccup's a rescue dog,' Charlie explained. 'Maybe that's why she's so protective.'

Hiccup turned up at Naomi's brother's house one day and moved into their garden shed. But no matter how they tried to coax her in for a cuddle, she stayed out of reach. Only Naomi and her sister-in-law could get close to the dog.

Naomi's resolve to stay pet-free melted as she got to know Hiccup. She wasn't an emotional gusher like a Labrador or a golden retriever, and she came across like she didn't need anyone, but over time Naomi proved to her that she meant no harm, and Hiccup let herself be loved.

'Honestly, Hiccup and Naomi have a lot in common,' Charlie said.

At the end of their hour together, Scarlett left Charlie and Barkley to practise in the twilight. Barkley was still confounded by the snacks falling from the sky, but he was working out that it might somehow be related to Charlie.

Scarlett popped two more paracetamol and braced herself to meet Gemma. She wasn't sure how she'd feel seeing her pregnant sister. She knew how she felt *thinking* about her, though, and that was ugly enough.

She'd had nearly a week to wallow in the news since Gemma dropped the P-bomb. Feverish, delirious and stuck in bed, there was nothing else to do but poke and prod the sensitive spots to see how much they really hurt.

'Best not kiss,' Scarlett warned her when they met in front of Shannon's gallery. 'I don't think I'm infectious, but believe me, you don't want what I've got.'

'I'm just glad you're feeling better!' Gemma said. 'Hello dogs!'

Fred and Ginger wriggled for their auntie. She was grinning like the cat that got the cream. 'How do I look?'

She was pleased with herself all right. 'You look fine, why?' Scarlett examined the wool camel coat over Gemma's dress. 'Do you think something's wrong?'

Gemma laughed. 'You and Jacob! It's very sweet that you want to wrap me in cotton wool. Nothing's wrong, and you don't need to fuss over me just because I'm pregnant.'

'I wasn't,' Scarlett said. 'I meant do you think your outfit looks weird or something?'

'No…' Gemma stared down at herself. 'Why, do you think my outfit looks weird?'

Scarlett sighed. 'I told you, you look fine. Let's go in. Shannon's inside already.'

Gemma grabbed her arm. 'What is wrong? And don't say nothing. I know you.'

Scarlett looked into her sister's worried face. *You haven't got the first idea about me,* she thought bitterly. *Look at you, with your glowy complexion and list of things you can't eat now and that little baby inside you, like it's the easiest thing in the world. You have no idea.* 'There's nothing wrong, Gemma. I've just been in bed for the last week. I'm sorry if I'm not jolly enough for you at this very second.'

Scarlett's snarky retort seemed to satisfy her. 'I'm sorry. Of course.' She tucked Scarlett's scarf into her coat collar. Scarlett pulled it out again. 'We don't have to stay out late. I'm exhausted these days anyway. This pregnancy stuff is no fun!'

You should try the alternative, thought Scarlett. *It's not exactly a barrel of laughs from where I'm standing.*

Something had turned sour in her. It wasn't only that she wanted what Gemma had. Everyone felt envy at one time or another. She'd coveted everything from handbags she'd spotted on the Tube to Scarlett Johansson's cleavage. And feeling anger, well, that was normal too. Nobody liked being denied what they wanted.

But this was much worse than that.

She didn't just want to be pregnant like Gemma. She wanted Gemma to be unpregnant. She wanted it so badly that she nearly choked on the bitterness.

'Right, do me a favour,' Gemma said, oblivious to her sister's mental sabotage. 'Don't mention the pregnancy to Shannon yet. Only our nearest and dearest know.'

Her words pricked Scarlett's conscience. She wouldn't wish herself on her worst enemy, let alone her sister.

Shannon turned a deep shade of pink when she saw them. 'You really didn't have to come!' she said, kissing their cheeks. If Gemma noticed that plague-ridden Scarlett let Shannon come within five feet, she didn't say anything. 'We could have met at the restaurant.'

'I want to see your paintings!' Scarlett said. And she really did. Despite being friends for almost five years, she'd only seen a few of Shannon's pieces. 'Rufus raved about them, you know.'

Shannon flushed deeper. 'He was just being nice.'

'I'll be the judge of that. Let's see them.'

'They're not square,' Shannon said as she led them to the opposite side of the gallery.

'Squares are for losers,' said Scarlett. 'These are beautiful. Really, they're so good!' She noticed little blue dots on some of the cards beneath. 'Have you sold some?'

'Four. Can you believe it? Two are anonymous buyers!'

Scarlett gasped. 'It's Mr Darcy! No, wait. Does he know you're an artist?'

'No, and nor does he know my name or that I've got a degree show. Nice try, though.'

'Who, then?'

'I've no idea. I'm just glad they've sold.'

Shannon and Gemma were both on good form, but it was no use. Scarlett wasn't enjoying the night. She was too… what was it? Sad? No. Envious? That wasn't quite right. Pissed off. That was it.

They hadn't even been trying! Gemma and Jacob. Her pregnancy was an accident, like dropping a dish or stubbing a toe. No, those would be bad. As easy as walking into Selfridges just as they're handing out free Crème de la Mer samples.

So why not for Scarlett? There she was after nearly a year, throwing down enough folic acid to make her baby bionic, and still weeing on sticks in vain every month.

Shannon didn't seem to notice Scarlett's mood and if Gemma did, she didn't let on. 'It was great to have Rufus at the opening,' Shannon said as their main courses arrived. The Italian waiter made a big show of pointing his giant pepper grinder at them. He may as well just have unzipped his flies.

'You know Julian loves him,' she continued. 'Everybody did. Well, how could they not?'

The dogs shifted at Scarlett's feet under the table. The restaurant had welcomed them like long-lost friends. They even got their own bowl of spaghetti, though they were cross with Scarlett for having the waiter bring it without sauce or meatballs.

'I practically had to tackle one of my classmates to keep her from taking him home,' Shannon said.

'What?'

Shannon's hands flew to her mouth. 'That came out wrong! I didn't mean he was flirting. Not at all! She's the flirt. Shameless. Rufus was perfectly behaved.'

'Who was this woman?' she asked.

'Honestly, Scarlett, it was nothing.'

'Who is she, Shannon?'

'She's called Roxy and nobody likes her.'

'Except Rufus, clearly.'

'No! It was the other way around. I shouldn't have said anything. I guess… I guess I just thought it's nice to hear that another woman thinks your husband is hot, that's all.' She looked beseechingly at Gemma.

'It *is* nice,' Gemma said. 'It's flattering, right, Scarlett?'

'Well, that depends on the circumstances. I'm not crazy about this woman throwing herself at Rufus when I'm not there. Did she know he was married?'

Shannon nodded. 'Oh, yeah, I made sure I told her.'

Shannon told her? 'Rufus didn't tell her himself?'

'Scarlett!' Gemma said. 'You're making a big deal out of absolutely nothing. So what if someone flirts with

Rufus? He's a big boy, right? He can handle himself. You know he'd never let anything happen.'

Why was she being attacked when Rufus was the one flirting with strange women? The idea made her ill. 'That's not the point.'

'Well, what exactly is the point, then, do you mind telling us? Because you're making Shannon uncomfortable. Talk about shooting the messenger.'

Who did Gemma think she was to tell her how to feel about her own husband? Suddenly she was the expert on marriage just because she'd fertilised an egg?

'The point, *Gemma*, is that I can hardly get Rufus to look at me anymore, so excuse me if I'm not leaping with excitement when some stranger tries to get off with him.' She gulped the last of her wine and poured some more as Gemma and Shannon sat back in their chairs. 'You have no idea what's going on in my life, so just stop telling me what's a big deal. You don't get to advise on marital problems. You can't be an expert on that *and*...' She pointed to Gemma's midsection. 'That.'

Gemma shot her a warning look. 'Don't.'

'Don't what? Tell Shannon that you're pregnant? She's pregnant. Isn't that just great? It's just fucking great.'

Nobody knew what to do when Scarlett burst into tears. It wasn't the usual reaction to your sister's impending motherhood.

Finally, Gemma scooted round the table to hug her sister. 'You daft mare, what is wrong with you?'

'That's just it, I don't know!' she wailed. 'I have no idea what's wrong with me. I'm supposed to be pregnant by now. *I'm* supposed to be pregnant, Gemma. Not you!'

'But I didn't even know— You've been trying? Talk to me, Scarlett! How long?'

Scarlett sniffed. 'Eleven months.'

'I should leave you two,' Shannon said. She grabbed her scarf and started winding it round her neck. 'This is family stuff. You've got things to… I'll go.'

'No!' Scarlett said. 'Please stay. I need you.' That had never been truer than at that moment. She took a deep breath. 'I need you both.'

She wasn't sure whether talking would make her feel better or worse, but either way, she suddenly couldn't stop. All the hope and disappointment and worry poured out of her. She told them every last detail, from the first happy month she and Rufus started trying through to the last wee stick she'd buried in the bin. She knew the time had come to get tested.

The idea horrified her. To know for sure seemed worse. She'd rather hold that tiny sliver of hope, even if it did cut her hand when it slipped away at the end of each month.

By the time the waiter tentatively slid the pudding menus into their huddled conversation, Scarlett was wrung out.

'Right, I know I shouldn't be angry with you,' Gemma began.

'You're angry with me?!'

'I am! Scarlett, how could you keep something like this to yourself? What on earth were you thinking, trying to go through this alone?'

'I'm not alone. I'm going through it with Rufus.' But that wasn't quite true, was it? Before they started trying, she'd believed he wanted a baby as much as she did. Sure, he was devastated every month when she told him they'd failed again. But he wasn't thinking about it nearly every minute like she was. He didn't feel sick with longing every time a woman walked past with a newborn nestled in the sling across her chest. He didn't avoid his favourite café because the entrance was blocked with prams that he'd probably never need. And he didn't hate every teen mum he saw with such ferocity that he sometimes had to stop himself from shouting in the stranger's face that it wasn't fair.

He wasn't the crazy one.

'I think I'm infertile,' she finally said.

As the words came out, she knew it didn't feel better talking about it. It felt like a terrible confession and there weren't enough Our Fathers in the world to give her absolution.

Now it was out there, officially, for other people to see, so it must be true.

Tears filled Gemma's eyes. 'I'm sorry I'm pregnant,' she whispered. 'When I think what you must have been going through when I told you. I wish I could take it back, or at least tell you in another way. I wish… It's still early. It might come to nothing.'

Scarlett stared at her sister. She was forcing Gemma to wish for a miscarriage to make her happy. What kind of monster was she?

'Don't talk like that, Gemma. I want you to be pregnant.'

She didn't, though. God help her, she really didn't.

Chapter 15

Scarlett was pretty sure she knew how Rufus would react when she told him what she wanted, but she couldn't let a little thing like absolute dread put her off. There might really be something wrong. Better to know and put them both out of their misery. There was just the small matter of his part in the process.

It took her most of the weekend and a few glasses of wine to work up the courage. *It's like dunking underwater*, she thought, *after wading in to the freezing part. On the count of three.*

One, two, three.

She didn't move a muscle.

Fine, then, the faster the better, like ripping off a plaster. Onetwothree.

Nope.

Super slowly?

Nothing doing.

Finally, while they sat beside one another on the

sofa with plates piled full of takeaway pad thai and green papaya salad from Chiang Mai, she plunged. 'I think we should get an appointment for tests with the GP.'

Rufus's fork stopped midway to his mouth. His eyes searched her face. He didn't need to ask what kind of tests. This was exactly the kind of pressure he'd said he didn't want. But what was she supposed to do? They desperately needed a way forward. 'I just think… we should. They're only blood tests for me… it's a little more invasive for you. I'm sorry.'

He shrugged. At the idea or his involvement in it? Either way, it didn't look like an outright no.

'You'll do it?'

'Why are you frowning at me? That's the same look you give me when I've done something stupid.'

She was frowning because this wasn't the reaction she'd expected. 'So, you will do it?'

'You mean me and a stack of porn in the broom cupboard? I'm not crazy about it, but, for you, I'll spunk in a cup. I can handle it.'

'Literally. Ba dum bum.'

Setting down his dinner tray, he gathered her into his arms. She breathed deeply for the first time in hours.

'I'm sure there's nothing wrong,' he whispered into her hair. 'Sometimes it just takes people longer. Please don't worry, Scarlett. Even if there is some issue, and I don't think there is, then there'll be a solution. Whatever happens, we'll deal with it together, okay?'

When she let herself cry, it was with relief as much as worry. Rufus stroked her hair, clenching her with his free arm, until she dried her eyes.

Finally, they were starting to feel like a united front again.

She made an appointment for the end of the week.

The GP ordered blood tests for Scarlett and a little cup for Rufus. Doing something, anything, was better than doing nothing.

'Are you thinking about it?' Rufus asked her a few nights after the appointment.

'Constantly.'

'Me too. Worried?'

'Shitting myself.'

'Me too.'

As they clung to each other, it felt a lot like healing.

Rufus held her hand when she rang their GP's office. By the time she'd listened on hold to Elton John's 'Rocket Man' for the fourth time, her tummy was in knots.

But the receptionist wasn't to put them out of their misery. She said the doctor wanted to see them.

Scarlett didn't hear what Rufus said as she hung up. Her mind had already galloped ahead. It was familiar terrain, potholed with all the fears that had scarred her imagination for months.

'I said it doesn't necessarily mean bad news, darlin'. The receptionist isn't trained to explain tests, is she?'

'I guess not.'

'That's the only reason we need to go in. I'm sure of it.'

The confidence in her husband's face did make her want to be as hopeful. She smiled back. 'I guess so.'

The GP gestured to the chairs in front of her desk. Her salt-and-pepper hair was pulled into a loose ponytail and her round wire-framed glasses made her look more like an art teacher than a doctor. She had the same calm air of someone you'd want with you in a lifeboat. 'Thank you for coming in.'

Scarlett nearly said, 'Thank you for asking us' before she remembered that this wasn't a social call.

Rufus held her hand so tightly it was cutting off her circulation.

'I'm Doctor Figg. I wanted to talk though your results with you.' She didn't look at her screen, where Scarlett knew all the answers were. She must have memorised them in preparation for meeting them.

'I'm sorry they told you to ring for the results. I prefer to talk to the couples in person, since they're usually concerned that there's a problem. It's nerve-racking to get even good news over the phone.'

Rufus's grip loosened a bit. It could be good news, then. Maybe the ulcer Scarlett was working on would be for nothing.

'The blood test results came back just fine, Scarlett. Your FSH, LH and progesterone levels are normal, and the chlamydia test was negative.'

Rufus planted a kiss on Scarlett's temple. 'What are the…?' he asked.

'Tests?' Dr Figg finished for him. 'FSH measures Scarlett's ovarian reserve. It was six point two, which means she is still producing eggs. It's not a test of the quality of those eggs, just an indication of quantity. The LH, or luteinizing hormone, checks whether ovulation is occurring, and it is. The progesterone test is another way to look at ovulation, and that's normal too.'

'So that's good,' he said. 'That's great, darlin'.'

She saw the relief on his face, but she wasn't so sure they could relax yet. 'Just because my test results are coming back normal, doesn't mean I'll automatically get pregnant, does it? I mean, sometimes you don't know why a woman isn't getting pregnant, right?'

Dr Figg nodded. 'Nobody agrees on the exact percentage, but it's thought that ten to twenty per cent of infertility cases are unexplained by the tests you underwent. It could have to do with the quality of the eggs, which, as I mentioned, wasn't tested, or whether the hormones are sufficient for implantation, or any number of other reasons. But that's not the case here.'

'You mean our problems are explainable?' Rufus asked.

'I think so, yes,' said the GP.

Scarlett felt her tears welling up. All week she'd tried to think about the best-case scenario. Would it be better to know for sure what was wrong with her? At least then they might be able to do something about it. On the other hand, what if they couldn't? Then she'd rather cling to some hope for a while longer.

Her tears spilled over. This was it: the moment she might find out she couldn't have a child. She'd imagined the conversation a million times already. It always kicked her in the gut and viciously scrubbed out the future she and Rufus wanted.

She'd always assumed that one day she'd headline as a mother in the role of her life. Motherhood was meant to be part of who she was.

The issue was so tangled up in how she felt about herself that it wasn't easy to unpick. Did it make her feel like more of a woman? Or rather, did the prospect of infertility make her feel like less of one?

Despite what Rufus liked to think, her boobs weren't there for his amusement. They were part and parcel of the baby-making kit. She had all the equipment. What if she never got to use it?

She stared at the GP. She could intellectualise it all she liked, make bargains with Fate, whatever. This woman was about to tell her whether she'd ever be a mother.

'I'm sorry,' she said, reaching for the Kleenex on Dr Figg's desk.

'It's perfectly understandable,' she said. 'It's never easy hearing test results when you think something might be wrong.' She took a deep breath. 'Rufus, you'll be pleased to know that your chlamydia test also came back negative.'

He laughed. 'I should hope so!'

Scarlett squeezed his hand again as they shared a smile.

'So, as to the results of your sperm analysis, there are three things we look at under a microscope: motility, morphology and sperm count. Motility means how well the sperm are able to move.'

'Whether they're strong swimmers,' he said.

'Right. Morphology looks at the shape of the sperm,' she went on, 'which can affect fertilisation rates. And the last thing we look at in the sample is the sperm count.'

'And how'd I do?' Rufus asked. To the GP he probably sounded like he was enquiring about the lunch specials rather than their future, but Scarlett heard the wobble in his voice. He was trying to keep it together too.

'Now, I don't want you to worry too much yet, but there were no sperm detected in the sample. There can be several reasons for this, including a faulty test, so the first thing we'll do is get another semen sample, and I'd like to do some blood tests as well. As I said, please try not to worry, though I know that's easier said than done.'

Rufus blew out the breath he'd been holding. 'That sounds bad. Is it because of my underwear? It's true that loose is better, right? I could switch to boxers, or no underwear if that's best, or—'

'We're going to look at all possibilities,' said the doctor. 'A new semen sample and some more blood tests are the next step. Those can give us more information.' She turned to her computer to tap out the blood test referral.

'But how can that be?' Scarlett asked. 'He definitely... when we have sex?'

Dr Figg nodded. 'Ejaculates, yes, and that's semen. It's the carrier, if you like, for the sperm. You can only see how many sperm there are under a microscope.'

Scarlett knew there'd be lots of time later for all the discussion this news demanded, but right now she needed to say something to make Rufus feel better.

But what was she supposed to say? Could Rufus really have *no* sperm? No, the test must be wrong, like Dr Figg said.

That's what she told him when they were leaving. 'I'm sure samples get mixed up all the time, or maybe they left it out too long or something. You'll see, Rufus. It'll be okay.'

Did she believe that? She didn't know. Part of her couldn't reconcile her strong, gorgeous, and yes, manly Rufus with the doctor's results. And part of her, she was shocked to admit, kept thinking, *Thank god it's not me who's at fault.*

He was quiet as they left the GP together. Scarlett understood. She knew exactly how it felt to think your body was betraying your future.

'I could cancel my class tonight,' she offered.

'No, I don't want you to do that. I'm okay, really. We'll know more after the tests. There'll be a simple explanation, you'll see.'

He seemed to be telling himself that as much as

her.

'I love you,' she said as they kissed goodbye at the train station. She really didn't want to have to go to London, but she couldn't cancel on her puppies.

'Love you too. See you later.'

Thoughts churned through her mind all afternoon. Well, mostly it was just one thought.

Her ovaries worked! She'd been so convinced that she was deficient that she'd never stopped to think how she'd feel if Rufus was the one with the problem. As it turned out, the relief actually made her feel giddy. Because even though being an infertile couple would be heart-breaking – and she'd have to unpack that whole idea later if it turned out to be true – it was miles better than being the one responsible.

As ugly as that sounded, it was how she felt.

Scarlett heard Shannon's voice as she got back to the house after puppy class. 'I'm home!' Shannon and Rufus were perched on the kitchen stools with what was left of the chocolate cake Rufus had made. 'Are we having a party?'

'What time is it?' Shannon asked. 'I didn't mean to stay this long.'

'Time flies when you're having fun,' Rufus said, carrying their plates to the sink.

Shannon hugged Scarlett goodbye. 'I'm so glad your tests were good,' she murmured.

'Thanks,' she said. Rufus missed the look she gave him. On the phone he'd sounded like his normal self. All three times that she'd rung. But she wanted to look him in the eye to be sure.

She was looking him in the eye now. 'You told

Shannon about the tests?' she asked as soon as Shannon had let herself out. 'Don't you think it's... I don't know. Private, I guess.' It was still too raw, too intimate for Scarlett to want to share. Even with best friends. They needed some time alone, just the two of them, to process the news together. 'It's between us,' she said, knowing she wasn't conveying her feelings very well.

He looked confused. 'You're the one who told Shannon that you wanted us to get tested. Am I supposed to keep my results secret now? Are you that ashamed of me?'

'No, of course not! That's not what I mean. Rufus, I'm not ashamed of you at all. I just thought we'd go through this together right now, you and me, not with an audience. You can talk to whoever you want, if it makes you feel better.'

What kind of horrible person was she, telling him he couldn't talk to his best friend just because she wasn't yet ready to? 'I'm sorry,' she said.

'No, I'm sorry, I'm overreacting.' He put his arms around her. 'Blame the hormones.'

She giggled into his chest.

'Maybe that's why I'm shooting blanks.'

She stopped laughing.

Chapter 16

Shannon definitely hadn't planned on yesterday. Rufus wasn't usually even home when she got back with the dogs. She'd nearly had a heart attack when she let herself in and he'd shouted from the living room.

'How are my dogs?' he'd asked as they launched themselves towards the sofa like furry juggernauts.

'No, dogs, you're wet!' she'd scolded. 'Don't let them up there till I can dry them off.' She got a towel from the kitchen closet and made a grab for Ginger. 'I'd have rung the bell if I'd known you were in, instead of using my key. Your key. The key,' she finished lamely.

'Nah, don't worry. I came back after my appointment. It didn't make sense to go all the way back to the office.'

Ginger stood still for her towel rub. It didn't hold a candle to a tummy scratch, but it'd do till she could beg another one of those.

'I was just going to gorge on cake. Want some?'

She sized up Fred, who thought he was clever

staying just out of arm's reach. She threw the towel over his head, walked over and picked him up. Not so clever.

'Please stay,' Rufus said. 'Please.'

They were sitting for less than a nanosecond before Rufus launched into the GP's appointment. 'No sperm were detected,' he said quietly. 'None. Not even one little trier. I am completely and totally impotent. Devoid of seed. A non-father forevermore.'

What an ugly word. Im-potent. Lacking potency. Powerless.

Wait a second, though. Was that the right word? Shannon thought impotent meant he couldn't get it up. Was that an issue as well? Crikey, she did not want to ask.

'I'm guessing from your silence that you're as shocked as I was.'

'No, not shocked. I'm just trying to figure out the right thing to say. So you *can* get it up?' Just to clarify the situation.

'Jesus Christ, Shannon, don't you think that's a bit personal, even for us?'

'I'm just saying that no sperm is different from being impotent. I'm pretty sure that impotent means little Rufus isn't rising to the occasion.'

'Little Rufus?'

'Or whatever size Rufus you prefer. That's not information I ever want to know, by the way. All I'm saying is that there's no reason to feel worse about it than you already do, right? If everything else functions okay, then that's good. The doctors just need to figure out the sperm thing.'

'Just, Shannon? It's not that easy. I've been googling it.'

'Oh, you haven't. Nothing good ever came from googling medical conditions.'

'I know, but I just feel so—'

'Impotent?' She risked a smile.

He laughed, then said, 'I can't believe I'm laughing about this.'

'Sorry, should I not make jokes?' This was new territory for them both.

'No, don't stop. It's exactly what I need. These past months have been so bloody serious, I can't tell you. I'm fed up with it all, to be honest. It seems like the only time I have fun anymore is when I'm with you.'

This was an uncomfortable conversation and not only because Shannon felt disloyal to Scarlett for having it. Scarlett and Rufus were her touchstone for relationships that could go the distance. If they couldn't make it, what chance did anyone else have? 'You're not thinking straight, Rufus. I know you have fun with Scarlett, I've seen you.'

He shook his head. 'There's always an underlying current, even before these tests. Earlier on when we weren't getting pregnant it felt like a failure. Now it still feels like a failure, only it's my fault, so I'm the failure. I can see it every time she looks at me.'

His face crumpled so suddenly that at first Shannon thought he was going to sneeze.

'I'm sure that's not true!' she said desperately as tears slipped into his stubble. 'She loves you. You love each other. You'll get through this, I promise.'

He shook his head and sighed loudly. 'Thanks, Shannon. It's all been a shock, you know? I'll try not to be all doom and gloom about it till we know for sure. This wasn't what you expected when you dropped the dogs off, was it? Sorry 'bout that.'

'No, that's okay.' What were friends for?

'At least stay for a bite to eat. I'll cook us

something.'

Hours later, Scarlett came home to find them in the kitchen.

Shannon rang Scarlett the next morning. 'What's your day look like? Are you around later? It's just that I could use some advice about the pugs.' She might not make time for herself, but Shannon knew Scarlett would always clear her diary for the business.

'I've got puppy classes this morning and Max and Charlie from six. Afternoon works for me, though.'

That's perfect, thought Shannon. 'I'm picking them up at two. I could meet you at the park at around ten past?'

She felt like James Bond. Or Jane Bond. Anyway, she had a secret mission: Operation What The Hell Is Wrong With My Friends.

She had to hurry to Sampson's house. She liked to show her face before the owners left for work. Otherwise they suspected she didn't get there till their pets were fit to burst.

She could hear Sampson's gravelly bark from the end of the road.

His owner opened the door. 'He's looking forward to his walk this morning,' she said as Sampson squeezed by her. 'Obviously.'

The dog ambled to the pavement in front of the house, sat down and stared at her with his droopy sad bulldog eyes.

By the time Shannon and Sampson got to the poodles' house, their owners were gone. The dogs had a little surprise waiting for her, though. The fruit bowl was tipped upside down on the kitchen floor, next to a carefully gnawed pile of skins and pits.

That was a lot of mango working its way through delicate poodle systems. 'You know you're going to pay for that in the park.'

No, their looks said. *But grab a few extra bags, because you will.*

They'd only just got inside the park gates when Fifi detonated. 'You couldn't even go on the grass?' Shannon muttered. The runny yellow grenade wafted its noxious fumes from the pavement. Stinkageddon.

She was just smearing up as much as she could with the plastic Tesco bags she had, when a shadow passed over her. She looked up, right into Mr Darcy's green eyes. 'Bad day?' he asked.

'Shitty, actually.' What did one do with a handful of diarrhoea in such a situation? 'The other one's going to go off any minute. Mangoes.'

'Ah. I'd offer to help, but it looks like you've got things in hand.'

She laughed, though she wasn't sure he'd meant to make a joke. 'Thanks.'

'Well, 'bye.'

''Bye.' He continued on with his greyhounds while she crept to a nearby bench. She'd actually talked to Mr Darcy! She hadn't been nervous at all. How could that be when she blushed at the supermarket when the clerk asked whether she wanted cashback? Was it because she'd been distracted by Fifi's outpouring?

Hopefully that wasn't the answer. She really didn't want to have a relationship that only worked when scooping up bowel movements.

A relationship. Imagine if that happened!

Sampson stared up at her with his tongue sticking out between his bottom two teeth. *Well done, lass. That was the hardest part.*

She rang Scarlett as she watched the poodles sniffing the low iron railing nearby. 'Hey, guess what just happened? I talked to Mr Darcy. I actually talked to him, and he talked back!' She could still hardly believe it.

'I've been waiting for this call for months,' Scarlett said. 'Finally! I need all the details, but I'm just about to start puppy class now. Tell me everything when we meet, okay?'

'Of course. I'll pick up the pugs and see you at the gate.'

Even the lingering whiff of poodle poo didn't dampen her smile as she tipped her face to the sun. Sampson laid down with a grunt and closed his eyes.

Now she had a new emotion to add to the anticipation that bubbled inside her whenever she saw Mr Darcy. She wasn't a hundred per cent sure, since she hadn't felt it in so long, but she thought it might be hope.

Shannon rang the bell at the pugs' house. 'They're nearly ready! I'm just looking for the golden tiara.' Anastasia swept off up the stairs trailing her jade silk dressing gown and four wrinkled dogs. It was the same routine every time Shannon arrived. Different accessory, same mad dash to find it.

Those poor dogs. As if pugs didn't look silly enough without being in costume.

That was what Shannon wanted to talk to Scarlett about.

'Here we are!' Anastasia said, holding the tiny tiara aloft. 'I knew I had one. Come here, my precious.' She scooped up one of the little black dogs. 'We're going with a tea dance look today.'

Shannon tried not to pull a face. 'Mm-hmm, very nice.'

Shaggy and Scooby, both fawn pugs, panted up at her. They weren't phased by the tartan tuxedo jackets or the straw hats they wore.

Daphne and Velma wore tulle dresses, one pink and one yellow, which shone against their shiny black coats. Daphne's tiara was a little crooked.

'Don't forget the cards,' Anastasia said. 'And tell anyone who takes a photo—'

'I know. Hashtag Supercalipugalicous.' She stuffed the business cards Anastasia handed her into her big bag. 'We'll be back in two hours.'

She closed the door on the crazy lady and led her dogs around the corner. 'Time for another costume change, boys and girls.'

They might have to look ridiculous at home but Shannon was boss in the park. She hated seeing animals in costume. Every year from Halloween through to New Year's she had to stay off Facebook to avoid seeing grumpy cats in Santa hats or dogs dressed as pirates. 'That's better.' Stuffing the tiny tuxedos and frilly frocks into her bag, she walked them to the park where Scarlett was already waiting.

'No outfits today?' Scarlett said.

Shannon answered her by opening her bag to unleash the pink tulle.

Scarlett picked out one of the dresses. 'Oh god, I see what you mean.'

'I just feel bad having walked them like that for so long before I got the nerve to take off those stupid outfits. These aren't even the worst of it. Sometimes they're the Spice Girls.'

Scarlett put her arm round Shannon's shoulders.

Because of their height difference, it was an awkward embrace. 'Don't feel too bad. It's the owner who should be ashamed of herself.'

When Shannon first met Anastasia, she thought what most people probably did when they saw her mad hair, kimonos and dogs. Another eccentric dog lover with too many photos of herself and her pets. But there was more to Anastasia than that. Her blog, for one thing. It was one of the most popular in the country and she posted photos and videos nearly every day. Shannon hated to think about how much she'd spent on costumes for the pugs over the years. Liberace's closet probably wasn't as full as Anastasia's spare bedroom.

Sometimes Shannon got the feeling that the dogs were more props than pets. 'Don't get me wrong,' she told Scarlett as they circled the park, 'they want for nothing. It's just that they're constantly being dressed up and filmed in weird situations. Last week she put them in a mini kitchen and had them pretending to bake tiny cakes. She called it the Great British Bark Off.'

Scarlett snorted. 'You've got to admit that's pretty good. Do you think she loves them? Do they get enough attention?'

Shannon wasn't quite sure how to answer that. 'She's definitely obsessed with them and her groomer is there nearly every day. Between the outfits and grooming and me, they're getting a lot of attention but, I don't know, it just doesn't seem like a healthy situation. I think Anastasia's the one really getting the attention. That blog is just a way to say *look at me* all the time.'

'Yeah, probably. Have you ever heard her shout at them, or do they seem fearful of her?'

'No, never. But isn't it psychological cruelty to make them wear those outfits?' She still had the scars from childhood when her mum had made her wear her cousin's hand-me-down dungarees. Her too-long arms and legs stuck out of them, earning her the nickname she didn't shake till college. Scarecrow.

'If there's any question about mistreatment,' Scarlett continued, 'I'll be the first one to ring the RSPCA. But as they're getting exercise every day and it sounds like they are well looked after, I think we should just keep an eye on things for now. You're doing the right thing, though. At least they can keep their dignity in the park.' She kneeled down to pug level as they wriggled around her. 'Who's who?'

'The boss-eyed black one is Daphne and the other black one is Velma. Shaggy is the bigger fawn one, and that's Scooby. Careful, he's a slobberer. They really are sweet dogs.'

Shannon had such a soft spot for little dogs. She'd always wanted one growing up, but she and her brother had to make do with their cat, Sniffles. Sniffles didn't even want to be a cat, let alone a dog, so he was pretty unsatisfying as far as pets went.

Scarlett brushed off her jeans as she stood up. 'I know this walk isn't really about the pugs.'

So much for Shannon's future in Her Majesty's Secret Service.

'Tell me everything about Mr Darcy,' Scarlett said.

'Only if you tell me everything about the fertility tests you and Rufus took.'

'That's extortion.'

'That's concern, Scarlett. I'm worried. This is hitting Rufus hard. I need to know how you feel about it.' It wasn't the first time that she'd seen Rufus cry, but he didn't usually let his feelings out quite so much.

'What time do you need to get the pugs back?'

'We've got plenty of time. What about you, Scarlett?'

At first, she didn't think she'd answer. That hurt. If the shoe was on the other foot, she'd tell Scarlett everything.

'I hate seeing Rufus so upset,' Scarlett finally said. 'I'm afraid of what'll happen if the tests come back with the same result. He's upset enough as it is. We both have to help him through whatever's coming.'

'We will,' Shannon said. 'He's my best friend. You both are. I'd do anything for you.'

Just as long as everyone stays loving and supportive, she thought. But what if they don't?

She supposed she'd always known that her social life was precarious. Growing up, it balanced on the rocky outcrop that was Rufus. They didn't need anyone but each other, friend-wise at least. Then he met Scarlett and Shannon's group of friends doubled all at once. But what if one of them started resenting the other, or worse, what if they started blaming? Then who was she supposed to side with?

Chapter 17

Things looked peaceful at Margaret's house when Scarlett turned up for their session. The front curtains were drawn closed and Biscuit didn't even bark when Scarlett rang the bell. That was promising.

She waited a few moments, listening for the shuffle of feet, before ringing the bell again. They'd switched to mornings, so maybe Margaret was having a lie-in.

No, there were footsteps. Margaret's son, Archie, flung open the door. 'Mum's not in, but you're welcome to wait. She should be back any minute.' He beckoned her into the hall. 'Would you like a drink?'

'No, thank you.' She followed him into the living room. The big flat-screen TV on the wall had the cricket on.

'If you'd like anything at all, just let me know. Please make yourself comfortable.' He settled on to the sofa while Scarlett undid her coat and found a chair.

Maybe Archie had a twin. One with his volume

turned

down.

They both heard a car pull into the drive a few minutes later. Archie clicked off the TV before bounding from the sofa. 'Excuse me, please.'

'Mum!' he bellowed. 'I'm late.'

Margaret hurried through the door after Biscuit. 'Hello, Mrs Deering, I'm so sorry! I meant to get back before you arrived.' She went to the windows and drew back the heavy curtains. 'Archie, it's so gloomy in here!'

'I've missed the first part of the match, thanks to you,' he said.

'I am sorry!' She glanced at the TV. 'Couldn't you have watched it on Sky?'

'Why don't I just sit at home then and watch Sky all the time, and not ever see my friends?!'

The little turd, thought Scarlett. He *was* watching it on Sky.

'All right,' Margaret said. 'Here are the keys. Will you be warm enough in that?' Her hand found the sleeve of his cotton jacket, but he pulled his arm away. 'Do you need some cash?' She pulled twenty quid from her purse. He stuffed it in his pocket on the way to the front door.

When Margaret slumped to the sofa her bright red wool coat rode up at the shoulders, engulfing her ears. She kept batting the collar away from her face.

'Don't you want to take your coat off?'

'Of course. What am I thinking? Actually, I don't really like this coat,' she said, taking it off. 'It's always shifting around or pulling in the wrong direction. I feel a bit like a letterbox in it. But Arthur gave it to me and he gets so sullen if I don't wear it.'

As if Margaret's wardrobe choice was a personal rejection. Arthur's ego had brittle bone disease.

When Margaret's phone rang, she stabbed at the

buttons. 'Hello darling?'

'Mum, this car stinks of dog,' came Archie's voice over the speakerphone. 'It's disgusting. Why don't you give Biscuit a bath?'

He hung up.

'I did, in fact,' she explained, putting her phone back in her pocket. 'We've just been to the groomer. She needed her glands done. I'm afraid Archie's right. She did stink up the car, but she's all clean now.'

Scarlett could see that. Biscuit's ears looked extra fluffy and she had the ever-so-smug look of a freshly washed dog.

'Would you like a drink?' Margaret asked. 'I'm going to make a pot of tea. Come into the kitchen. We never sit in here.'

She usually drank coffee now but she'd been raised by her mum on tea, so she didn't discriminate when caffeine was on offer.

Margaret bustled around the kitchen making conversation while she rinsed out the pot and gathered real china teacups and saucers. As she was reaching into one of the high cabinets, she knocked the sack of sugar. It hit the floor in a sweet tidal wave. 'Bugger. Do you take sugar?'

When Scarlett shook her head, Margaret nodded to herself. Then she scooped as much as possible from the floor back into the sack, picked out a few pieces of fluff, and swept the stray crystals into the bin.

'I don't understand how someone can be so polite to others and beastly to me,' she said, sniffing the milk before pouring it into a delicate pitcher.

'Ha, believe me, it happens to everyone.' Scarlett was thinking about the last week around Rufus. How could someone closer to her than anyone else in the world, who'd shared her most intimate moments, act like he didn't want to be in the same room? She thought she knew every facet of the man. This discovered fragment was painful to the touch, and she had no idea how to smooth it. She'd been cheery till her cheeks ached. She'd tried cajoling him out of his moods, despite feeling like shite herself. The more she tried, the more jagged his edges became. She just wanted to make him feel okay again. Then, maybe, they'd be okay again.

It wasn't that he wouldn't tell her what was wrong. Every day he told her. They shouldn't have taken those tests, he'd said. It was better not knowing.

Would he feel the same way if she'd been the one with the bad results?

'I try to make everyone happy,' Margaret continued, unwittingly echoing Scarlett's thoughts. 'But everything I say seems to set Archie off.'

Scarlett dragged her mind back to Margaret. This was her session after all. 'Maybe that's the problem,' she said. 'You're too nice for your own good.'

'I don't know how else to be,' she answered. She had, once upon a time she said, had her own mind. In that dim and distant past, she thought she might have been an outgoing young woman with some ambition. She'd be foxed if she could remember now what those ambitions were. Wife and Mother were the only titles she'd answered to for decades and she wasn't quite sure what had happened to the rest of it.

She glanced at Biscuit. 'Your whole family is a pain in the arse,' she said. 'And you. You're no better.'

Biscuit turned away to stare out the bifold doors into the garden.

The breeze had a warm edge as they worked together outside. The daffs and crocuses had given way to pink, purple, fuchsia and white stocks all along the borders. Their sweet heavy fragrance mixed with the scent of freshly cut grass. Margaret's was the kind of garden Scarlett had always wanted. She'd have to adopt Margaret to look after it, though. She was hopeless with plants.

'I've been practising all week, like you said, Mrs Deering. Watch this. Biscuit, sit.'

Biscuit gave Margaret the spaniel equivalent of a whatever-face. *What do I look like, your performing monkey? I think not.*

'Blasted dog. She did it before.'

'It takes time, but she'll get there,' Scarlett said.

'Well, I haven't got much time left. Oh, that sounds melodramatic. I just mean that, well, it's Arthur, you see. He says I've spoiled the dog. Honestly, I haven't, though. He thinks if I can't even get an animal to behave when he's paying for a professional trainer, well, then I really am hopeless.'

The more Scarlett heard about this Arthur, the more she wanted to strangle him. 'Margaret, take it from me, you are not hopeless. What proportion of dogs do you think I've met who don't listen to their humans? I'll tell you. A hundred per cent. If their dog minded them, then they wouldn't need my help. And if Arthur thinks he can do better, he should be here to try.'

'Oh, I'd love to see that!' Margaret said. 'That's not the deal with us, though. He's the breadwinner. I do everything else.'

Love, honour and do thy laundry, Scarlett thought. Margaret needed to renegotiate her terms.

They hadn't been training long when Margaret had to take a call from the caterer. Their sessions always seemed to be a series of interruptions with some training in between.

'Octavia.' She made a scowly face at her mobile, but her voice stayed perfectly reasonable. 'I thought the quote was £8.99 per head. I'm sure it was in your email... Oh. Really? Bowls? Are you sure they're more efficient than plates? I didn't think a serving table would be that expensive. Aren't they just folding tables? No, no, of course I'm not telling you how to do your job. It's just that we'd agreed a price and now it's not long till the party. I see. I guess I didn't read all the Ts and Cs. We do, Octavia. We're so grateful that you can do it for us. When do you need payment?' She sighed. 'Okay. I'll just have to explain the increase to Arthur. Hmm? Yes, I suppose I could just send it from my account. No, you're right. All right. Thanks ever so much again. Thank you. Bye.'

'Bloody caterers,' she said to Scarlett. Then she looked horrified. 'I'm sure they're very nice as people, though. It's just that I'm already at the top of our budget.'

'I know a good caterer,' Scarlett offered. 'We used a great company for my parents' anniversary party. Two sisters. I could give you their details.'

'Oh gosh, no, thanks ever so much. What would I tell Octavia?'

'You could tell her to get stuffed!'

Margaret laughed. 'I haven't got that kind of courage. I haven't even told Arthur about the other price increases,' she said. 'He'd be furious. Not at Octavia for the price rises, but at me for letting the budget get out of hand. It doesn't matter if she's taking advantage or that he keeps coming up with expensive new ideas and more guests who I don't even know. I just have to make it all work.' Not that her family had any confidence that she could do it.

'For once I'm not going to let them be right.'

'But if there's no more money?' Scarlett asked.

Margaret confessed that she'd been skimming off the house account to save up for the shortfall.

'The party's not till June and if I don't bankrupt us first, I'd love for you to come. I mean, of course if you're busy, or don't fancy it, I understand. It's just that it'd be nice to have another friendly face there.'

'I'd love to come, thank you.' Getting Rufus out of the house might show him that life did carry on in spite of his reproductive system. That was a lesson she'd had to learn herself months ago.

Chapter 18

Rufus was slouched on the sofa when she got home. The dogs were in position beside him. 'Killing the bad guys?' The video game was on.

'Mm.' He craned his neck when she stood in front of him.

'Glass of wine? There's that red that Shannon brought. I'm having one.'

He pushed pause on the game. 'Sure, thank you.'

The dogs followed her into the kitchen. 'I know you've eaten already,' she told them.

Ginger sat primly. Fred glanced at her and did the same, wagging his tail.

'Shameless.' Throwing them each a treat, she filled a wine glass, took a few big sips and topped it up. 'One for you and one for me.'

As soon as they'd swallowed their treats, they went back into the living room for more tummy scratches. Such fickle animals.

All the way home from Margaret's she'd thought about Rufus's reaction to the tests. God, she'd thought about nothing else for the past week! She knew first-hand what the idea of infertility did to someone's confidence.

Maybe he needed to be re-manned. Like being resurfaced, but with testosterone.

She kicked off her shoes. Then she unbuttoned her blouse and fluffed her hair. *Come on, you can do better than that.* Smiling to herself, she shimmied out of her jeans and peeled off her shirt. *You're not even trying.*

She walked starkers into the living room. 'Here's your wine.'

The dogs watched her standing there, but then they also followed her into the bathroom when she pooed, so a little nudity never fazed them.

Rufus, on the other hand, did a double take. 'You weren't training the dogs like that?'

'Mm-mm, I put my hair up.'

He smiled. 'I'd like to have seen that.'

She moved towards the sofa. 'You can see me now from the comfort of our sofa.'

A blast of gunfire erupted from the TV. Rufus dove for the off button. 'What's got into you?' He sat up straighter.

Sitting astride him, she leaned in to kiss his soft lips. He took her face in his hands. She sank so gratefully into the feeling.

'Dogs, go away,' he murmured when he came up for breath.

Scarlett could feel their soft fur on her calves, one on each side. They didn't budge. 'Dogs, go!' she said.

You go. We were here first.

'Put them in the kitchen?' she suggested.

He groaned. 'Do I have to move?'

She didn't want anything to break the spell, but she never liked Fred and Ginger to see them having sex. 'I'll go. Don't move.'

Carefully she picked them up, one under each arm, and hurried to the kitchen. 'Be good,' she said, throwing them a handful of treats and closing the kitchen door behind her.

Rufus hadn't moved, though his jeans were undone when she got back. 'That's cheating. I'm supposed to do that for you,' she said, suggestively she hoped. She'd never been very good at sex talk. She'd once had a boyfriend who kept up a running commentary in bed. She'd tried it a few times, but just ended up sounding like a conductor on the London-to-Reading commuter train. *The next stop will be foreplay in approximately six minutes. Please mind your step when climbing aboard.*

Sexy.

Kneeling in front of Rufus, she got his jeans off. 'Come back up here,' he said, gently lifting her shoulders till she was sitting on him again. He pulled his T-shirt over his head.

Despite being as gym-phobic as Scarlett, Rufus's body was toned. Plus, he had the smoothest skin she'd ever felt. She really wanted to feel more of it.

Pulling him sideways so they were stretched out together, she slid her hand down his chest to his tummy and into his briefs.

But there was no nice hard-on waiting there. There wasn't even a soft-on.

Scarlett tried not to squirm, but she hated touching a flaccid penis. When she and Gemma were children, Gemma had thrown an enormous slug into her hair. In her panic to get it out she'd squeezed the soft, cool moist animal in her hand. That was exactly how her hand felt in

Rufus's pants.

But she couldn't snatch her hand away. Rufus knew the slug story. He'd make the connection.

Suppressing a shudder, Scarlett redoubled her efforts. Rufus did too, it seemed. Within a few minutes things were moving again in the right direction.

'I want you now,' she said, stumbling over the uncharacteristic words. *Remember to keep your belongings with you at all times. The next stop is intercourse in approximately one minute. Thank you for choosing Southwest Trains.*

She pulled him on top of her, but no matter how he approached the situation, they couldn't get the party started. 'Hang on, let me move up,' she said. 'There, is that? How 'bout if I—?'

When they first got together he seemed to be always at attention around her. What a difference a few years made.

'No, stay there,' he said. 'Let me— I can— I just need to…'

But no matter what they tried, sex was not on the cards for them.

We regret to inform passengers that the eleven-fifteen express has been cancelled, and this is the last service for the evening.

She fought back her tears. His lips might have said yes, and his hands claimed he was turned on, but his genitals told the truth. Even naked in the comfort of their own living room, she couldn't get Rufus to have sex with her.

Her face flamed with shame at being so physically unwanted. Her very best wasn't enough for him.

'I'm sorry,' he whispered. 'I can't even— I'm hopeless.' His expression was thunderous.

His words cut through her humiliation. He must feel like a total loser too. Of course he was blaming himself. It probably wasn't the time to add to that.

'It's all right,' she said, stroking his hair away from his face. 'This happens to everyone when they're stressed.'

'Does it really?' he asked. His question was somewhere between a plea and a challenge.

'Oh, yeah, all the time,' she bluffed. She needed to relieve his worry. If she didn't, then she might end up with a garden slug in bed for the rest of their marriage. 'A lot, actually,' she said with a meaningful nod. 'It happens to me sometimes you know.'

He pushed himself up on one elbow. 'You're telling me you can't get erect.'

She thought fast. 'You know sometimes when I get up to go to the loo just before we…? I, erm, I add a little lubricant.' She shrugged like it was no big deal. Hopefully the room was dark enough that he couldn't see her blushing at the lie. As long as he didn't ask her to show him the lube. She really didn't want to have to repurpose her lip balm.

But he seemed satisfied with her answer.

'Could we just kiss for a while?' she asked him. 'You know I love how you kiss me. I could do that all night.'

That was completely true.

'Thank you, Scarlett. You're amazing, you know.' He pulled on his briefs, took her hand and led her to their bedroom. She respected his pants as the no-go area they obviously were and, with the pressure off, they explored each other's bodies till the early hours.

She woke tired, but happy. That had been one of the most sensual nights they'd had in months. Up, down, over, under, everywhere. She hadn't even gone to sleep properly on her pillow. For some reason she was halfway down the mattress with her feet hanging off the end. What a session. Smiling to herself, she turned over to face Rufus.

She came face to crotch with his erection.

He looked so peaceful sleeping. She listened to his deep, even breathing. Tentatively she reached over. Nope, she definitely wasn't dreaming.

His breathing quickened as she stroked him. He let out a little sigh as he started moving against her hand. His eyes were unfocussed when they opened. He smiled.

'Shall I?' Scarlett was so turned on that she might cry if he said no.

He answered by pulling her on top of him.

There were no slugs in bed that morning.

Chapter 19

Charlie and Max were already at the centre when Scarlett got there. 'Charlie's got an offer on his mum's house!' Max called when he saw her. He sounded as giddy as a schoolgirl. His bromance with Charlie was coming along nicely.

She reached down to give Barkley's head a good scratch. 'That's fantastic, congratulations.'

Charlie shrugged. 'The buyers are offering the asking price and they're not in a chain. The new kitchen really helped, thanks to Max.'

'It'll happen quickly, then,' she said. That should be good for Charlie's bank account, but she wondered what it would mean for his living situation.

As if answering her question, Max said, 'I've told Charlie he can stay with me if he needs to. I've got the whole house just for me and Murphy. It'd be awesome to have a housemate, yeah?' He pulled his sweatshirt over his head. The lipstick pink polo shirt underneath was wet around the neck and shoulders where the rain had soaked through.

'Nice shirt,' said Charlie, looking down at his own pink polo.

'Good taste, mate. Next time we should ring each other first so we don't look like twins.'

Charlie glanced at Max's arms bulging from his shirt, then at his own normal human-sized arms and tummy. 'We need name badges, it's such an uncanny resemblance.'

Scarlett scattered a few squeaky toys around the floor and got Max and Charlie to drop their dogs' leads to let them play. 'Charlie, whenever Barkley passes by a toy without picking it up, get in there fast with a treat. You've laid the groundwork for him to seek permission, so this is the next step. And Max, Murphy's going to get excited about playing with Barkley. Sorry about that, Barkley! When he looks like he's going to mount, say "Oops, time out", and lead him away to a corner to let him calm down. "Oops" can be your no-reward marker. It tells him that behaviour won't get him a treat.'

As they watched the dogs play, Max told them about his date with Violet. 'She wasn't quite my type so I don't know if we'll see each other again. Oops, time out!' He walked Murphy to the corner.

'Good. Give Murphy a minute to compose himself.'

Barkley watched his playmate go to the corner. He looked at Charlie. He looked at the squeaky toy and sat down.

Charlie threw him a treat. 'Well done, Barkley!'

'I feel like her photos might be a few years old,' Max said from the corner.

'How old was she?'

'Erm, I'm guessing maybe fifty.' He caught Scarlett's expression. 'It's all right, I'm talking to a few others online. I'll find my soulmate eventually!' He shrugged off the date, but Scarlett caught his hurt expression as he turned away. Poor Max.

As soon as Max let Murphy loose, he ambushed Barkley again, landing on him in a furry heap and panting with joy at the chance to show his affection.

That wasn't the reward Barkley had hoped for.

'He's not getting better, is he?' Max asked as he led Murphy to the other corner. He looked miserable. 'Every week I think he is and then he goes off on one again. He'll have to have the snip, won't he?'

'It's not a straightforward process, Max. We're training him, but he'll still be unpredictable sometimes. Just like people are. I do think we're making progress, so don't give up yet.' Scarlett would love to tell him it was going to be okay, but she didn't want to oversell the changes they could make. 'You should stay flexible about the options, okay? We've still got a few sessions to see how much he'll improve.'

She bet he wouldn't have the same objection to surgery on something other than Murphy's testicles. Women didn't feel their femininity threatened when their dogs were spayed. They just got on with it. Bloody sensitive men.

'Barkley is fixed, isn't he?' Scarlett asked. Maybe knowing Barkley was in the same knacker-free boat would make Max feel better.

'Mum had him done when he was a puppy. I wish his eating was as easy to fix.'

Barkley started licking the linoleum.

But Charlie had a bigger problem to worry about: the tightly-wound ball of furry hostility who turned up at the end of class with his girlfriend.

Scarlett could see Hiccup's flanks quivering with nerves and hear the little Jack Russell growling from where she stood.

'Naomi's giving me a ride home,' Charlie explained. 'It's okay, Hiccup.'

Scarlett couldn't just ignore Hiccup's distress. 'Naomi? It sounds like Hiccup is feeling stressed. That's why she's fidgeting and growling like that. She's trying to scare us off. Try backing her away a little bit. Don't pat her or talk to her. You just want to move her away from the thing that's making her nervous. When she calms down, give her a pat and lots of encouragement.'

Naomi led Hiccup back into the hallway. Her growling stopped nearly as soon as she turned away from them.

Scarlett still didn't get Naomi's appeal for Charlie. He was so friendly and she was so… not. There was nothing rude about her, but Scarlett had probably known warmer ice-cube trays.

Charlie offered Scarlett a ride to the Tube station after the session. 'It's still peeing it down,' he said. 'We can at least keep you dry.'

Hiccup growled at her all the way to the car.

'Do you mind sitting in the back with Charlie?' Naomi asked when they reached the old tan Saab. 'I'm not sure it's a good idea putting the dogs together in the back.'

Just try it, Hiccup glared at Barkley.

Barkley was all for riding in the back. When Charlie opened the door, he dove for the opposite side, where a vintage box of Kleenex lived. It was like his birthday and

Christmas had come all at once.

Charlie got in the other side to shift to the middle. 'Sorry, buddy, shove over.' He attached the dog seat belt and clipped Barkley in behind the driver's seat. Denied his Kleenex starter, Barkley settled for the next best thing.

'Barkley, leave the window alone, that can't taste good.' The glass was already opaque from previous saliva sessions.

Barkley wagged his tail. *What's taste got to do with anything?*

Hiccup glowered at him from her guard post beside Naomi. When she whined, Naomi reached over to scratch her shoulders. It calmed Hiccup. It seemed to calm Naomi too.

She shouldn't have rewarded the dog for being territorial, but Scarlett didn't say anything. Naomi wasn't a client, after all.

Barkley had stopped obsessing over the window to focus on the rubber bit where it slid into the door. Where others saw a mode of transport, Barkley saw a smorgasbord on wheels.

'He's not eating the door, is he?' Naomi called.

'No,' Charlie sighed. 'He's licking it. He thinks it tastes good.' He pulled a squeaky toy from his bag. 'Here, try this.'

Scarlett smiled. Charlie was definitely getting the hang of the training.

When Naomi stopped at the light, he reached between the seats to stroke his girlfriend's arm. It was a friendly gesture, but Hiccup launched herself at him. She was clipped in to her dog belt so she didn't get very far. But it was far enough to frighten a yelp out of Barkley, who'd forgotten there was anyone dangerous riding with them.

'I'm so sorry!' Naomi shouted over Hiccup's frantic barking. 'She thought you were coming up here, I guess.'

'No, it was my fault, I shouldn't have stuck my hand near her.'

'Don't be silly. It's Hiccup who can't behave.'

In the rear-view mirror Scarlett saw Naomi's eyes well up as they pulled away from the light. 'He's a friend, Hiccup. A friend. Why can't you understand that?'

Things were still tense when they got to the Tube station to drop her off. It would probably be a chilly journey home for the couple. 'Thanks for the ride!' Scarlett said. 'Charlie, see you on Thursday. Naomi, hopefully I'll see you again soon too.'

As she dug out her Oyster card and hurried out of the rain into the station, she realised she'd meant what she'd said. If anyone needed help with their dog, it was Naomi. If not for her own sake, then for Charlie's. Otherwise Charlie might end up living with Max after all.

Chapter 20

Scarlett and Rufus made their way to their GP's surgery. The weather seemed too warm, too sunny and pleasant for it to be one of those depressingly defining moments of truth. It was more like a day for a picnic. If they got the news they hoped for, then maybe she'd suggest one after their appointment.

Dr Figg wore the same owlish glasses and patient manner she'd had in their first meeting. Scarlett scrutinised her expression for any clues, but the GP was good at her game. She gave nothing away. 'Thank you for coming in. We've got all your test results back, Rufus, and they confirm the initial semen test.' Rufus grabbed Scarlett's hand. 'The condition is called azoospermia, which just means the absence of sperm in the semen.'

'So it's not a low sperm count?' Scarlett asked. Azoospermia. It sounded like an album U2 would have released in the nineties.

Dr Figg shook her head. 'No sperm were identified. Now, there can be a number of reasons for this, and many are treatable. It might be a transport problem, if the testicles are producing sperm, but they're not getting into the semen.'

'You're saying there could be leaves on the track?' Rufus asked.

'In a manner of speaking, yes.' She shifted a notebook to the other side of the desk and started drawing an upside-down willy. Rufus squeezed Scarlett's hand as she tried not to smirk. 'Sperm is transported from the testes to the urethra through these little tubes. A blockage can prevent the sperm from mixing with the semen before it leaves the body. And a blockage is treatable.'

Okay, that was good.

'Or it may be, for example, that there's a hormone imbalance affecting the production of the sperm in the testes.'

'And that's treatable too?' Rufus asked.

'Yes, there's a good response rate from hormone therapy. I want to refer you to a urology specialist, if that's all right?' She turned to her monitor to generate the referral request.

Scarlett studied the trays of blue-, yellow- and purple-topped test tubes on the corner of Dr Figg's desk. She tried to take in the news, but could only wonder what the different coloured tubes were for. So many possible blood tests. How many would Rufus have to take before they found an answer?

'And what about Scarlett?' Rufus asked as Scarlett stood to leave. She sat back down. Clearly, they weren't finished yet. 'How do you know there's not something wrong with her too?'

Dr Figg didn't flinch, though Scarlett did. 'Scarlett's initial tests came back normal, Rufus, remember? There's nothing at this point to indicate a problem.'

'But you said yourself that those tests don't measure the quality of her eggs, do they? So maybe that's really the problem. Or there could be something else wrong that you didn't test for yet.'

It was obvious from Dr Figg's tolerant smile that she'd heard protests like this before. 'Just because there's a problem, Rufus, doesn't mean there's anything wrong with you. I know this must be distressing to hear, but it doesn't mean there's anything wrong with *you*. You've got a medical condition, that's all. The urologist will do a complete physical examination. He'll run blood tests and additional semen tests to find out what's causing your azoospermia. Then together you can look at options for treating the condition.'

Numbly Scarlett left the surgery with Rufus clutching the urologist's referral letter. They didn't hold hands on the walk back.

Chapter 21

Shannon carefully peeled off Daphne's royal blue briefs and undid her cape. 'You'll always be my superhero,' she told the wriggling pug. The costume joined Shaggy's Spiderman outfit and Scooby's puffy green Hulk suit in her bag. 'Come here, Velma.' She peered into the dog's brown eyes. 'You actually look like you enjoy being Batman.' She couldn't leave the tiny clothes on, though, no matter what Anastasia would have liked.

Freed from the pressure of crime-fighting, the pugs squirmed and pranced underfoot. They didn't really need leads since they rarely moved more than a few feet from her. But they were only little dogs. A speeding bike could turn one into a pug pancake.

She checked her phone. No missed calls. She rang Scarlett again but it went straight to voicemail. What was going on with her? She'd been sure she'd ring straight after their GP appointment. That was days ago. It was

Rufus who'd finally rung her today, after his appointment with the urologist.

He'd only texted her in the morning to say he was going. 'How'd it go?' she'd asked.

'About as good as you'd expect when someone cuts off a bit of your bollock.'

'Ouch. Why did he do that?'

'Yeah, ouch. It's one of the tests.'

'Are you all right?'

'It's no picnic.'

'I'm sorry, Rufus. Can you sit on some ice or something?'

'That's supposed to make me feel better? I'm glad you're not my urologist.'

'Believe me, so am I,' she'd said.

She was so preoccupied thinking about her friends that Mr Darcy was nearly upon her before she noticed him. He wore a Pink Floyd T-shirt with his fleece tied round his waist. His greyhounds loped beside him, their sinewy legs ready to speed them across the park as soon as they were off their leads. Her gaze fell on her own charges, all of whom were standing on the sun-warmed pavement with their tongues lolling.

She caught his smile as she looked away from him. Was it for her? She glanced back at him just as she remembered she was wearing her dorky specs.

She couldn't snatch the glasses off now.

He half raised his hand. She half raised hers back, ready to fake an itch on her chin in case she was mistaken.

'Your poodles have shrunk,' he said as he approached.

'The wash was too hot.'

'Are they friendly?'

When she nodded, he knelt down to pug level for a scratch. As Mr Darcy sank his hand into the furry rolls across Scooby's shoulders, the dog wriggled so violently that he fell over. Soon they were all at it, tipping like dominoes. 'Not so steady on their feet, are they?'

The little show-offs. 'The first time they did it I thought they'd all had ear infections,' she said. 'Or strokes.' Anastasia taught them to throw themselves over like fainting goats. Now they did it for attention. 'If you stop scratching, they'll stop doing it.'

She risked another sneaky peek at Mr Darcy as he patted the dogs. His eyelashes were as thick and dark as they'd looked from a distance, and he had those big eyelids like the models in the eyeshadow adverts. She didn't need her specs to see that he really was gorgeous.

He stood up. 'I've seen you here before.' It was a statement.

He'd noticed her too. Unflattering visions played through her mind as she thought back over the last several months – scrambling across the pavement collecting the spilled contents of her handbag, toting piles of poo like office workers carried their takeaway lunches, and staggering through the park lugging a lazy drooling bulldog.

Neither of them seemed to know what to say. They watched the pugs circling round Mr Darcy's feet. She noticed that his T-shirt wasn't Pink Floyd. A prism shone through the silhouette of a cow's head. Dark Side of the Moo.

'I guess... see you around?' he finally said.

'See you.'

On the way back to Anastasia's she thought of at least half a dozen clever things she could have said to keep him talking. If she could have kicked herself and walked at the same time, she would have.

She tried Scarlett again after she'd dropped off the dogs. Finally, her friend picked up. 'Are you okay?'

'Fine, why?

'I mean after Rufus's appointment. And you didn't ring me back. Hello?'

'Sorry. He told you what the doctor did? He must be getting sick of blood tests.'

Shannon laughed. 'I wouldn't mind those as much as the examination!'

'I know. Worse than going for a smear test.'

'At least with a smear test they don't cut off a chunk of your testicle! I would have had a heart attack as soon as I heard the word biopsy… Are you in a tunnel or something? Scarlett?'

'No, sorry. He told you what the biopsy was for?'

'It's amazing that they can look for sperm like that, isn't it? Or maybe it's not. I'm no testicle expert. I guess you will be, though, before this whole thing is done. How are you feeling? I know how Rufus feels, but what about you?'

'I think we're in for a long road ahead.'

Shannon had no idea what to say to make Scarlett feel better. It *was* going to be a long road.

Chapter 22

A young woman answered the door when Scarlett rang Margaret's bell. 'Mummy's out the back.' Whereas her son Archie had Margaret's athletic build, her daughter was plump with wispy blonde hair cut into a lanky bob. She must favour her father, which made Scarlett even more baffled about the man's appeal.

Scarlett followed her through to the kitchen.

'Mrs Deering!' Margaret cried. 'You've met my daughter, Cleo?'

'Very pleased to meet you,' Cleo replied. 'It sounds like you're helping Mummy tremendously with Biscuit. Well done!'

She managed to make Scarlett feel welcome and talked-down-to all at once. She must get that from her father too. 'Margaret is doing really well with the training.'

'Thanks to you!' Cleo said.

'No, thanks to Margaret, actually. Training is only as good as the person spending time with the dog.

Biscuit's progress is all down to your mum.'

'Aren't you a clever mummy?' She kissed the side of Margaret's head. 'I'm off. Nice to meet you, Mrs Deering.'

Margaret stuffed a pile of whites into the washer beneath the worktop. 'Bugger,' she said, shaking the empty bottle of fabric conditioner.

'Oh, I never bother with that,' Scarlett said. It was enough that their clothes were clean. Often musty-smelling from a few days left in the washer, but technically clean.

'Arthur notices, believe me. It was on the list too, I just didn't have the cash.' She rooted around in the shopping bags on the table till she found what she was looking for. Popping open the lid on some hair conditioner, she squirted a blob into the washing machine.

'L'Oréal. Because he's worth it,' Margaret said, turning to fill the kettle. 'Tea, yes?'

Scarlett stifled a snort. 'Thank you. How has Biscuit been?'

'Do you know what? I don't want to jinx things, but she's actually listening to me sometimes.'

Scarlett returned her smile. 'That's because she's starting to see you as top dog. We'll reinforce that now, and we can work on any other behaviour issues she's having. The heavy lifting is done, so this is where we get to do the fine-tuning.'

'I'm really so grateful to you, Mrs Deering.' Margaret pulled an armload of washing from the tumble dryer and folded it as she talked. 'It's nice to have something going well around here. Archie's taken the car back to school and doesn't seem to want to return it, no matter how nicely I've asked. I know he wants his freedom, but I really do need that car.'

Scarlett looked around the large kitchen. Margaret had a lot of house to run. 'So how are you managing without it?'

'Supermarket delivery, and I've been taking taxis a lot, though there really isn't money for that.' She ran her hand through her hair. No matter how frazzled Margaret got, she always seemed to have time for her hair and make-up. Now knowing her a little bit better, Scarlett guessed that came standard as part of the Perfect Wife package. Peering at her own reflection in the bifold doors, she smoothed her hair.

Outside, Biscuit was still no model student, but at least she'd mostly stopped viciously barking whenever Margaret corrected her. 'From now on, Margaret, Biscuit will have to earn.'

'Great, we need all the bloomin' money we can get.' Biscuit nosed Margaret's hand. She patted the dog's head.

'Starting with attention,' Scarlett said. 'Whenever Biscuit wants something – a pat, a treat, her breakfast, a walk – I'd like you to make her sit. When she makes her demand, if you give in to her automatically then she'll still think she's boss. Okay? Let's grab some toys. When she reaches for one, make her sit before you give it to her.'

'Sit. Biscuit, sit. Sit, Biscuit. Sit. Biscuitsit.'

Biscuit stopped reaching for the toy in Margaret's hand and turned away from her owner in a perfectly executed snub.

But stubborn as she was, she was still a dog, and dogs liked to play. After a moment she made another bid for the squeaky orange turtle in Margaret's hand. 'Sit, Biscuit.'

The dog took her time, but eventually she did.

'Ooh, that's my bum ringing.' Margaret grabbed for

her phone as Biscuit chewed her squeaky turtle prize with delight. 'Hello, Octavia. Yes, it'll be painted by the weekend. I wasn't planning to… It's just that I didn't think you were setting up until closer to the party. It's still a month away. No, I know how busy you must be. Of course. Will all the tables be set too? I guess we could eat in the kitchen. Oh. The fishbowls as well? I sort of thought they'd just come on the night. How often will I feed them? Will you supply— No, of course. I can pick up some food.'

She put her hand over the phone, closed her eyes and took a deep breath. 'But that payment isn't due till after the party. I thought that's how catering worked. You're paid the final amount after you've done the catering… I'm sorry, I'm not trying to tell you how to run your business.' She listened to Octavia speaking. 'It's gone up by how much? Including VAT? Plus. I see. No, I didn't know about El Niño. It has that much effect on prices? I feel sorry for the farmers, then… How do they survive from wheat to wheat? No, you're right, drought is definitely no laughing matter.'

She looked completely downhearted as she hung up. 'Wherever am I going to find the money? And how the bloomin' heck am I supposed to paint our hallway by tomorrow?'

With a sigh, she sat heavily on the grass.

'Isn't the grass wet?'

'Yes, it is.' She sighed. 'I can't do anything right. I can't even sulk right.'

Scarlett offered to help Margaret to her feet. 'It sounds to me like you've bent over backwards to accommodate this Octavia person. What kind of caterer sets up for a party a month in advance?'

Margaret showed Biscuit another toy. 'Sit, Biscuit.

Good girl. Let's face it, Mrs Deering, she's shovelled shite over me for months because she knows I'll take it.'

'Then stop taking it. It doesn't sound like you can afford to pay her any more anyway. How much *have* you paid her?'

'Just the small deposit. I've been putting off the next payment. She asked for it early, though it's not due till tomorrow, actually.'

Scarlett thought again about the lovely caterers they'd used for her parents' anniversary. 'You shouldn't be fitting in with the caterer's theme, Margaret. They're supposed to be fitting in around you.'

'I know. I ended up hyperventilating in Homebase at the weekend. I got so anxious about choosing the right colour for Octavia. Do you have any idea how many shades of purple paint there are? They had to take me into the break room to calm down. It's all a bit much, to be honest.' She frowned. 'It's all a bit too much. I'd love to never see that woman again.' She laughed. 'Arthur might have a stroke if I fired her. Blimey, it would feel good, though… How would it work, practically, I mean?'

'I guess it depends on what your contract says. When we did our parents' party it was for a fixed price. It sounds like your contract doesn't have that.'

'If only I had a contract! Then maybe I'd understand why there are all these price increases. But Octavia wanted to keep things flexible.'

'Margaret, without a contract you've got no guarantee that she'll even show up to cater your party. You could end up with a house full of people and no food on the night.' She shrugged. 'On the other hand, there's nothing saying you can't fire her either.'

'How might I do that, exactly? Firing her?'

Scarlett knew she was giving a desperate woman a

push, but if anyone needed it, Margaret did. 'If there's no contract, then you just tell her you won't need her for the party. That's it. You'll probably lose your deposit, though.'

'But maybe gain back my sanity.' As she paced the length of the garden, Biscuit, newly outranked by her mistress, followed at her heel. Those two might end up making a good team after all. 'It's my party,' she said to herself. 'I don't want the flippin' Arabian Nights in here or fishbowls all over the place. I didn't even want a party. Who wants to celebrate a decade of wrinkles and menopause? Do you know what I wanted for my birthday, Mrs Deering? A spa weekend. I've never had one in my life. They look so nice and relaxing, shuffling round in your dressing gown and slippers all weekend. Imagine sleeping in as late as you want and someone else doing the cooking and the laundry! That's all I wanted. Not this bloomin' party.' She grabbed her house keys from the ceramic bowl beside the hob. 'I'm sorry, I know this isn't normal, but if I pay you extra, would you come with me to tell Octavia we don't need her?'

Scarlett didn't need to be paid overtime for that!

Their Thelma and Louise double act lacked a little something without a car, but they did their best to keep the spirit of the adventure going on the Tube.

'Did we have an appointment?' Octavia asked when she met them at the garage door where they'd been buzzed in.

'No, sorry. I mean, no, we didn't.' Steely intention might have propelled her there, but Margaret's apology habit was hard to break. 'I've come to let you know that, thank you ever so much, but we won't be needing your catering for the party. Thank you, though. Very much. Thank you. Bye.'

Scarlett could hear Margaret's voice quivering, but she'd done it!

Octavia's black eyebrows turned down. 'Of course you need me, Margaret. Arthur hired me for your party. We've been planning it for months. I'd say you need me very much.'

Margaret's shoulders slumped till her handbag slid to the crook of her arm. She put her hand over her mouth and nodded. 'Octavia, you're right, I do need you,' she said between her fingers. 'I've got nearly a hundred people coming to my house expecting a party. I've never had a party for that many people before and I wouldn't know where to start doing that on my own.'

The caterer's smile was triumphant. She knew she'd won.

Then Margaret straightened her back. 'I might need you, but I very much don't *want* you, or your constant price increases. You should be feeding us caviar off gold spoons for the money you're charging. So please take this as formal notice that I won't be hiring you for my party.'

'How are *you* going to pull off a party for a hundred people? Have you thought about that? Does Arthur know you're firing me? I bet he'll have something to say.' Octavia crossed her bony arms.

'I don't know yet how I'll do it, but I'll figure it out. And no, Arthur doesn't know I'm here. But Octavia, he also doesn't know that you've asked for triple the money. How do you think he'd feel about that?'

It was Octavia's turn to look shaken. 'Who are you?' she snapped as if just noticing Scarlett.

'This is my friend, Scarlett.'

'You're the dog walker.' It sounded like an accusation.

'She's my friend,' Margaret corrected her. 'Now, I

think we're finished here.' She flashed Scarlett a wobbly smile as they turned to leave.

'Good luck with your party,' Octavia said to their backs. 'It's going to be a total disaster.'

'At least I won't have any flippin' fish to worry about,' Margaret mumbled. 'Now all I have to do is figure out how to throw a party in a month,' she said to Scarlett.

'You can do it, Margaret.'

'Do you know what? I'm starting to think maybe I can.'

Chapter 23

Rufus was killing bad guys again when she got home from Margaret's. The blinds were still drawn in the living room. She peered at Rufus in the glowing blue gloom where he'd made himself a nest on the sofa from the duvet. 'Have you moved at all today?'

On screen he paused the stubbly man on the quad bike. 'I answered the door when the takeaway came. Does that count?' As he stretched, one hairy leg poked out from under the duvet.

'Did you open the door to him like that, in your pants?'

'I have a robe on. What time is it?'

Scarlett laughed. 'Almost dinnertime.' She opened the blinds to banish the pall hanging over the room. Stale man and curry. 'I picked up some bits for us.'

They were more than bits. She'd tramped all over north London for Rufus's favourite foods: the smoky baba ganoush and nutty falafel from the Lebanese restaurant near her old flat, where they always gave her a free box of gooey baklava, the rosemary and sea salt focaccia from the Italian deli, paper thin slices of prosciutto and peppery salami, and those giant bright green olives that were impossible to eat in one bite. She got Medjool dates from her man at the corner shop, where she couldn't resist a few ripe avocadoes to mash up with fresh lemon juice and sea salt.

The plastic shopping bags were starting to cut into her hand. She turned towards the kitchen to put them down. 'I'll make us martinis while you shower.'

'Scarlett, that's nice, but I'd really just like to relax.'

She turned back. 'And I'd really like to have a nice night with my husband. Why can't we both get what we want?'

He might as well have put the back of his hand to his forehead, the way he sighed. 'You're not going to make me go out, are you?'

She took a slow, deep breath before answering. 'I just said I've got us a load of food.' They didn't have to go out to have fun. She was literally bringing fun to him on a plate.

The martini glasses were in the high cabinet with the bread maker, the iron and all the other gadgets they never used. The glasses had been a wedding present from Rufus's parents. Those people knew their way around the bottom of a Gordon's bottle, but after a few weeks of nightly martinis, Scarlett and Rufus had put them away for the sake of their livers.

They did used to have fun together. She was sure she remembered long nights of silliness and comfort. That might be a bit homely for some, but she'd loved knowing every Friday night that they had a relaxed weekend ahead of them.

Once she'd poured large measures of gin over the

ice in the cocktail shaker, she threw Fred and Ginger each a treat. 'There's no reason we shouldn't still have fun like we used to, right, dogs?'

They stared at her. Fred tilted his head. *Yeah, sure, start with another one of those snacks.*

The drinks nearly overflowed the glasses when she poured them from the ice-cold shaker, but a few slurps got hers down to a manageable level. But then Rufus's glass looked much fuller. She siphoned off a few sips from his glass too.

Rufus padded back into the kitchen in his jeans and favourite blue hoodie. He smelled of lemony shower gel.

'It's been ages since we've had these.' He took a big sip of his martini.

They had been romantic once, hadn't they? Naturally romantic? She thought so, but the last year had muddled everything up in her head. There were only so many on-demand sex sessions one could have before the shine wore off.

'Put on some music, will you please?' she asked. 'Something dancey.'

'Getting your groove on? You should drink martinis more often.' He went to the iPod on the shelf.

Exactly her thoughts. She found little dishes for all the food and piled them on trays. 'Let's eat in the living room,' she said as Beyoncé sang about single ladies.

Scarlett bounced from the kitchen with a tray. 'Grab that one, will you?' She grinned as she laid out the morsels and fluffed the dented sofa cushions.

Rufus attacked the baba ganoush. 'Why don't we eat this all the time?' A plop landed on the table as he scooped more bread into the dip.

Scarlett swiped up the plop with her finger and popped it into her mouth. 'Mmm. It's divine.' Though to be honest her tongue had gone a little numb from the gin. She took another sip. 'Let's dance.'

'Let's eat,' he said, not moving.

That sofa was becoming attached to his arse. 'No, come on,' she whined. 'It won't go cold. Dance with me.' She drew him to his feet. 'What's wrong?' His funky chicken was half-hearted to say the least. 'Is it your incision?'

Rufus's face went funny.

'It's only been a week, I guess. How long does it take to heal?'

'How do you know about that?' he murmured.

'Shannon told me. Since you didn't bother.'

She gazed at him, sipping her drink.

'Look, do we have to talk about it?' he finally said. 'Our conversations don't always have to revolve around my medical shortcomings.'

Fair enough. She tried to remember the fun little anecdotes she'd thought of on the journey back from London. Before their night went totally off the rails.

'Want to play cards? Or Pictionary? A board game would be fun!' Even she didn't believe what she was saying. Shannon had never mentioned any raucous Scrabble tournaments with Rufus. She doubted they figured into his top ten nights out.

She didn't bother getting a game out. What was the point? Why was she jumping through all these hoops anyway trying to be Rufus's entertainment? It was obvious he wasn't having fun.

'Could you please just stop acting like everything is normal?' he asked. 'Everything is not normal. It's about as far from normal as it's possible to be.'

'We'll get through this,' she said.

'How, Scarlett? How exactly are we meant to get

through this? We aren't sterile, are we? I am. You can still have children. I'm the one shooting blanks.'

'I can't have them without you, Rufus.'

'As if I haven't got enough pressure. Thanks for that. Thanks for reminding me.'

She slammed down her glass. 'I can't win with you! One minute you tell me to stop acting like everything is normal and the next you yell at me when I do. I can't believe you didn't tell me about the biopsy. How do you think I feel when you shut me out like that?'

He swallowed hard. 'Jesus, could I be more of a dick?' He reached for her. 'I'm so wrapped up in my own shit that I've been an arsehole to you. I just feel so, I don't know, hopeless. In every sense of the word. There's nothing you can do to help me with this, and I'm really sorry about that, but there isn't. They're my feelings. I am sorry you're having to deal with them too. You don't deserve any of this.'

'Just don't shut me out, Rufus. I mean it. We're dead if you do that.'

Although he wasn't being cagey with everyone, was he? He'd talked to Shannon about those first tests, and the biopsy. Who knew what other deep-down private things he was sharing with her.

That hurt.

Chapter 24

Summertime finally came to the park. Blowsy cherry blossoms gave way to a canopy of green running up to the ornate wrought-iron gates, and inside the rhododendron were blooming. All along the borders their papery flowers popped with colour against deep green leaves. On sunny days like these, Scarlett couldn't imagine having a better job.

Charlie jogged over with Barkley waddling behind. 'Would it be all right if Naomi stuck around for class today?' He couldn't stop smiling.

Scarlett glanced at the young woman at the edge of the grass. Her hand found Hiccup's wiry coat as the little dog eyed them. Instead of ignoring Scarlett like she usually did, Naomi returned her smile. The ice queen was melting. 'Has she decided to join us?' she murmured to Charlie in her best ventriloquist impersonation. *Azz zhe decided oo oin us?*

'Not exactly. She dropped us off and I said it would be good to hang around for a while just to see what the session is like. Maybe if she realises how much it helps then she'll try it? Would that be okay?' His face was as optimistic as Barkley's was when there were treats within snaffling distance.

'It's more than okay, Charlie. It sounds like there's hope yet.'

She bent down to scratch Barkley's ears. 'Have you been a good boy?'

'Mostly,' Charlie answered for his dog, who was exercising his right to remain silent. 'He ate a whole box of Kleenex. Not just the Kleenex. The box too.'

Barkley didn't look at all embarrassed by this. Charlie might have to accept that Barkley would always have a penchant for paper goods. If they could just get him to stop snacking on things that put him in hospital, then that would be progress.

'Alright, mate!' Max waved energetically as he joined them. 'Alright, Scarlett?'

'Someone's full of beans today.'

'Wait till you see who I'm meeting after class. It might be a perfect night! I was thinking of bringing Murphy on the date, what do you think? Women like dogs, yeah?'

Imagine Murphy's joy at the prospect of a ménage à trois. 'Mightn't it get complicated if he's with you? I'd let him sit out your first date, if I were you.'

Max nodded. 'Her flat might not allow dogs anyway.'

Someone is certainly confident of his chances, thought Scarlett.

'Though that wouldn't work in the long-term. It wouldn't be fair to leave him alone for whole weekends… though I guess we could stay at mine.'

'Just checking, this *is* a first date you're talking

about?' Charlie asked, throwing a treat to Barkley when he sat.

'Am I getting ahead of myself again? Typical me!' Max sang. 'It's just that I have a really good feeling about this. Wanna see her?' He dropped the lead as he fished the phone from his pocket.

Murphy wasn't about to miss out on a chance like that. He was on Barkley faster than mangoes through the poodles.

'Murphy, no!'

'Get between them if you can,' Scarlett reminded him. 'Try distracting him with Bunny Wabbit.'

Barkley was not amused by the assault.

Max's face crumpled as he watched Murphy panting out his lust. Bunny Wabbit hung limply in his hand. 'He's not improving! Every time I think he is, he goes and does something like this. You should have seen him earlier. He went after the sofa arm this morning. I mean he really went at it.'

'Max, I think we need to be realistic. The humping isn't always just a habit. I know you really don't want him neutered, and you should keep working with him, but we're getting towards the end of the course. Maybe it's best to have a solid plan in your head. This is about Murphy.'

'Scarlett's right,' Charlie said. 'You don't have to give him the snip if you really don't want to, but then you could never let him off the lead. And you said yourself that's not fair to Murphy. It might be a choice between two shitty options.'

Scarlett hated seeing her clients disappointed, and not only on a professional level. They were always more than clients by the end of the course. 'He has improved, Max, don't forget that. You control him much better now.'

'I know,' Max said. 'He's not as bad as he was, but I can't trust him off the lead yet.'

'We'll work really hard on the training for the next few weeks and then give him a chance to prove himself. How about that? We'll devise some tests for him in the later sessions. That's fair, right? If we're happy that he's controllable, then maybe he won't need to be neutered.'

'Murphy's Last Stand. And if he fails…' Max didn't finish.

They all watched Murphy panting into the sunshine.

Murphy wasn't the only one needing distraction. Maybe Max would feel better to know he didn't have the only difficult dog. 'Charlie, I'd like you to walk slowly towards Naomi. I'll hold Barkley. Sort of sneak up without looking like you're sneaking.'

Charlie inched his way towards Naomi, freezing in place every time Hiccup glared at him. He practically stared at the sky and whistled.

Hiccup growled her warning. 'Wait till Hiccup stops growling, Charlie, then go a bit closer. If she doesn't stop growling, then Naomi, I want you to walk her away. Just a few steps, though, like you were doing before. Throw her a treat, Charlie, when she seems settled.'

Poor Barkley stared at his human. *What's the meaning of this betrayal? You've mixed up your dogs, Charlie. I'm over here.*

What if he gave *all* his treats to the ungrateful little beast? Didn't Charlie remember what had happened in the car? *She tried to kill us, Charlie. KILL US.*

Hiccup didn't like the situation either, but a treat was a treat and, as they rained down, she found she could stomach the idea.

'Do you think you could help Hiccup?' Naomi

asked shyly. Charlie tried to contain his grin.

'I think so, yes,' Scarlett said. 'I'd suggest some one-on-one sessions.' She didn't really have time to take on another client, but she couldn't very well say no when Charlie's future depended on it. 'Shall we meet again and see how we get on?'

'How many sessions do you think she'll need?'

'You'll usually see progress with just a few. Once a dog catches on, her behaviour can change really fast. After that it's all about reinforcement. Are you worried about Hiccup?'

Naomi reddened. 'It's just that… she has to get better.'

'I'm sure she will,' Scarlett said. She wasn't fazed by the urgency in Naomi's voice. She was used to desperate clients. They often came to her as a last resort. 'I know it's tough right now, especially when you're around Charlie and Barkley, but there are techniques we can try to help Hiccup overcome her mistrust.'

'No, what I mean is: she *has* to get better. The police have said she has to. She's got an ASBO,' Naomi confessed. 'A dog ASBO. If she doesn't stop being aggressive, they might even put her down. I can't let that happen!'

Scarlett stared at Hiccup.

The furry, foul-tempered little felon whined as tears sprang to Naomi's eyes. 'I'm sorry for being emotional,' she whispered.

It seemed that Naomi wasn't quite as steely as Scarlett had assumed. 'That's totally understandable. Let me email you tonight with some dates I could do. Could you do something in the daytime?'

'Any time. We have to fix her.'

Chapter 25

They might be seeing a different doctor in a different room with comfier chairs, but Scarlett had the same dreadful feeling as she stared around the waiting area. It was a lot plusher than their GP's surgery, with pale grey deep-pile carpet and muted walls. There were no brightly coloured Blu-Tacked reminders to parents about vaccinations and breastfeeding clinics or plastic crates of toys. Urology was for grown-ups.

'This is nice,' Scarlett said, noticing one of the paintings.

Rufus looked at her like she was insane.

'The decor, I mean. The surroundings.'

His smile was faint. They were both tired of keeping up appearances.

When he squeezed her hand, it made a farty noise from the sweat slicking their palms. They both sniggered. Maybe not so grown-up after all.

A man around her dad's age opened one of the office doors. 'Would you like to come through?'

Rufus made the introductions as they went into his office.

Mr Woodwin's apply pink cheeks and laughing blue eyes were too jolly for someone who handled people's bits. His sparse greying close-cropped hair did add to his general look of competence, though.

'Right, well, you'll be anxious about the test results, so let's not delay.' In the brief moment that he looked first into Rufus's eyes and then Scarlett's, she knew the news wasn't good.

She seemed to float above them as Mr Woodwin told the couple tightly holding hands that Rufus's condition was rare. She heard him say it wasn't a delivery problem but a production one. Non-obstructive azoospermia. The few sperm they found in the testes sample had maturation arrest and sperma-something-else. It was a double whammy. She was aware that Rufus asked if it was curable and listened as Mr Woodwin explained that they didn't like to use words like curable.

'Well, what word would you use, then?' he asked.

Mr Woodwin's cheery demeanour didn't waver. He was used to delivering bad news. 'There may still be some assisted reproduction options.'

'What the hell does that even mean?'

'Rufus! I'm sorry, Doctor— Mr Woodwin. Assisted reproduction?'

Mr Woodwin kept smiling. 'Sometimes non-obstructive azoospermia is caused by a hormone imbalance. A problem with the hypothalamus or pituitary gland can cause this, but that doesn't seem to be the case here. Your hormone tests all came back within the normal ranges. And it's not from trauma or a physical abnormality like an undescended testicle.'

'Then what *is* causing it?' The anguish in Rufus's question was palpable.

Mr Woodwin shrugged. 'We don't know. I understand how frustrating this is, but in some cases, there just isn't a clear reason for the difficulty. What we can do is look at some alternatives like artificial insemination using donor sperm. That's not my area of expertise, but of course I'd work closely with a fertility specialist if that's a route you'd like to look into. Rufus, Scarlett, I'm sorry I haven't got better news, but there *are* other options to become parents. Do you have any questions?'

Scarlett could barely hear Rufus speak. 'Is there any chance for me to father my own child?'

The compassion on Mr Woodwin's face was as absolute as it was heart-breaking. 'There may be a chance, and I have to stress *may*, but you'll need to weigh up the pros and cons of any treatment. They are very intensive and sometimes extremely invasive.'

This coming from a man who'd already carved out a piece of her husband's scrotum.

'As I said, in my opinion there isn't an identifiable cause so there won't be a definitive treatment. Anything that's tried would be an informed shot in the dark. That's not technically a medical phrase, by the way.' Mr Woodwin sighed. 'I'm sorry. It's never easy to hear news like this. I suggest you take some time to think about it before making any decisions about the next steps, okay? I'll send a letter to your GP this week so any other doctor you talk to will have the full picture so far.'

So far. That didn't sound like the end of the story to Scarlett.

'Mr Woodwin said we could get a second opinion,' she said as soon as they left his office. The sunshine was at odds with the morning they were having. It seemed wrong to feel the warmth on her back, as if it was just an ordinary day. She sipped from the water bottle she carried in her bag, then offered it to Rufus.

She didn't expect his response. 'Jesus Christ, Scarlett, what's the point?' For a split second she thought he was talking about the water. 'I've already had two sperm tests, a biopsy and all the hormone tests. Another doctor would just do the same to me. He won't find anything different.'

'He might, though. We can't give up, Rufus. Not

when there might still be a chance.' She was talking to herself as much as him. 'If there's any chance of having your baby, I want to take it.'

'But don't I get a say in what happens? Maybe I don't want to be your sperm donor at all costs.'

She couldn't believe what she was hearing. 'Jesus Christ, Rufus, I don't see you as my sperm donor! Is that really what you think of me? You're my husband, who I want to have a baby with. We're supposed to be in this together. You're being too pessimistic. Shouldn't we at least get another opinion? An opinion isn't too invasive, is it?'

He reeled away from her. 'Let's see. I'm made to wank into a cup, again. No, that's not too bad compared to, say, sticking a needle into my ball sack. Oh, which I'll also have to do again. Who knows? Maybe this time they'll put a little camera up my willy or something. Just to be sure I'm completely sterile. Excuse me for not rushing over to sign up for that.'

Her grip was awkward when she pulled him into her arms. 'We will do this together. I promise. If we can't do it the normal way, then we can look into artificial insemination. There'll be a way, Rufus. We will have a baby.' She wondered why she didn't want to cry when a few months ago the idea of not having a child had her in floods. Maybe she'd used up her quota.

'If there's one thing I am sure about, Scarlett, it's that I don't want someone else's child.'

'Not even if it's mine?' she whispered.

'Yours and some random stranger's? I'd feel even more like a loser then, knowing we had to pay some bloke to give you what I can't. Can't you see, Scarlett?'

Yes, she could. She could see that the man who was supposed to love her was threatening to keep them from having a baby because it hurt his ego. 'What happened to being in this together?'

He didn't answer.

'You meant it when you thought it was my fault, didn't you? Now that it's not, suddenly it's every man for himself. Is that it?'

He couldn't look at her.

'Where does that leave us, then?'

'I honestly have no idea,' he said.

They didn't speak as they went back home.

She rang Shannon as soon as Rufus left for the train station. 'I need you,' she said when her friend answered. 'What are you doing?'

'It doesn't matter. Are you home? I'll be there in twenty minutes.'

The tears came then, in great big pity-filled splashes on to the marble worktop that they'd picked out back when they thought they'd be together forever.

Chapter 25 ½

'Take Stevie and Nick here, for example,' Mr Darcy was saying as he stroked his thumb over one of the greyhounds' sleek fawn-coloured heads. Shannon tried not to stare at his hands. They were nice hands. The kind of hands that would be warm to hold.

She blamed the weather for her interest in his hands. The clear sky and mild breeze were churning her tummy with anticipation. The weather always did that at this time of year. Sunshine was starting to push the darkness to the edges of the day and it was warm enough to ditch her tights. That always seemed like a time for optimism. 'I guess their owners were Fleetwood Mac fans?' she answered Mr Darcy. 'Fleetwood and Mac would have been worse, you know.'

Mr Darcy had adopted his dogs two years earlier after their music-loving owners realised they couldn't give the greyhounds the exercise they desperately needed. He'd never have taken them on, he'd said, if he'd had an office job. But being a freelance IT programmer meant working from his sofa. Since walking helped him think anyway, the dogs got their exercise while he found solutions for his coding problems.

'People think it's hilarious to name their pets like that, but do they ever think about the consequences?' he said. 'We're the ones left shouting stupid puns across the park every day. "Come here, Block and Tackle."'

She laughed longer than she needed to, but she wanted to encourage him. When it came to awkwardness, he was even worse than her. 'I don't know why people do it.' She glanced at the pugs. 'What happens if these others go before Velma? Then she'll just be a weirdly named dog.'

Her pocket started ringing. 'I'm sorry, I've got to take this call. Hi, Scarlett.'

'It doesn't matter,' she said into the phone. 'Are you home? I'll be there in twenty minutes.' She gathered up the pugs' leads and stuffed her phone back into her pocket. 'I'm really sorry, but I've got to get to my friend's. They're… She's… I've got to go.'

His expression creased with concern. 'Oh, well, okay. Actually, I had – do you… I was just wondering…'

But Shannon was already hurrying towards the gate.

'I'm Josh,' he called after her.

She spun round. 'I'm Shannon. I… erm… Bye.'

Josh. She tried it out on her tongue as she walked towards Scarlett's. Joshua. No, definitely Josh. It wouldn't be such a bad name once she got used to it. She was making progress, right? Never let it be said that she wasn't a mover and shaker.

Yeah, right. More like a creeper and a crawler.

It was, though, the most progress she'd made with a man in years. If, by progress, she could count having brief conversations with someone whose name she hadn't found the courage to ask. At least he'd saved her that trouble.

Foreboding crept up Shannon's neck when Scarlett flung herself on her at the front door. Scarlett wasn't normally a flinger.

She wasn't a sobber either, but just then, rules were being broken all over the place. 'It's all right,' Shannon murmured into her friend's shaking shoulder. 'It will be all right.' She hated platitudes like that, but what else was she supposed to say? There'd be time for solutions later.

Scarlett pulled away with a raggedy breath. 'Come into the kitchen. Fred and Ginger will love the pugs.'

But the Westies were less keen on their houseguests than Scarlett had thought. They ran at the pugs, which just made them wriggle and fall over. They really were hopeless at being dogs.

'Rufus couldn't get away fast enough.' Scarlett bashed the kettle against the tap as she filled it. 'So much for being in this together.' The tea mugs clattered on the marble worktop.

'You are in it together! I know Rufus, and he loves you.'

But as she listened to what happened, the first tiny doubts trickled into her mind. The doubts came faster as Scarlett talked, until they were a deluge that threatened to wash away her certainty about her best friends.

'He's just in shock, Scarlett, I'm sure of it. Of course he'll consider adoption or a sperm donor if there's no other way. He wants a baby as much as you do.'

Shannon's heart sank when Scarlett shook her head. 'He wants his baby, not some donor's. No matter that it would still be my baby. That's not enough for him, apparently.'

They sat in silence waiting for the kettle to boil as they watched the dogs wriggle all over the floor. 'It's too early for you to even be talking about donors,' Shannon finally said. 'You've just now found out. You need time to think things through. That's what the doctor said too, right? Don't put so much pressure on yourselves when no decisions need to be made right now.'

'It's too late, though. We have talked about it and Rufus has made his position clear.'

'You can't judge him by what he said when he was upset. He'll change his mind.'

Scarlett poured out the boiling water. 'Maybe. The problem is, Shannon, now that I know how he feels, how could I trust that he won't change it back later? Like, in the middle of the process, or when I'm pregnant?'

Shannon had no idea how to help Scarlett and Rufus. She only knew that she had to. They couldn't break up. Sure, if they did, they might move on eventually. They could meet new partners and live happily ever after, but what about her? Assuming she even survived the split without taking sides and permanently alienating one of them. They were the constants in her life, and it was full because of them. Now that art school was finishing, she didn't have much else. Her world was whittled down to a fine point. Scarlett and Rufus were teetering on top.

Chapter 26

Life went on for Scarlett as if the urology appointment had never happened. The sun still shone and the rain fell, politicians still argued in Parliament, she still stepped in puppy wee and ran low on milk for her coffee every few days. Nothing had changed. Everything had changed.

She and Rufus were only skimming along the surface. They didn't have conversations. They simply exchanged information, without any sharp edges, true, but without any feelings exposed, either. It was only on close inspection, Scarlett knew, that their banter rang hollow.

'I don't know what you mean,' Rufus said when Scarlett brought it up. 'I thought we were having fun.'

They were cooking dinner together. 'We are. But something feels different.'

The sound of the chef's knife clattering on to the chopping board made the dogs prick up their ears. 'I don't know what you mean. We're cooking like we always do. What's different?'

'It's just a vibe. Are you okay?'

'You mean aside from constantly being asked if I'm okay?'

'I'm just worried about you.'

'I know. Yeah, I'm okay. Hey, come here.'

She eased into his arms. Maybe she was overreacting. He had calmed down since the appointment. He was more like the old Rufus than he'd been in months. A tiny part of her wondered if he felt relieved to have an answer finally. As devastating as it was, maybe he was moving on.

If only she could.

He went out with Shannon most nights now. Each morning she rang Scarlett to dissect their conversation. Despite these autopsies, Scarlett was no closer to understanding her husband.

How could he keep her from having the child she wanted so badly? Because that's what his refusal was doing. Sure, technically she could overrule him and get a sperm donor anyway. Then he'd probably leave her. He'd definitely resent her. That wasn't what she wanted either.

Rufus's defunct testicles were holding her happy family baby dreams hostage. This was no Stockholm syndrome. She had little sympathy for her captors.

She arrived at Margaret's house the next day half expecting to see her up a paint-spattered ladder, but the front hall was still pristinely white. She hadn't changed her mind about the caterer.

Biscuit stood beside Margaret as she opened the door. 'Mrs Deering, come in! Come, Biscuit.'

To Scarlett's astonishment, the dog did what she was told. Margaret's smile was triumphant. 'Not bad, eh?'

'She's like a different dog. The new techniques have really helped.' Scarlett squatted down to give Biscuit a good rub. She deserved it. 'I don't think you'll need many more lessons after today. Good girl, Biscuit!'

Margaret's face fell. 'Oh, I hope we will, Mrs Deering! I so enjoy our sessions.'

Scarlett laughed. 'So do I, but I'd be taking your money for no reason if we continued when Biscuit doesn't need more training. This is a good thing. You've done a wonderful job retraining your dog. You should be very proud.'

She shrugged. 'S'pose.'

'Don't worry about that now. Shall we have a cup of tea first?'

Margaret perked up as she filled the kettle and chose a selection of biscuits from the stack of tins in the cabinet.

'How are you getting on finding a new caterer?' she asked as Margaret poured water over their teabags. The delicate stacks of bone china no longer came out of the cabinet. They used big hefty builder's mugs now.

'I've given up the search,' she said, stirring in the milk. 'It's too late to find anyone now so I'm on my own.'

She didn't sound unhappy about it. 'Are there still a hundred people coming?'

'Oh, yes, and the list is growing all the time. Arthur can't stop inviting people.'

Scarlett would be having heart palpitations if a hundred people were about to turn up at her house. 'Erm, what *are* you going to do?'

'I'll just have to do the food myself.' She shrugged. 'My only plan so far is to get everyone so pissed that I could serve beans on toast and no one would notice. I've found a Prosecco wholesaler who's doing me a very good deal. He's got a decent bottle to start with and a more economical option for later.' She winked. 'So get your drinks in early. I am so pleased you're able to come. I've also invited my WI friends, and I do like a few of the neighbours, so it won't be so bad.'

Scarlett frowned. 'How many of the guests are actually yours?'

'I could count them on two hands and a bloomin' foot. The rest are Arthur's colleagues and the children's friends.'

'I see why you're not too bothered about how it turns out, then.'

'Oh, no, Mrs Deering, I feel sick about the whole thing going pear-shaped! I'm just doing the best I can, that's all. It's no use complaining when people deal with worse all the time and just get on with things.'

Scarlett wished she could bottle Margaret's attitude. She'd be drunk on it. 'Who's going to serve all those people, though?'

'I'll have to hire someone, I guess. I just need to find waiters who'll be happy with everyone's undying gratitude and not much else.'

It was clear as Margaret put Biscuit through her paces in the garden that she probably only needed one more session to solidify their training. Scarlett was always a little sad when this day approached. Granted she didn't like Biscuit as much as some dogs but she had grown more than a little fond of Margaret. 'You've done so well with Biscuit,' she told her. 'As I thought, our sessions are coming to an end.'

Margaret sighed. 'I'll really miss you.'

'I'll miss you too, Margaret, but we'll do one more session, maybe after the party. And I'll see you there anyway.' She really *didn't* want to say goodbye to the woman. 'There's nothing saying we couldn't still meet up sometimes, if you'd like. I mean as friends?'

The smile that beamed across Margaret's face told Scarlett her answer. 'As friends... Scarlett. Thank you.'

She rang Shannon as she was leaving Margaret's. She could think of one person who'd do anything for undying gratitude if it meant being in the limelight. 'Make sure you text him to tell him I'm ringing, okay? He may not pick up an unknown number.'

'What, Julian, pass up the chance to talk to strangers? You are joking, right?'

'Darling, leave it all to me!' Julian trilled when Scarlett told him what Margaret needed. 'What's our theme?'

'I'm not sure she has one. You can ask her when you speak.'

'She must have a theme, darling, otherwise how will we all know what to wear? I know, I'll make a mood board for her! There's nothing better to help clients visualise ideas.'

'Okay, but remember, Julian, she hasn't got a lot of money for props and things.'

'Not to worry, darling, my friends and I can raid our dressing-up boxes and I'm a genius at upcycling. You'll be amazed at what I can do with everyday household items... and I'm not bad at decorating either, ha ha ha ha ha!'

Rufus didn't want to go to Dad's for dinner and Scarlett didn't want to push him on it. Their truce was uneasy, but at least it was holding. *Fake it till you make it*, she thought sadly as she drove to pick up her mum.

Julia waited out front as Scarlett pulled up behind

her car. She'd assumed her mum's car was in the shop or something. Otherwise she could have driven herself to Dad's. She must just want the company. Or she knew that Scarlett did. 'Why are you outside?' she asked.

'I'm enjoying this evening.' She adjusted her pink cardigan over her dress. 'It finally feels like summer, don't you think? Thanks for driving.'

'No problem, though I may not stay late, if that's okay, with Rufus home.' She'd never been one to plan her schedule around her husband. Yes, they spent a lot of time together, but she had her own life too. Lately, though, she'd been reluctant to leave him.

'It's fine, sweetheart. We'll leave whenever you like.'

Julia hadn't sounded the least bit surprised when Scarlett rang after the urology appointment. 'He just needs some time to rebuild his ego,' she'd said. 'This kind of thing is hard on a man. He'll come around, you'll see.' Scarlett wasn't so sure her mum knew what she was talking about, given that the only relationship in her life had ended in divorce.

Gemma was definitely on Scarlett's side, but then she was also extremely hormonal about anything that stood in the way of her sister having a baby. 'He's just going to have to get over that silliness,' she'd said. 'For both your sakes.'

They stood together in Felicia's kitchen. 'You're really showing.' Scarlett reached out to touch Gemma's tummy. 'Do you get sick of people doing that?'

'I don't mind when it's family or my friends. It's just annoying when strangers do it. I wouldn't walk up to a woman on the Tube and honk her boob, yet they think they can rub my tummy.' Her expression clouded. 'Is it getting harder seeing me like this?… Or easier?' The last question was hopeful.

'No, not harder.' It wasn't getting easier either, but it wouldn't do any good telling Gemma that. It wasn't like she could change the situation. Fate, that bugger, had cruel timing.

She'd gone back and forth over telling Dad and Felicia about Rufus's results. Her mum had to be told because she was her mum, and Gemma because there'd be hell to pay if she didn't. Dad and Felicia would want to know, of course, but what purpose would it serve? It'd just make them feel bad for her.

But it felt wrong to exclude only them and they were as sympathetic and supportive as she knew they'd be. Basically, everyone was being great about it except the one person who got the last say.

'You're home early,' Rufus said as she bent to the sofa to kiss him.

'Didn't miss me, then?' The question came out harsher than she meant. Or perhaps it came out exactly as harshly as she meant. She couldn't tell anymore.

'Was dinner good?' he asked.

'Felicia sent some home for you. You've eaten?' Oh, the mundanity.

'I had a burger with Shannon. I'll bring that to work tomorrow for lunch, though.'

So he'd been out again. 'Have fun?'

His smile was relaxed, easy. Rufus 1.0, before his operating system changed and all her favourite programmes stopped running. She tried not to mind that it was Shannon who reset him. 'We went to that handmade burger place in the Oracle. I'm full of meat.'

'Full of something anyway.' She slumped down next to him. 'What are you watching?'

'The dogs wanted *Doctor Dolittle,* but we've seen it so many times. I'm broadening their horizons with *Die*

Hard with a Vengeance.'

'Which you've seen how many times?' It seemed to be on telly at least once a week.

He covered Ginger's ears. 'Shh. They don't know that. Without you here they outvote me.'

'Then you need me.'

He planted a wet kiss on her cheek. 'Of course I do.'

Her tummy flipped when she felt his lips. It was probably just a trick of the mind, like a phantom limb. Those feelings had been amputated.

And yet she so wanted to believe that everything was okay, that they were just like any other couple jostling with their dogs for space on the sofa. In a little while they'd argue mildly over who'd take them for the last walk of the night. One after the other they'd go upstairs to clean their teeth. She'd put away the jeans or clean clothes piled on the bed and throw the decoration-only cushions into the corner. Rufus would put on his reading glasses and open his book. They'd sleep, wake and do it all again. Routine. It was easy, comfortable… secure. Was this what people meant by papering over the cracks? She could see the appeal.

She snuggled down further into the crook of his arm when the film came back on, but as it played across their flat-screen telly, she found she wasn't really watching it. That's because Rufus was stroking her tummy. 'Full of good food?' he asked.

'Mm-hmm.' It wasn't really a question to be answered. And it wasn't an innocent gesture, either. Rufus knew exactly how it turned her on when he did that.

He'd better not be teasing.

Her hand found his thigh. He wasn't the only one who knew how to press buttons. She knew what he liked too. When they were first together they used to stroke each other like that for hours. Such tantalisingly slow, not-quite-innocent foreplay landed them in bed every time.

They kept their eyes on the screen as Bruce Willis beat people up. Scarlett heard the change in Rufus's breathing. He moaned when her hand found his crotch. She smiled into the blue telly light. No slugs.

They turned to each other at the same time to kiss. Ginger jumped off the sofa to leave her humans to their weird rituals. 'Let's go upstairs,' she said.

'No, here.' He was pulling up her jumper.

She glanced through their large front window to the street beyond. 'At least turn off the TV so no one can see in.' Though part of her liked the idea that someone might be watching. What had gotten into her?!

Their lovemaking was slow, passionate and giggly in turns, and it felt so familiar and carefree that Scarlett wanted to cry with relief. Every time she looked into Rufus's eyes he smiled back. When he closed his eyes he became more urgent, then faster.

She knew when he was about to come, and not because he told her, like a few exes had done in the past. As if that kind of thing needed an announcement.

'Oh my god,' he gasped into her shoulder. 'Shannon!'

Neither of them moved. Rufus's body lay on top of hers, completely still. He'd better hope he'd died. For a moment she couldn't speak.

'I love you, Scarlett,' he murmured, still not moving.

'What did you say?'

'I love you?'

She shoved him to the floor. 'No, before that.'

'I don't know.' He looked up at her. 'Nothing?'

'Try again.' She felt the bile rise in her throat. Felicia's Cajun chicken threatened to make another appearance. 'What did you say?' She pulled her legs up to her chest.

He grabbed his pants to shimmy them back on. Not easy from a sitting position, but he was awfully vulnerable with his willy waving about like that. 'I didn't… I was… I was out with Shannon tonight. That's all. It was a slip of the tongue.'

'A slip of the tongue, Rufus? Really? Exactly where has your tongue been slipping?' This couldn't be happening. She knew the tears would come later to flood all the whys, whens and whatfors. Right then, she was so angry she wanted to kill him. 'You just said my best friend's name as you came.' The words sounded hard and cold. Like she felt. 'How could you?'

'I haven't, Scarlett. Come on, you've got to believe me. It's not what you think!'

It took her mind a second to catch up. So far it had only registered the words and set the alarm bells ringing. Now it was starting to work out their meaning. Oh god, she really was going to throw up.

She didn't have time to do more than lean over the arm of the sofa. Dinner hit the floorboards.

'Don't you dare,' she said as he moved towards her. She pulled her jumper over her head, not bothering with her bra first. She didn't want to be uncovered in front of him.

Was this how her parents felt when they divorced? Was there an edge that they couldn't step back from? She'd never asked. She'd always thought they weren't a good blueprint for her relationship. Maybe she was wrong about that. Maybe they were a very accurate one after all.

He put his head in his hands as he spoke. 'Nothing's going on between me and Shannon.'

'You've just shouted her name while having sex with me.' She wasn't sure who she felt more betrayed by.

He pulled himself up on to the sofa and found his shirt. It went on inside out. 'I don't know why. You've got to believe me. Maybe it was just because I haven't exactly found things easy with us lately and I've just come back from seeing my mate.'

She stared at him in horror. *He* hadn't been finding things easy?

'But that doesn't mean I cheated on you. I'm just saying that there's been so much tension these last months. Even before the doctors, when we were trying. Goddamn it!' He wiped his hands over his face. 'There's a lot of pressure with you, Scarlett. It's been all about a baby for months and then all the tests and I know how disappointed you are in me. I know. I can see it all the time. When I'm out with Shannon I can forget all that. It's relaxing. I guess I was just relaxed now with you. For the first time in a long time. Isn't that good?'

She thought about that for a moment. 'What kind of twisted... You're not seriously blaming me for this?'

'No?' It was more of a question than an answer.

'Well, obviously you are or you wouldn't have said it.' She took a deep breath. Ten minutes ago they were having sex. Giggling, naked together. An hour before she was wondering if she'd been overreacting. She'd dared to hope things weren't as bad as they'd seemed. She'd doubted her instinct.

Fate, you heartless bastard.

Never in a million years did she think she'd say the next words. 'I want you to leave. I can't have you around me right now, not after this. You need to go.'

Part of her wanted him to refuse, to beg to stay so they could find a way through it together. She'd probably still kick him out, but she needed to hear him want to stay.

Instead he nodded. 'I understand. I'll get some things together. Scarlett? I'm so sorry.'

'Don't even think about going to Shannon's,' she spat.

He turned. 'This isn't about Shannon.'

'I mean it, Rufus.'

'I'll be at the Travelodge.'

Chapter 27

Scarlett dozed off a little before dawn with a dog gently snoring on each of the goose down pillows she'd splurged for when they'd picked out their bed. Fred and Ginger couldn't believe their luck when she'd hoisted them to the mattress, though she took most of the fun out of the sleepover by sobbing all over them.

Four words ran through her head. It. Hurts. So. Much. She thought the words. She shouted them and she snivelled them into already-soaking Westie fur. She couldn't wrap her head around what had happened. It had happened, hadn't it? This wasn't some terrible dream where Fred was about to stand on his hind legs and sing 'Somewhere Over the Rainbow'. It wasn't something she would wake from.

She hadn't misheard him. He'd admitted that. Oh. My. God. Shannon. Another four words to obsess over. Rufus's words.

For better or for worse, her husband had said them. After they'd stood in front of all their family and friends and made promises and she'd never felt anything as solid and sure as his love. He'd said them.

What happened?

For richer, for poorer, they'd made it through hard times. Through parents' health scares and the sleepless nights when they'd stretched to buy the house. One would lose their nerve, buckle or crack under the weight of emotion, only to be gathered in by the other and convinced everything would be okay. Because they were in it together.

In sickness and in health, no matter what, they were supposed to be in it together.

Until death us do part.

Or until he shouts another woman's name during sex, in which case he goes to live at the Travelodge.

If she'd ever needed her best friend, it was now. How utterly kick-in-the-head ironic was that?

How was she supposed to confide in Shannon, the woman who figured in her husband's sexual fantasy? His eyes had been closed, as she now remembered it. Who, exactly, was he imagining he was having sex with? Obviously, he was having no problem performing with her.

Scarlett would go mad if she didn't talk to someone, though. The Westies weren't giving her the answers she needed. She put on last night's clothes and brushed her teeth again, but she could still imagine the sick.

It was pouring when she reached Gemma's London office. Her sister worked in a giant glass box. The rain streaming down its windows reminded Scarlett of going to the car wash with their dad as a child. It was the highlight of their Saturdays together, snug inside the old Volvo belting out 'Singin' in the Rain' in performances that would have made Gene Kelly wince. Scarlett loved the force of those spinny brushes as they buffeted the vehicle and the soapy water pouring over them, knowing they were safe inside.

She'd give anything to crawl back into that car. She called Gemma's work number.

'What's wrong?' Gemma said when she picked up. 'You never ring me at work.'

True, as she thought about it. Gemma had always rung Scarlett during the day instead. 'I need to see you. Can you come out for coffee? I'm downstairs. In your lobby.'

Her sister took one look at her and said, 'Right, it's Rufus?'

'What the hell, Gemma, how do you know already?!' Her words ricocheted off the marble floors. A few people stared.

Gemma grabbed her arm. 'Know what?' she hissed. 'I don't know anything. You look like shit, though. I just assumed.'

Scarlett realised she hadn't brushed her hair or washed her face. She must look like Medusa on a bender. 'Nice to see you too.'

Gemma made a sourpuss face. 'Yeah, well, it's not a social call, right? Let's go. There's a coffee shop around the corner with downstairs seating. Nobody goes down there unless they have to.' She looked Scarlett up and down. 'You look like you have to.'

'Why aren't you more upset?' Gemma asked when Scarlett had told her. It had only taken a few seconds. That didn't seem possible, but then her entire relationship had disintegrated in seconds too.

'Do you think I got these eyes by not being upset, Gemm? I'm sick. I must have dehydrated myself crying last night.' She searched her sister's face. 'I'm not overreacting to this, am I?' She'd give anything for the answer to be yes.

'If Jacob had done that he'd be in the hospital right now. No, not the hospital. They'd need dental records to identify his body. You definitely aren't overreacting. Although… What do you actually know? I mean, concrete facts. Now's not the time to jump to conclusions.'

'You are not taking his side.'

'No way! He's a shit bag. He's the longest-serving mayor of Shitsville, the twentieth-generation crown prince of Shitistan. Darth Vader of the Shitstar.' She smiled at their childhood game. They used to go on for hours like that when their parents cheesed them off. 'We know he's guilty of saying her name, but do you think there's anything really going on between them?'

Scarlett pushed away her coffee. 'He claims not, but he would, wouldn't he? He says he's relaxed around her, and that they were out last night, so when he was relaxed around me he accidentally said her name.'

'Right, while having sex with you. Uh-huh. Do you believe him?' She pushed Scarlett's cup back in front of her.

Scarlett pushed it away again. 'You obviously don't. I don't know.'

She had known it was risky to tell Gemma. Epic grudge-holding Gemma. She might never forgive Rufus.

When she realised that that would only matter if Rufus stayed in their lives, she felt sick again.

'All right, let me ask you another question. Do you believe Shannon would do this?'

'My gut says no. Am I being naïve? I should trust my husband more than my friend, right? Not that I can trust anything.'

Gemma reached for her hand. 'You will. You'll just have to work everything out in your own mind first. Will you talk to Rufus?'

'I can't right now. This is all tangled up in everything else that's going on.'

Gemma rummaged in her bag till she found what she wanted. 'Here. Just because you feel tragic doesn't mean you have to look like a bag lady.'

Scarlett ran Gemma's brush through her hair.

Much as she wanted to take a duvet day (or month), she couldn't ring in sick to her life. There were still dog classes every day, her family to think about, her best friend to avoid…

She let the call go through to voicemail again, where it joined the messages from Rufus. Let him tell Shannon what happened if he wanted to. Clearly she was on his mind all the time anyway.

Gemma was right. Scarlett didn't actually know whether anything had happened between them. That didn't stop the humiliation from pulsing through her every time she thought about her husband shouting her best friend's name as he climaxed.

She needed to take a leaf from her own instruction manual. Distract, distract, distract.

Seeing Murphy's tail semaphoring his excitement at the community centre door did bring a faint smile to her face. Work was exactly what she needed.

'Sawasdee krab!' Max cried when he saw Krishna tucking her yoga mat into the batik print bag she always carried.

'Namaste,' she said back, pushing a curl of grey hair

away from her face. 'There's an excellent energy in the room tonight!' She namaste'd her way out through the throng of OAPs waiting to start the senior ladies' bingo next door.

There might be good energy, thought Scarlett, but the pong of enlightenment was stifling. She opened all the windows. 'What did you just say to Krishna?' she asked Max.

'Oh, that? It's hello in Thai – from when I had a girlfriend from Bangkok. She taught me some phrases for when we went back to visit her family, but we broke up before I got to go. On the bright side, though, I got to learn a new language!'

That man could put a positive spin on a dysentery epidemic. *Sure, I shit my pants, but I went down a belt notch!*

Then Charlie and Barkley turned up. Scarlett had managed to squeeze in a session with Hiccup between her weekday puppy classes, but it would be better for everyone if Naomi could do a session after Charlie and Max instead. Now that Scarlett had her nights free – possibly for the rest of her life – there was nothing stopping her from asking. 'Will Naomi meet you later?'

'Yeah, she'll pick me up,' said Charlie. 'It sounds like Hiccup's lesson went okay. Maybe there's hope for the little terror yet.'

Scarlett was careful to stay neutral on the subject. Naomi's jaw had clenched and unclenched throughout their session, no matter how much Scarlett tried getting her to relax. How that woman hadn't yet ground her teeth to dust, Scarlett couldn't imagine. She'd scrutinised Hiccup for the tiniest signs of progress and seemed devastated when Hiccup didn't listen… which was most of the time. Yet Scarlett did spy a few glimmers of hope in between the bared teeth and raised hackles. Maybe things weren't as bad as Naomi feared.

'Although...' Charlie held up his arm. The dog's teeth had ploughed an angry furrow into his skin. 'I had the nerve to try getting into bed with my girlfriend last night. Don't know what I was thinking.' He sighed. 'I don't know what I *am* thinking. How am I ever going to marry her?'

Max beamed. 'Marry! No way, mate!' He shoved Charlie's shoulder and nearly knocked him over.

'Yeah, well, it'd be easier if it was her parents who hated me. At least she doesn't live with them. And they don't bite.' He gently prodded Hiccup's reminder that he wasn't top dog in Naomi's life.

But Max's romantic streak wasn't dampened just because Charlie might need a tetanus jab. 'It'll work out, you'll see. Where? When? How are you going to propose?' Max leaned forward so as not to miss a single detail.

Charlie fidgeted. 'I haven't worked that out yet.'

'The details don't matter, mate, the important thing is that you found Naomi and she's The One. You are so lucky. I'd give anything to be in your shoes.' Max practically swooned.

'I've just got to get Hiccup on my side. How hard is that going to be?'

It seemed like a rhetorical question.

Charlie wiped his face with his sweatshirt. 'Sorry I'm so sweaty. We jogged here. Well, we walked a lot too, but there was definitely some jogging.'

Scarlett gave Barkley's ears a good fondling. 'Was Barkley too distracted to jog all the way?'

'Nah, I'm too unfit. I haven't been able to exercise since Mum died. Barkley was ace!'

'Well done, mate.' Max nudged his shoulder. 'I

think Murphy is doing better too.'

They all watched Murphy as he strained at his lead to greet Barkley with a nose to the behind. Barkley looked perfectly happy to say hello from a distance.

'This whole fitness thing is getting critical,' Charlie said. 'It's now or never.'

Max nodded. 'Don't I know it? There's not much longer to get my beach body ready.'

Scarlett's beach body looked exactly like her sit-on-the-sofa body. But in a swimsuit.

'I've got a month before my next doctor's appointment.' Something about the way Charlie said it sounded serious.

'They'll do another ECG,' he explained. 'To monitor my heart. Not that there's definitely anything wrong, but with my mum's heart attack…'

'I didn't know that's how she passed away,' Max said. 'She wasn't that old?'

Charlie shook his head. 'These things sometimes run in the family, apparently. Mum's mum was only in her thirties. So at least Mum got longer than that. There's a chance I didn't inherit the dicky heart so I really do need to get fit. Mum cleaned every day and that definitely kept her in good shape, so maybe it staved off the inevitable for a few years. I've got to work harder at it, though I have slimmed down a bit.'

'I noticed, mate!' Max said, sticking his thumbs up. 'You're looking good. If you ever want to jog together, I'd be up for that. I don't run that much so I'm probably as unfit as you.'

Charlie and Scarlett both glanced from Max's biceps to his powerful legs.

'It would be good practice for the dogs as well,' Scarlett said. 'They're getting to the point now where they should be able to put into practice everything you've been teaching them… We can have a little test today. Think of it as a pop quiz to see how well they're doing.'

'I wish we'd studied more, Murph,' Max said.

'It's nothing to worry about. Now, Charlie, I've brought loads of toys that Barkley hasn't seen before, so he'll be extra curious about them. Let's see how strong his self-control is.'

Both dogs strained at their leads as rubber toys bounced all over the floor. She often wondered whether the dogs enjoyed the training. They certainly got a lot of treats. Maybe that made up for having to work for them.

The pair bounded for the toys as soon as they were let off their leads.

'Barkley!' Charlie cautioned.

Barkley's rump hit the linoleum like it was drawn there by a magnet. He waited. Charlie waited. 'Good boy, go on.'

He lunged for the squeaky mushroom, which Scarlett had nicked from the house. Then he spotted the hamburger. He loved hamburgers even more than mushrooms. He sat and looked at Charlie. 'Go ahead.'

It took a few tries, but eventually he got hold of both toys. He turned to Charlie with his wide-open mouth full of rubber.

'Well, what do you want me to do?' Charlie asked his dog. 'Spit one out.'

Barkley might have, if he hadn't noticed the red fire hydrant.

'How many toys do you think he can shove in there?' Max wondered.

'This is the dog who got an entire roast chicken in his mouth,' Charlie reminded them.

Barkley's golden ears flopped forward as he stood

over the hydrant, staring as he tried to work around the laws of physics. He seemed to be trying to levitate the hydrant with his glare.

'Call him over, Charlie, and get him to drop the toys so he can pick up the new one.'

Meanwhile, Murphy played catch with himself. The setter tossed a squeaky toy into the air, then missed it by a mile, slipping all over the lino in the process.

Scarlett's grin widened. Aside from the pleasure of watching a dog being silly, Murphy was distracting himself. The training was actually starting to work. Between tosses he raced around in a victory lap with his tail tucked under. Snatch, throw, miss, race round. The more he ran the more high-spirited he became. She could hear him giving off throaty little growls as if the toys had dared to come alive to evade him. His tongue lolled as he raced faster and faster. Barkley watched him for a few seconds before sitting down to wait for the whirlwind to subside.

'Max, Murphy may be getting a little overexcited. See if you can calm him down. Remember your techniques.'

But Murphy wasn't interested in Max's techniques. He dodged left and right when Max tried to catch him. Oh good, keep away from the human!

Scarlett noticed just as Murphy did that the door into the hallway was open. He cocked his head as someone shouted 'Bingo!'

'Max, get the door!'

It was too late. The dog shot into the hall, and straight into the senior ladies' bingo night. Scarlett didn't need to hear the startled shouts to know what was happening in there.

They found Murphy straddling a grey-haired

woman. 'Murphy, no, bad dog!' Max hauled his pet off the nana. 'I am so sorry!' he said, brushing off the soft blue arm of her cardigan, where Murphy had concentrated his attention.

'Oh, that's all right, young man,' she said, adjusting her glasses where they'd slipped sideways. 'I haven't had that much attention in years!'

Barkley ambled up behind them with the hydrant between his teeth, wondering what he'd missed.

The mood was subdued back in their own room. Even Barkley seemed to lose interest in the squeaky toys. 'He needs the snip,' Max said, pulling his dog into an embrace as he sat beside him on the lino. 'He can't be trusted off the lead.'

Charlie patted Max's shoulder. 'I'm really sorry, buddy.'

Max murmured into the silky red fur on Murphy's shoulder. 'I don't want to do it to you.'

'Do you think it might make you feel better to talk to a vet first,' Scarlett wondered, 'to find out what's involved? It's really a straightforward procedure. Murphy would be sedated and have painkillers. It won't hurt him.'

'How do you know?' Max snapped. 'How many times have you had your bollocks cut off? I'm sorry! I know you're only trying to help and at least you gave him the chance to turn things around.'

She sat on the lino too. Charlie joined them.

'You know what would help?' Max said, straightening up. 'If you came with me when we go. You too, Charlie, would you?'

Scarlett nodded, rubbing Murphy's ear. 'Of course. You'll schedule the procedure, then, and tell us when?'

'I might have some questions first.'

'We can find out whatever you need to know.'

The dog lolled his head towards Scarlett and trained his big brown eyes on her. Then he caught her in the face with his tongue. That sweet, doomed dog kissed the judge who'd just condemned him.

Chapter 28

'What are you doing here?' Scarlett demanded. How much more direct did she have to be for everyone to just leave her alone? She'd clearly ignored every single voice message for a week. If she didn't want to talk on the phone, why on earth would she want to be trapped in her own house to do it in person?

The dogs were acting like they'd been reunited with the long-lost friend they'd never thought they'd see again. But then they nearly wet themselves when they heard the tin opener before every meal.

'I'm taking the dogs out.'

Handy excuse. She never came this early.

'Scarlett, can't we talk? I'm worried about you.' Shannon's expression was pleading. 'Rufus just rambles on the phone and I can't make any sense of it. What is going on with you two?'

All the uncertainty of the past week slapped her in

the face. She could feel it, hot and stinging on her skin. She stuffed her paperback into her bag for the train journey later. 'If you've talked to Rufus, then you must be up to speed on things. I'm late. I've got to go.' She turned away before Shannon could see her tears.

'I want to hear it from your side.'

Her side?! Let's see. Her husband, who could barely get it up with her, had a screaming orgasm while thinking of her best friend. Yeah, right, that would feel great to admit… *to her best friend.* 'I can't. I'm meeting Gemma at the hospital for her scan.'

'Scarlett, if you don't want to talk to me, please at least tell me you're talking to someone?' Shannon's voice wobbled. Guilt, maybe. 'You shouldn't go through something like this alone.'

'I'm not alone. I do have other friends besides you. I've got to go now.'

It took most of the walk to the station to calm down. She wasn't angry with Shannon, exactly. She was furious that it had happened, though. Rufus conjuring up Shannon when he was naked might not be her fault, but now Scarlett had to spend the rest of her life wondering at what point he'd started preferring his best friend to his wife.

Her emotions were all mixed up with events. She'd run in circles inside her head so many times that she no longer knew what she thought about any of it. The only thing left were her feelings.

Disbelief. Humiliation. Fury.

She definitely wasn't ready to talk to Shannon.

Gemma had rung in the middle of breakfast with her request. 'Jacob's had an emergency at the hospital and

Mum and Dad are both working. Could you come with me to the hospital?'

Scarlett had stopped buttering her toast. 'What's wrong?'

'Nothing, it's for my twenty-week scan... I'm really sorry to ask, but it's too late to reschedule. I don't want to go alone. They might find something wrong, right?'

'I'm sure they won't!' Scarlett could feel her heart thumping in her neck. *I don't know if I can do this on top of everything else.*

'They're checking for abnormalities, Scarlett. That's what the scan is. What if they find something? You don't have to be in the room or see the baby, but maybe you could just sit in the waiting area? Or outside even, if that's more comfortable? I might need you when I come out.'

She was early to the hospital but standing there was better than having to face Shannon. She never thought she'd be grateful to look at someone else's baby scan rather than talk to her best friend.

The A&E department, she knew, was just around the corner. She'd once spent a night in its care. She didn't remember being driven there by one of her clients, and even her overnight stay was fuzzy. She did remember asking if anyone else had ever been concussed from being tripped by a dog. It happened all the time, said the doctor, though she'd suspected he was joking. They did a CT scan when she failed at touching her nose, but they let Rufus take her home when the scan came back clear. Her brain was the same as always – no less and no more. Rufus had stayed home from work to look after her. He got in all her favourite food and they ate in bed.

She pushed the memory away when she saw Gemma jogging from her car.

'Are you supposed to run?'

'You do know the baby can't fall out, right? Thanks for meeting me.' She glanced away. 'I know it's not easy, Scarlett. Do you want to come in or…?'

That was the question Scarlett had asked herself all the way to the hospital. She very much did want to be there. If only she could guarantee that she wouldn't hate her sister again when she saw the baby she was carrying. The last few months had helped dull those feelings, but if they came back while she was in the room, she'd spoil Gemma's scan and look like the world's worst sister in front of the sonographer.

'I'll come in and see how it goes, okay?'

Gemma grabbed her hand. 'Thank you. I'm shitting myself.'

They held hands all the way in to reception.

Her heart began to race when the nurse called Gemma's name. If only she knew how she'd feel when she saw the baby. Then she'd know whether she should be there or not. Intellectually she could tell herself she was about to glimpse her niece or nephew for the first time. Up to now, that was something only Gemma and Jacob got to do. What a magical gift to be invited into the circle with them.

She just wasn't sure if her emotions would listen to reason.

The sonographer had Gemma lie on the bed and pull her stretchy jeans away from her tummy. 'Pull your top up too, please,' he said. 'We don't want to get the gel on your clothes.'

'You look like you've had too much pasta,' Scarlett joked when she saw Gemma's tummy.

'Pasta *and* pudding, right?' she said as the sonographer put the wand to her tummy. She wasn't looking at Scarlett, though. She was staring over her shoulder at the monitor.

'There's your baby,' the sonographer said as psychedelic blobs started emerging and melting on screen. 'Hang on, it's hard to make out.' He dug around on Gemma's side. 'I'll see if I can get a better angle for you. Then we can see what's going on.'

Images kaleidoscoped in and out until something baby-shaped appeared. 'There,' he said gently.

Scarlett's eyes were glued to the screen too. This was the moment she'd coveted for herself. She waited for the ugly response. But where was the anger? When would the resentment hit her?

She examined her reaction. She peered into its corners and crevices. She shined the light in, looking for shadows. Sadness was there. And something that felt a lot like self-pity. She wanted to whisper 'Why not me?' to the sonographer.

'It looks so much like a baby,' Gemma mused. 'With a big head. Is that normal?'

Scarlett couldn't miss the worry in her voice.

The sonographer nodded as he looked intently at the screen. 'I'll do the measurements in a minute.'

'Look, that's our nose!' Scarlett said. 'God, Gemma, it's your profile, isn't it? How amazing! And is that the spine?'

'All the bones show up white. There's the hands and fingers.' He pointed. 'And the thigh bone, see?'

Scarlett waited to be resentful or angry, but even the sadness receded as she stared at Gemma's child. 'I'm sorry Jacob's not here,' she said.

Gemma turned from the screen. 'I'm glad you are.' There were tears in her eyes as they both looked back at Scarlett's niece. Or nephew.

'Do you know the sex, Gemma? Do you want to

know?'

'Could we see?' she asked the sonographer. 'My husband wants to know too.'

'We can try.' He moved the wand around. 'Sometimes it's not very clear.' He tried another spot. 'And if we don't see a willy it doesn't necessarily guarantee it's a girl. They can be notoriously shy… oh. Well. That's pretty definitively a boy.'

'A boy!' Gemma said.

'Did you have a preference?'

Gemma nodded. 'Healthy.'

They watched the sonographer as he turned the monitor away from them and set about his analysis. 'He's looking for things that could be wrong,' Gemma quietly explained. 'Spina bifida and things like that.'

'Down's syndrome?' Scarlett asked.

'No, I did a blood test for that and it's fine.'

'You didn't tell me that.'

Gemma shrugged. 'Well, it was early on. There was no reason to worry you.'

'That's not why you didn't tell me.'

'It doesn't matter.'

It was amazing, really, that Gemma didn't hate her for ruining her pregnancy. It was supposed to be the happiest time of her life, to share with the people she loved most, and there she was, afraid to talk to her own sister. 'I love you,' she said.

'Don't get sentimental. I'm very hormonal.'

A tense ten minutes later the sonographer pronounced Gemma's baby healthy. He was clearly pleased to deliver the good news.

Gemma laughed the way she always did when she was nervous and trying to cover it up. As the sonographer talked through everything he'd checked, Gemma's hand found Scarlett's. They stayed like that till it was time to go.

Chapter 29

Sampson's droopy eyes weren't impressed and his jowls even more downturned than usual as he watched Mr Darcy's greyhounds cavort round him. Speed and cunning might have been handy for tracking down dinner in the olden days, but they were, frankly, a total waste of energy in this era of tin openers and owners with opposable thumbs. Sampson's chin fell between his front paws with a wheezy sigh.

Shannon had to look hard to spot the joy in that dog, but it was there despite having a face like a smacked arse. When his compact rear end wriggled or he panted Pedigree Meaty Meals into her face, he was ecstatic. Warm breezes made him turn his face skyward with contentment, and rubbing his velvety brush-cut fur sent him into a blissful stupor. He could do without walking to the park, but he did enjoy lying with his nose in the grass once they got there.

She snuck another glance at Josh as he chased the greyhounds (must stop thinking of him as Mr Darcy). It was a given now that they'd chat whenever they saw each other. Awkward pauses still peppered their conversations, but it was a start. Well, what did she expect when the two shyest people in Berkshire county tried talking to each other?

'Fifi, Clive, come here,' Josh called. They pretended he was speaking Swahili. 'Do they ever play?'

'Only with each other. They're the most insular dogs I've ever met.'

As long as they stuck to dog-talk, the wheels of their conversations stayed greased. It was only when topics veered into real life that they got stuck.

'Fifi, Clive, come on, boy, come here, come on! Clive, come here, boy. There's a good girl, Fifi, come on!' Flapping his arms seemed to pump up his excitement like a bellows on a fire.

The poodles watched him descend into manic cheerleading.

'They won't listen,' she said. 'They may as well be cats.'

Eventually he gave up and jogged back to her bench, though he stared straight ahead when he sat down.

She did too. They could have been strangers waiting for the number nine bus.

A wood dove cooed in the tree behind them. The sound always made her think of summer.

'So, um, I was thinking,' he said, still staring into middle distance. 'Maybe we could, if you want, I don't know, get a coffee or something after this? If you drink coffee? Or tea? Or… water? Do you drink water?'

'I drink water.'

'Okay, then.'

'Okay.'

'After this?'

'Okay. Let me get Sampson moving.'

The bulldog's ears twitched at his name. He stared up at her.

'Come along.' She gave his lead a gentle tug.

Josh joined in with his encouragement. 'Sampson, come on, boy!' He sprang from the bench. 'Time to go…. we're going now, there's a good boy. Come on. Getup. Geeet-up.'

Sampson's gaze shifted from Josh to Shannon and back again.

Sighing, Shannon looped her bag over her head so it went across her body. With a weightlifter's squat she deadlifted the dog. 'You don't get any lighter,' she told him as he lolled on his back in her arms.

Pedigree Meaty Meal hit her in the face.

She might be skinny, but Shannon was strong. Carrying a stubborn dog will do that for a person. 'He usually gets uncomfortable like this after a while. Then he'll walk,' she explained.

Sure enough, Sampson decided to put his feet on the ground on the way home. They dropped him off, then the poodles and finally the greyhounds at Josh's house.

After the last of their four-legged conversation starters left them, Shannon had to wrack her brain for something to say. 'Do you drink coffee a lot?'

Or tea? Or water? Crikey, she was as bad as him.

'Not a lot,' he told the zebra crossing in front of them. 'I like hot chocolate.'

'Me too.'

'That's good. Hot chocolate is good. Chocolatey.'

'Maybe the café does it,' she said to the lamp post.

'Maybe.'

'With whipped cream. Maybe.'

They dove into the first open café they found. Any port in an awkward storm.

Why couldn't they just talk like normal people? *Come on, Shannon,* she urged herself as they ordered their hot drinks. *You can do this.*

'Do you like art?' she asked as they sat at the little round table in the wide bay window. She'd thought of the question on the way over, but they'd been too busy torturing the hot chocolate conversation to death. 'I do art.'

'You do? What kind?' He scanned the room like some of her work might be on the walls. It was one of those cafes with bunting and mismatched teacups on shelves.

'The usual kind,' she said. 'Paintings.'

'I like paintings.'

'Me too.' Another conversation was heading straight for the bin. For the first time since they sat, she forced herself not to see Mr Darcy when she looked at him. He was just a guy, like Julian or Rufus or any of her art school classmates who she'd managed to hold conversations with over the years. Pretend he's Rufus. 'I just finished my Fine Arts degree course in London.'

Rufus didn't have deep green eyes like Josh, though.

'Couldn't you have done it locally?' He spooned some of the cream from his hot chocolate into his mouth.

Rufus didn't have lips like him either. Josh's were shaped like a cupid's bow and naturally turned up at the corners.

'I could have, but Reading didn't accept me,' she said, pushing his lips from her mind. 'That's okay, though. I've been here all my life, so going to London made a nice change. We had our degree show there and everything. I was cacking myself, to be honest. All those people looking at my work.'

'I don't blame you! It's my worst nightmare... I play piano, but I don't do gigs. That's cacking territory for me too.'

Kindred cackers. Finally, they had some common ground that didn't involve dogs. Poo-covered ground, but still. Plus, he was creative! 'What's the opposite of musical? Oh yeah, tone-deaf, that's me,' she admitted. 'Would you be good enough to do a gig?' She reddened. 'I mean, how long have you been playing?'

'I started when I was eight.' He fiddled with the handle of his mug while she tried not to stare at his piano-playing fingers. 'My mum made me take lessons from our neighbour but I just fool around on it now. I can't imagine performing anywhere live.'

She laughed. 'We *are* alike.'

'I do have some songs on YouTube,' he murmured. 'Maybe you could listen if you want. Please, though, not when I'm with you!'

'Yeah, I'd like to hear them.' It probably wasn't the time to tell a classically trained pianist how much she loved cheesy pop songs. 'Do you see live music a lot? I don't really, though every time I do I tell myself I should go more often.'

He nodded, saying, 'I do the same thing with the theatre.'

'Or flossing your teeth.'

He frowned.

'I mean, I do floss my teeth. Just... not as... often... God, I'm sorry I'm so bad at this!'

Then he laughed. 'Not nearly as bad as me. Listen, Shannon, it's not like I can take my own advice, but maybe we could both try to relax. I promise I'm not scary, and I know you're not either. Just the opposite. You're quite lovely.'

That didn't sound scary at all.

Chapter 30

Scarlett hadn't seen Rufus in fourteen days, nineteen hours and (she checked her phone) about fifteen minutes. He'd left her at least twenty voice messages though, so she shouldn't have been surprised to find him sitting on their front step when she got home from Charlie and Naomi's sessions in London.

'You're actually doorstepping me?' she called from the pavement as Rufus came into view.

'It works for journalists,' he called back, rising to his feet.

'What makes you think I want to see you?'

'I know you don't want to see me. Your silence is deafening. But we've got to talk.'

That little phrase caved her tummy in. How many times had she heard it at the end of a relationship? How many times had she said it herself? 'I don't feel much like talking, thank you.'

'Scarlett, we can't go on like this. We're married. We've got to talk to each other.'

Her pace slowed. 'You know that's not true, Rufus. Your parents never talk to each other. It's worked for them for decades.' When he smiled she clamped her mouth shut. She wouldn't let herself fall into this banter. It was too easy, too normal and she was afraid to feel normal. Because as soon as she let her guard down, as soon as she dared to think there might be a way forward, the reality slapped her again. It left marks every time.

He looked too good to be feeling very terrible. His hair wasn't greasy or his stubble unkempt; he didn't look like he'd been living on a diet of takeaways and despair. She knew she couldn't say the same.

'I'd like to see the dogs, please. I've missed them.'

'Suit yourself.' She held her breath as she moved past him to unlock the door. She would not be undone by the whiff of lemon shower gel. 'You could have come earlier when I wasn't here.'

'I know.' To the delight of the dogs he followed her inside.

'Take them for a walk if you want,' she said as they danced all over his feet. Anything to get him out of the house so her heartrate could return to normal. As she passed the mirror in the hall, she wiped away some of the eyeliner that had smudged under her eyes.

Stop that! She forced her hand to stay away from her hair. Let it be lank and unfluffed. It didn't matter.

'I've got to go soon, so you can let yourself out,' she called over her shoulder as she headed for the kitchen.

'I know,' he said. 'Puppy graduation. Do you think I could come with you? Maybe take the dogs with us and have a day out with the family?'

She whipped round. He had the nerve to try smiling. 'What, and just pretend everything is fine all of a sudden? No, Rufus, you can't come with me. What are you thinking?'

'I'm not thinking, I'm hoping. Scarlett. We have to find a way through this.'

'I don't have any idea how to do that. Please, tell me how, will you? Because I can't just forget everything that's happened and go on as normal, being best friends with the woman you may actually want to be with.'

'I DON'T! Christ, Scarlett, can't you understand that? I don't have any interest in Shannon. I never have. We're mates, that's all. What I said was a mistake. It doesn't mean anything.'

Of course it meant something. Maybe not that they were having an affair, but it meant that something wasn't right. Besides, it wasn't just Shannon, was it? That may have been what had knocked the stuffing out of Scarlett, but it wasn't the only problem. It might not even be the biggest one. If he couldn't see that, then there wasn't really anything left to say.

'You need to go now,' she said.

His expression clouded over. 'Fine. I want to see the dogs regularly. They're mine too.'

She couldn't believe they were discussing custody. She willed her voice not to shake. 'Suit yourself. I'd prefer it if you didn't come when I'm here, but if you can't do that, then don't expect me to drop everything to welcome you.'

'Yeah, I can see that's not going to happen,' he said, clipping on the dogs' leads.

Scarlett loved puppy graduation more than any other day in her work calendar, and not even her crumbling life dimmed the joy she felt watching her students cavort in the warm weekend grass. Their humans couldn't be prouder if they'd been the ones graduating.

But today was all about the dogs. 'Milo,' she called the first puppy forward. Milo tripped towards her on the biggest paws she'd ever seen in a beagle mix. His owner claimed he'd been sired by a spaniel, but Scarlett suspected Milo's mother had had an affair with a Great Dane.

'Congratulations,' she said to Milo's owner as she handed him the diploma. 'And this is for Milo.' She squatted to puppy level so she could rub his soft brown ears. 'They're special treats that I think he'll love.'

As she called up each dog for their diploma and treats, she remembered how excited she'd been when Fred and Ginger were pups.

She and Rufus had talked a lot about getting dogs while they planned their wedding together. 'They'll be our trial kids,' Rufus had joked. 'If we manage not to screw them up, then we'll be okay parents.'

'You don't have a lot of faith in your girlfriend's training abilities,' Scarlett had said. Her business was expanding enough, at last, to let her believe it was a going concern. Going so well, in fact, that it was hard to keep up on her own.

'Fiancée,' Rufus had corrected.

'Fiancée, I mean.' She'd giggled, like she did every time she thought about marrying Rufus. They were doing all the planning together and, so far, they'd agreed on everything. He seemed to have a new idea every day that he could barely wait to share with her.

So she was amazed that he managed to keep his surprise from her till their wedding day.

They had a strict no-peeking policy that morning, with Scarlett sequestered in one part of the church and

Rufus in the other. 'Do you think Rufus has champagne too?' Gemma asked, knocking back the last sip in her glass.

'Don't drink too much,' Felicia scolded, 'or you'll fall asleep at the reception.'

'Not a chance,' said Gemma. 'I'm too excited. My big sister's wedding. Who'd have thought, after all the losers she's dated?'

'They weren't all losers,' objected Scarlett as she stared at herself in the mirror. She'd done that for most of the morning. Soft curls framed her face, floating out from beneath her grandmother's cathedral-length veil (something old). Despite the modern cut of her figure-hugging dress (something new) it suited perfectly.

They all jumped at the knock on the door. 'Scarlett?' her dad called. 'Are you decent?'

She could see his face beaming over the huge red bow on the box in his arms. 'I'm Rufus's emissary. He's asked me to give you your wedding day present.'

'Wow, that doesn't look like jewellery,' Gemma noted.

It definitely didn't sound like jewellery either.

Her face broke into a smile as she heard the scuffling and snuffling inside.

'You'd better take the lid off,' said her dad.

'What's he done?' Felicia said as she and Julia crowded around the box.

But Scarlett knew. As she opened the lid, two pairs of button eyes looked up. Set against their snow-white fur, they looked like toys. Their little black noses and pink tongues went straight for their new owner's hands.

'Those are the cutest things I've ever seen!' Gemma squealed, sticking her hand into the box to stroke their soft fur.

'This is for you.' Her dad handed over an envelope.

> *Dear Scarlett,*
> *Today is the first day of the rest of our lives together and I can hardly believe it's really happening. I love you more than I ever thought I could love anyone and can't wait to be your husband and build our life together.*
>
> *I hope you love our dogs as much as I do. They haven't got names so we can choose them together. I thought you might like something blue on your wedding day.*
> *I love you,*
> *Rufus*

Sure enough, tied around each tiny collar was a pale blue bow. 'Dad, tell him that yes, I do love our dogs already.' She buried her nose in their fur. Sod the make-up, these were their dogs!

She toyed with their pale blue leashes. 'Do you think I could take them down the aisle with me?'

Her dad nodded. 'I think that's the idea. You can try. What's the worst that can happen?'

'Will that be okay?' sensible Felicia asked. 'With the vicar, I mean?'

'It's their wedding day, honey. They get to do what they want. Rufus says there's a puppy minder in the back pew. He's thought of everything.'

'Then I'll do it!' Scarlett said. 'If they get tired or don't want to walk, I can hand them over to the puppy minder.'

What an entrance she was going to make!

Nerves fluttered in her tummy as she stood with

her dad in the vestibule listening for the organ to begin her entrance music. The puppies stepped all over her satin shoes in what would become their signature move. She was too happy to care about a few paw prints.

'Ready?' her dad asked, crooking his arm for her to take.

The puppies led the way, riding a wave of 'aahs' that threatened to upstage the bride. Their little behinds wriggled with excitement as they zigzagged up the aisle. Scarlett watched Rufus burst into laughter as he waited for them at the front. His eyes shone with tears.

The vicar's eyes looked less friendly, though. Bride or no bride, she knew she was in for a ticking off when she got to the front. But until then she was enjoying every single second.

The faces of everyone she loved in the world beamed back at her, and no one more so than Shannon. She stood at Rufus's side, taking her best woman duties very seriously to make sure everything went perfectly.

But she hadn't factored in Rufus's surprise. Just as Scarlett was about to reach the front of the church, Shannon's mouth made a little 'O'.

Scarlett looked down. One of the puppies was squatting on its tiny haunches, leaving a puddle on the floor of god's house.

When she heard Rufus exclaim 'Oh, Jesus', her eyes flicked from their peeing puppy to the vicar. His expression darkened even more.

Lifting the hem of her dress, Scarlett stepped around the puddle. What else was she supposed to do – blot it up with her train? Besides, nothing was going to stop her progress towards Rufus.

Her dad pulled his soon-to-be son-in-law into a hug. Then he kissed Scarlett's cheek and went to sit between Felicia and Julia in the front row.

'You are beautiful,' Rufus told her, chastely taking her hand. Kisses would have to wait till they had official permission. 'Nice entrance. Sorry, vicar, we'll get that cleaned up.' He signalled to the woman at the back who already had paper towels in hand.

It wasn't a wedding anyone would easily forget. They still put a little cheque in with their Christmas card to that church every year, but Scarlett wasn't sure they'd bought the vicar's forgiveness quite yet.

Chapter 31

She didn't want to turn up at Margaret's party on her own, but she couldn't very well ask to bring Gemma. Margaret wanted fewer guests, not more. Besides, she told herself (in her mother's voice), it would be character-building. At the very worst she'd be bored for a few hours. At least she wouldn't be sitting alone in her house.

She scanned through her meagre wardrobe choices, her heart sinking as her hand swept over the dress she'd worn the night Rufus took her out for that pricey meal in London. It was her best dress. She didn't want to go to the party looking like Biscuit's dog trainer. But she worried that memories would swamp her when she zipped herself into the frock.

Could clothes hold memories like that? She stared at the dress. There was only one way to find out.

Shimmying out of her jeans and T-shirt she pulled the dress over her hips. It was soft, not silk but silky. Its deep green fabric hugged her waist without being clingy and its flare at the hem made it swing with each step. She could wear her flat boots so her feet wouldn't hurt from standing.

Maybe the dress needed a good cosmic airing out anyway. She could exorcise the memory of dinner with Rufus by having fun at the party. And if she didn't have fun, she could be home in her jimjams by ten.

Scarlett heard the revelry even before she reached Margaret's house. Loads of people milled about in front, smoking and chatting with drinks in their hands. So much for Margaret's wish for an intimate gathering.

All the shrubs and the cherry tree were festooned in white fairy lights and every window glowed. It looked like the kind of party she'd always wanted to be invited to. She fixed her face into her I'm-already-having-fun expression and made her way through the open front door.

She could see why so many people were outside. There was no room in the house. She squeezed between the guests who lined the entrance, self-consciously trying not to rub up against anything too intimate.

Nearly all the men wore suits, and it was nearly all men. It looked like a sales conference with more atmosphere. Every so often she glimpsed a flash of something that wasn't worsted wool, but she didn't see Margaret.

She took her phone out. That should buy her five minutes or so before she looked as Sally-No-Mates as she felt.

She'd never been so happy to see a missed call from Max. She rang him back.

'Hiya Scarlett! I was just wondering if there's an antidote to Viagra?'

'Erm, Max, that's not really something I've got a lot

of experience in. If it's a problem, you may need to go to A&E.'

Max barked out a laugh. 'No, no, sorry! It's not for me. I just wondered if there's something that does the opposite of Viagra, you know, to dampen a sex drive instead of encourage it?'

She thought for a moment. 'I'd have to say wearing a onesie to bed. Or wedge heels. They're both guaranteed to dampen desire.'

'I couldn't make Murphy wear a onesie. Isn't there a pill or something?'

'Max, you're not actually thinking about giving a drug to Murphy for the rest of his life? Doesn't neutering seem kinder than that?'

He sighed. 'I guess so. Sorry to bother you.'

'I want you to feel free to ring any time. It's important that you're comfortable with the procedure. Okay?'

He'd already had several ideas for saving Murphy from the snip. What would he think of next?

Suddenly people started flowing away through the kitchen, as if someone had unblocked the plughole in a house-sized sink. As she allowed herself to be swept along on the tide, she gasped at the decorations. Pastel tissue-paper flowers of all sizes cascaded across the walls in great sprays and swirls. They tumbled from the mantelpiece and across the tables. They hung upside down in frothy pastel pops of colour from the high ceilings, with their sunny faces beaming down upon the heads of the crowd. The effect was womb-like and magical. It reminded Scarlett of being in one of those old-fashioned sweet shops.

As she reached the kitchen she saw two things: the reason for the flow of people, and Julian with his catering crew. The back doors had been flung open to the evening and guests were making for the garden. Fairy lights twinkled all along the fences and bamboo garden torches lined the walkway.

'Finally, some room!' Julian shouted, kissing Scarlett's cheek. 'We had to use the Christmas lights to make the back habitable. I just hope it doesn't rain or everyone out there's going to get electrocuted. Well? What do you think? Is it fabulous, or what?'

'It's amazing, Julian, really. How did you pull this off?'

'Thank you very much.' He curtsied in his lilac tutu. The others – boys and girls – wore colourful tutus as well, with contrasting stripy or polka-dotted knee socks and white vests. There was no mistaking any of Julian's crew for the guests. 'It was simple, really. Margaret got a job lot of tissue paper off eBay and we made all the flowers together. Team Margaret are very creative, you know.'

'Team Margaret?' she asked.

'Well, we're definitely not Team Arthur. What a pillock.'

'And the outfits? From your dressing-up box?' She wished she'd worn something more flamboyant. Looking around, she'd rather be part of Julian's tribe.

His long silky plaits shimmied when he shook his head. 'Loads of us have tutus, as it turns out. I thought I was more original, but alas, no.'

They both noticed Margaret coming towards them. 'I'm so pleased for her,' he said fondly. 'This is her triumph.'

Surely, Arthur and her children couldn't help but be impressed with what she'd managed to pull off in just a few weeks.

'Mrs Deering, hello!' They hugged. 'Your Julian has

been such a dream. Blimey, will you look at this place?' She glanced over her shoulder. 'It puts Octavia to shame, and she's supposed to be a professional.'

Scarlett followed Margaret's gaze. 'She's *here*?'

Sure enough, Octavia stood unsmiling beside a lanky man in a blue tartan suit and yellow cravat. Based on his expression, he couldn't wait for someone to point out his eccentricity.

'Can you bloomin' believe the cheek of that woman? Butter wouldn't melt.'

When one of Julian's team swooped by with a tray full of canapes, Scarlett popped a tiny puff into her mouth.

'These are delicious, Margaret,' she said between chews of pastry and crab.

'Only the finest for Arthur and his friends.' She winked.

As Julian rushed off to help with the drinks and Margaret went to greet new arrivals, Scarlett found herself gravitating towards the Aga in the kitchen. Biscuit lay curled in her basket, stubbornly oblivious to the human invasion. 'Don't worry,' Scarlett told the dog as she carefully squatted down in her dress, 'you'll have the house to yourself again in a few hours.'

Biscuit gently wagged her feathery tail as she looked up.

As much as she wanted to stay there in the corner with the dog, she knew she had to socialise at least a bit, if only so she could tell Margaret later how nice her friends were. She searched for a group who looked friendly, sure they'd be Margaret's friends instead of Arthur's business contacts.

She approached two middle-aged women standing in the opposite corner of the kitchen. They smiled invitingly when she caught their eyes. Both women wore the same kind of trendy jeans and soft-looking jumpers that Margaret favoured.

'You're friends of Margaret's?' she asked. 'I'm Scarlett. I've been training her dog, Biscuit.'

'Oh, we know Biscuit!' The Asian woman rolled her eyes. 'Margaret has to bring her whenever we meet. You've done wonders for that dog, I must say!'

'For them both,' said the pretty blonde beside her. 'Margaret is definitely more confident these days.'

'That's nice to hear,' Scarlett said. 'And Biscuit's behaviour is all down to her. She's been working really hard with her.'

Both women nodded. 'She works hard at everything. Look at this party – isn't it marvellous? She's always the perfect hostess.'

Scarlett swallowed her smirk, wondering how well they really knew Margaret. She felt privileged to have seen the inner workings of her household over the past few months, and to know she wasn't the only one who used Febreze or invoked the five-second rule for food dropped on the floor.

They chatted easily about Margaret and the Hampstead Heath WI as the tulle-swathed waitstaff kept their wine glasses topped up.

'That's Arthur?' she asked her new friends as a tall man with a shock of thick ginger hair loudly tapped his glass with his wedding ring.

'That's him.'

People drifted in from the hallway and the garden as he started speaking.

'Thank you, everyone, for coming tonight to celebrate Margaret's, ahem, mumble, mumble birthday.'

'Fifty!' shouted a man to their left.

'A lady never tells,' joked Arthur. 'And clearly you're no lady! Where is she? Where's my wife?'

Heads swivelled to find Margaret, who was lurking at the edge of the crowd.

'Come here, darling.' Arthur beckoned her to the middle of the room. Couldn't he see she'd hate that? 'Everyone wants to wish you happy birthday.'

Margaret blushed deeply as Arthur hauled her into the limelight. 'This is a fantastic party,' he said. 'And it's all down to one woman.'

Margaret smiled and started to say something just as Arthur cut her off. 'Octavia! Where's Octavia? She pulled together this whole party for Margaret. Isn't she wonderful?'

Scarlett heard Julian exclaim 'What the fuck?' just as Octavia rushed forward.

She wouldn't dare take credit! Scarlett would march up there herself to set the record straight if she did.

Octavia's face was aghast. 'You don't think I did this! Please, Arthur, paper flowers? It looks like a school class has been let loose with their scissors and paste.'

The room went silent. A few people craned their necks to get a better view of the decorations.

As Scarlett's eyes darted to Julian, she shook her head. Now wasn't the time to defend his handicrafts.

'It looks so contrived,' Octavia continued. 'Not natural at all. But I suppose that's Margaret's style.' Her pale, horsey face was contorted with malice.

Margaret found her voice. 'Our decorations look contrived? Please, Octavia, you're one to talk about looking unnatural. You've been tucked so many times you look like a hospital corner.'

The room gasped, but Octavia kept her cool. 'I haven't been involved in this party, Arthur,' she said again. 'I bowed out weeks ago. Over creative differences.' Her look challenged Margaret to disagree.

'But… then who did it?' Arthur asked. 'All the drinks? The flowers? Who catered?'

'Nobody,' said Margaret. 'No, I mean I did. Not nobody. I had to find a way to have the party after… Octavia resigned. Julian and his friends – they're the waiters – they did all the decorations and I got the wine from Oddbins, and do you know that Waitrose loans glasses for free?'

Arthur shook his head, clearly in shock. 'The food too? Did they make the little pigs in blankets? I loved those.' The room murmured its agreement. Scarlett could have eaten a whole plate of the things.

'They're from M&S.' Her look challenged her husband to make a big deal of that.

He blanched and took the bait. 'Margaret, pre-packaged food? Standards!'

Someone next to Scarlett whispered, 'But I love their chocolate fondants.'

Margaret drew herself up. She was nearly as tall as Arthur when she stood straight. 'Oh, give it a rest, will you please, Arthur? Don't act like you've got a Michelin-star palate. You've been eating bloomin' M&S ready meals for years and never knew the difference. All the food is from M&S and I think it's delicious. If you could have done better, you should have stepped in and catered your own damn party.'

Arthur seemed to notice all the people listening. 'Well, isn't that something? How about that, everyone? Margaret did this all on her own!' He managed to make it sound both insincere and condescending. 'I do wonder what she spent all the catering money on, though!'

That raised a hearty laugh from most of the men in

the room. None of the women cracked a smile, Scarlett noticed. A few looked openly hostile.

Scarlett watched Biscuit creep up beside Arthur. Spooked by all the noise, she started to bark.

She was just about to go to the dog when Margaret roared, 'Biscuit, go lay down!'

That not only silenced the dog, but the entire room. Biscuit slunk back to her bed.

'You were wondering where the catering money went?' she asked Arthur, making a big show of looking at the sparkling watch on her wrist. 'I thought it was time for a change, so I bought myself a birthday present. Though I won't be wearing it next weekend when I go to the spa I've booked myself.'

'How much did you spend?' he asked.

'A lot. Because you know what, Arthur? I'm worth it. I see that now. I do love you, but things are going to change around here. Does that surprise you?'

Scarlett's heart sank for her friend when Arthur shook his head. He wasn't about to accept a complete change of rules after nearly thirty years of marriage. She looked at the way his jaw jutted forward and his eyes glinted. That wasn't the kind of person who was told what to do.

Unfortunately for him, neither was Margaret anymore.

'Well, you seem to have a lot to say tonight.'

Margaret didn't answer. She continued to meet his eye.

'I've got something to say too.'

She seemed to deflate a little. He'd better not humiliate her in front of all these people, Scarlett thought.

He took Margaret's hands. 'I've completely underestimated you. You did all this. I'm afraid, in that case, I've been a bit of a knob. I'm sorry. I'm really sorry.'

Margaret smiled. 'It's all right, Arthur. You have been a bit of a knob, but I forgive you. Things are going to be different around here now, though.'

'Really? Does that mean you'll start cooking homemade food instead of M&S?'

'Definitely not.'

Arthur raised his glass. 'Ladies and gentlemen, please be upstanding for my wife. May you grace the world for another fifty years with your warmth, kindness, humour and… well, I was going to say honesty, but I guess I'd better say ingenuity instead. Frankly, darling, I can't imagine my life without you and I love you. Three cheers for Margaret!'

'Hip hip.'

'Hooray!'

Finally, it really did feel like the celebration that Margaret deserved.

Chapter 32

Shannon felt like Scarlett had stuck her in the heart with a chef's knife when she'd made that crack about having other friends. She deserved it, maybe. She was spending all her free time with Rufus. From Scarlett's point of view, that must look like she was taking sides.

And Shannon had to admit that she was taking sides, a bit. In all the years they'd been friends she'd never known Scarlett to be cruel. In fact, she'd say she was one of the kindest people she knew, building a business around helping dogs and their owners and taking Shannon on when she needed work. She was always going above and beyond for people. She'd even put her own feelings aside to go with Gemma to her scan. That couldn't have been easy.

Yet Scarlett was freezing Rufus out over something he couldn't control. There he was having to deal with finding out he'd never father children, and she was rejecting him for it. It wasn't fair.

Rufus might be reluctant to call Scarlett out on that,

but Shannon wasn't. Her friend was hurting too much to let it go on.

He answered his hotel room door in sweats and a faded grey T-shirt.

'Am I interrupting anything?'

'Just having some pizza,' he said, waving a slice at her. 'Are you hungry?'

He stepped aside to let her into the gloomy room. The TV was on with the sound down and there were clothes strewn across the chair and piled on the floor in the corner. A towel hung over the bathroom door.

'I like what you've done with the place.'

'I wasn't expecting company,' he said, picking up a beer bottle from the bedside table and smoothing the bedcover.

'Drinking alone?' Her tone was teasing despite the seriousness of the question. 'Don't they clean in here every day?'

'Yeah, they clean around my stuff. Pizza?' He offered her the box.

She tore off a slice. 'Mmm, extra grease. Planning to end it all by having a heart attack?'

The joke fell flat. 'Did you see Scarlett when you went over today?' she tried.

'No, she wasn't there. Have you seen her?'

Shannon shook her head. 'We haven't even talked properly. It's ridiculous, isn't it? We should go over. That's what I'm thinking.'

Rufus glanced away. 'She won't talk to me.'

'She can't ignore us if we're standing in front of her.' She hoped that was true. 'Come on, Rufus. This has to stop, don't you think? You can't live here forever.'

He shook his head. 'I guess I'll eventually get a flat.'

The way he said it broke her heart. 'You won't have

to do that. You two just need to talk again. Come on, come with me. We'll go together. Moral support.'

She could see him weighing up the proposition. 'Change into something decent first, though. Come on. You know you need to talk to her.'

He must have wanted convincing. They made their way to his house as Shannon tried to calm herself. What if Scarlett was horrible to them? What were they supposed to do if she slammed the door in their faces? Or phoned the police? She'd definitely cry if that happened. She might get angry too. Who did Scarlett think she was, exactly, to punish Rufus for something he couldn't help? And punishing Shannon for it too? She had a lot of nerve, actually.

'Will you use your key?' she asked as they walked up the path to the house.

He shook his head. 'It doesn't feel right. That's fucked up.'

It felt like progress when Scarlett answered the bell. She could see through the window that they were out there. 'You've brought reinforcements.'

'Hello to you too,' Shannon snapped.

'Sorry, hello,' she answered.

'Can we come in?'

'I can't legally stop you.' She walked back into the house and through to the living room.

'Get your coat. It's chilly in here,' Shannon whispered.

'I've had my coat on for weeks,' he murmured back as they followed Scarlett.

Shannon wished they'd worked out who was going to say what, because it was uncomfortable sitting there staring at each other. They could only fuss over Fred and Ginger for so long. Her eyes found Rufus's. *Say something,* she urged. But apparently, he'd lost his voice.

She really saw herself as the backup act for Rufus's show, but he seemed to expect her to headline on the main stage.

The hardest part about the last few weeks wasn't that Scarlett wouldn't talk to her or that Rufus was so upset. It wasn't even the way she felt pulled in opposite directions by her friendships. The thing she couldn't get her head around was that they were in this situation at all. She'd have bet everything she had that nothing could make Scarlett and Rufus stop talking to each other. It was as if completely new personalities had emerged from her best friends, as incomparable as a butterfly is to the caterpillar it was before. Only these emerging personalities were far uglier. And to think they'd been lurking there inside her friends. How could someone who you've trusted with your most intimate secrets and feelings turn so cold? It scared her to think that love could work like that. Maybe she was better off without it.

Rufus was still mute, leaving Shannon to fill the silence. 'Scarlett, I thought you and Rufus should talk.'

Scarlett sat back and crossed her arms. 'I don't think so.'

She thought fast. 'Well, will you at least talk to me?' She took Scarlett's shrug as a yes. 'I know you've been through a lot lately. Both of you have. And that's been really hard, but you and Rufus are in this together. I can't imagine two people who are more committed than you. I've known Rufus since we were seven and I can tell you that you are the love of his life.'

Scarlett snorted.

She stared at Rufus, willing him to speak up. Surely she wasn't going to have to do all the work. 'Hello, Rufus! Now would be a good time to say something.'

He slumped into the sofa. 'What do you want me to say? She knows she's the most important person in the world to me. I've told her. It doesn't seem to matter. Nothing I do or say is good enough for her.'

A flash of anger knocked Shannon off balance. Wasn't it bad enough for him to hear that his swimmers weren't even making it into the pool? Now he had to put up with his own wife betting against him. 'Scarlett, is this really something you can't get over? For his sake? I know it must be a shock, but really, you've got other options.'

'What other options have I got, Shannon?'

'There aren't other options,' Rufus said.

But Shannon cut him off. 'Sperm donation, for one thing. Or adoption. If you want a baby, there are ways for you two to have one.'

'I don't believe this,' Scarlett said, getting to her feet.

Shannon stood up too. 'Don't be angry! I'm just saying that you and Rufus love each other, so find a way to have a baby together.'

What did Rufus mean there weren't other options? She'd just thought of two right off the bat.

'You haven't told her, have you?' Scarlett's question was for Rufus.

'This was a bad idea.' Now everyone was on their feet.

'She doesn't know! Tell her, Rufus.' Scarlett crossed her arms again. 'Go on, tell her why you're at the Travelodge.'

'Stop taunting him!' Shannon cried. 'I don't want to hear you bashing Rufus just because he can't give you a child. You're being insensitive, Scarlett… no. No. You're being a bitch.'

Scarlett's mouth dropped open. 'Maybe I am,' she

said. 'But I think you should hear the full story before you decide. Rufus? Don't make me say it. Please.'

He rubbed his stubble. 'Shannon, Scarlett's right, you shouldn't blame her. This is all because I said something stupid.' He hesitated. 'Jesus. Okay. It meant absolutely nothing, but I accidentally said someone else's name when we were in bed together. I swear it didn't mean anything! Even so, I've really hurt Scarlett. Obviously. And I'll spend the rest of my life making it up to her if she'll let me.' His look pleaded with Scarlett, but she didn't seem moved.

As Shannon looked back and forth between her friends, her heart started to squeeze as she imagined what Scarlett must be going through. On top of all those months thinking she was at fault for not getting pregnant. And Rufus acting like he'd lost interest in her.

'You said… While you were…?' Well, that was just *perfect*. 'Have you been cheating, Rufus?'

He laughed, which seemed a little inappropriate given the circumstances. 'Of course I haven't. God, of course not.'

'Well, then, who is it? Whose name did you say?'

Was it Roxy the Rocket? She hadn't got her way with his body so she'd insinuated herself into his mind instead. No wonder Scarlett was mad at Shannon. She'd introduced them.

'Tell her, Rufus,' Scarlett said.

He stared at the floor, the wall, anywhere but the women. 'I said your name.'

It was Shannon's turn to gawp. 'You did what?'

'He said your name, Shannon,' Scarlett said bitterly, 'just as he orgasmed. "Oh my god, Shannon" was the direct quote.'

Shannon walloped Rufus so hard in the chest that

he fell back on to the sofa. 'You absolute bloody arsehole!' she screamed at him. Saying another woman's name to his wife in bed? How could he do such a thing to her best friend? 'Do you have any idea how much you've hurt Scarlett? Don't – just don't,' she said when he started to defend himself. 'You don't know. I'm sorry, but you haven't got a clue what that feels like, what it does to your self-esteem when you're already feeling insecure. Rufus, how could you?'

And how dare he say *her* name while he had sex?! 'And you've dragged me into this!'

Oh, blimey. He couldn't think of her in that way, after all their years together, could he? No, he couldn't. This was the guy who thought nothing of scratching his balls in a full hand-down-the-pants assault in front of her. There was no romance between them.

Her eyes sought Scarlett's. She couldn't think she had anything to do with what happened. She'd never even contemplated Rufus as a living, breathing male, even when her bed had seen less action than Mother Theresa's. Rufus was just Rufus. She didn't even like thinking that he had a penis. To her, he was a Ken doll, smoothly asexual.

'I feel ill just thinking about this,' she said to Rufus. 'Scarlett, I'm so sorry this happened. You know it means nothing though, right?'

'Does it?' Scarlett said. 'I'm not so sure. As long as you're in his head, where does that leave me?'

'But I don't want to be in his head.'

'That makes two of us, but here we are.'

Chapter 33

Scarlett sobbed again all over Fred and Ginger after Rufus left with Shannon. Not that they'd had a choice about leaving. She'd kicked them out. There wasn't anything more to say and besides, she couldn't stand the look of pity in Shannon's eyes. Oh, the poor wronged wife, it said, I'm sorry your husband prefers *me*!

They weren't just angry tears, though, or humiliated ones. She recognised the feeling that enveloped her as she heard the door click shut behind them. Hello, old nemesis. Here to remind me that I'll never have children? Once again, her motherhood was out of her hands, but the thing she hated most was that it was in Rufus's hands. And he was strangling it.

She woke knowing she'd have to start measuring out her future in terms of the activity she could use to fill each day. She'd go nuts otherwise. The puppies had graduated, but she still had dog classes in London today and tomorrow, then her sessions with Charlie and Naomi tomorrow night. Which left tonight yawning in front of her.

She rang her dad's mobile. 'Can you and Felicia come for dinner tonight? Around seven?'

'What's the matter?'

'Nothing, why?'

'Because the last time we came to yours for dinner I think Nick Clegg was in the coalition.'

'New government, new dinner,' she said. 'Can you come?'

'Sure, only do me a favour? Have something nice and fattening for pudding. Felicia's not letting me eat any sweets, but she won't hurt your feelings.'

'Sure, Dad.' She had to end the call as she choked up. Her dad might not appreciate Felicia's restrictions, but Scarlett saw them for what they were: little I Love Yous.

Julia answered her phone just as Scarlett got to the shop. 'I'm having Dad and Felicia round for dinner tonight,' she said. 'I'm about to text Gemma. Can you come too?' She threw a couple of red peppers into her basket along with a head of broccoli. 'It's just pasta.' With enough Parmesan cheese, her attempts usually turned out okay.

'I've got a brainstorming meeting at five that I can't move,' Julia said, 'but I could be on the train back by six-thirty. Shall I bring pudding?'

'Dad's asked for something decadent. Felicia's not letting him eat sweets again.'

'Well, I'm not going to be the one to go against Felicia's wishes.'

Those two never broke ranks, especially against her dad. 'Come on, Mum, let the poor man live a little. A slice of cake won't kill him.'

She was just putting a tray of vegetables into the oven to roast when the doorbell sent the dogs hurtling towards the front door. Wonders would never cease: her family was early.

Oh. Not her family.

'Scarlett, I know you can see me,' Shannon said through the frosted window. 'We need to talk.'

'Now's not good for me,' Scarlett answered through the closed door. 'I'm having people over for dinner.'

'Two minutes, that's all.'

She wrenched open the door. 'You don't need to be Rufus's mouthpiece, you know. He can speak for himself.'

Shannon smirked. 'We both know how good he's been at that so far.'

The ghost of a smile twitched at Scarlett's lips. 'I can't believe he didn't tell you what really happened.'

'You can see why, though. Not that I'm defending him! He says I've bruised his sternum.'

'He deserved a kick in the head,' Scarlett said. Shannon had been right. He'd betrayed them both with the same words. She must be wondering what he was thinking too.

They stood looking at each other as the dogs tried to get their attention.

'How will we get past this, Scarlett? I mean with Rufus. What do we do to make it all right?'

'I wish I knew. It's not just about what happened. It's everything. I've got a lot to think about. I'm sorry, but you can't help me do that.'

Shannon nodded. 'I'm here when you're ready, okay? Whenever you're ready.'

'Yeah, okay, thanks.' A sudden thought stopped her from closing the door. 'It's not really you, you know.'

'I know. I love you too.' Shannon turned, waving over her shoulder, and let herself out through the little front gate.

Gemma was late, but she came with chew toys for the dogs, so at least they forgave her. 'You always spoil them,' Scarlett said.

'That's because I love them, don't I? Don't I?' She crouched down to wriggling dog level. 'Who's a good dog?'

'I wouldn't get so—'

Ginger jumped just high enough to catch Gemma in the mouth with her tongue.

'—close when you're talking. That's one of her favourite tricks.'

'That's disgusting.' She rinsed her mouth out in the sink.

Scarlett shrugged. 'They're dogs. Thanks for coming. It hasn't been a good few days.'

Worried looks shot between her mum, her dad and Felicia.

'Let's go into the living room,' she said, grabbing a bottle of wine and the glasses.

It took no more than a minute to tell them everything. How was that possible, when it might take a lifetime to get over?

'That's a lot to have to deal with,' Julia said. 'On top of everything else.'

'At least you've got us to talk to about it,' Gemma said with a wink. She knew full well how cringy it was talking to their parents. 'It's lucky you've got your family.'

'But that's just it!' Scarlett said. 'This is exactly what I'll never be able to do! I can't have my own family. No daughter is ever going to be embarrassed by me or hate me when she's a teenager or pretend she doesn't know how the ink stain got on my red leather jacket or the empty bottle of gin got under the car seat. I can't have what you've all got!'

Everyone was quiet for a moment.

'I wasn't crazy about the ink on my jacket,' Felicia finally said. 'But my darling, you can have those things if you want them.'

Scarlett knew what she was saying. Technically, nothing stopped her from using a sperm donor or adopting a child. Nothing except the loss of her husband.

But what kind of life would they have together if they did make it through this? She knew herself. She'd resent Rufus. Things got rocky enough when they were trying together for a baby, and they were on the same side then. There was no way they'd make it as opponents.

For the first time she was thinking the unthinkable. She definitely knew she wanted a baby. Rufus definitely knew he didn't want help from an adoption agency or a sperm donor. He couldn't father a child and she couldn't fertilise her own eggs.

So which was she supposed to give up? Her marriage or motherhood?

Staying busy kept Scarlett's whirring mind from driving her nuts. Just about. No wonder some people became workaholics. The more she immersed herself in the dogs, the less space she had for her own life. Which suited her fine.

Max still rang up most days with excuses. He hadn't

booked the vet and had cancelled their sessions rather than face Scarlett in person.

Charlie kept turning up with Naomi, though, and they worked as if their love life depended on it.

'Let's start with another test today for Barkley,' she said to them once they'd dropped their bags. 'I bet he'll get a First.'

She carefully extracted her advanced training secret weapon from her bag.

Barkley glued his eyes to the aluminium foil as she unwrapped it. Dog treats? Leftover sandwich? Was it even edible? It didn't matter – could he get it into his mouth?

Chicken! It's chicken!

Everybody, the lady's got chicken! He looked from Charlie to Hiccup.

Hiccup wasn't as impressed with the big reveal.

'Now we'll see what Barkley is really made of,' said Scarlett as she tossed chunks of boiled chicken around the room. Barkley whined at the end of his lead.

'It's like passing his Master's dissertation,' Charlie said.

'More like his PhD,' said Naomi. 'Good luck, Barkley!' She squatted down to pet Hiccup while Charlie got into position at one end of the long room.

The treats were strewn near the edges of the floor, which left a corridor down the middle. 'First I want you to try to make it from one end to the other without Barkley getting any of the chicken.'

They crept at a snail's pace with Barkley on a short lead. His hind legs quivered. Whines floated up to the fluorescent lights. Scarlett could hear Charlie murmuring 'Leave it' under his breath.

But Barkley kept his eyes trained on Charlie's face.

He wanted that chicken very badly, but now he knew how to ask for it. After an age, they got to the doorway.

'Well done!' Scarlett whooped. 'Good boy, Barkley!'

'Good boy, Charlie!' Naomi said. 'That's some seriously impressive training.'

Charlie couldn't look more pleased with himself. He reached down to give Barkley's ears a good scratch. 'You are a champion, Barkley.'

Barkley graciously accepted his praise, although *champions deserve chicken…*

'Now walk him back and this time, go close enough to the chicken for him to get it. But make him sit first. Think of it as his victory lap. He gets all the chicken!'

Barkley executed a perfect request every time.

'He's passed,' Scarlett said. 'With flying colours. Congratulations to you both. I know it was a lot of work, and I'm really proud of you. I think he's ready to jog in the park now, don't you?'

'I might even go tomorrow before work,' Charlie said.

Scarlett thought back to the dog she'd first met. She hardly recognised that obsessive Labrador who'd chewed window casings and snaffled down fag packets. Just look at him now. She'd really miss the goofy Labrador after classes ended next week. She wondered if Charlie might grant her visitation rights.

'Now that we know Barkley has changed his habits,' she told Naomi and Charlie, 'if you'd like, we can spend your last few classes socialising the dogs? That way hopefully they'll be able to live together.'

Scarlett realised what she'd just said when Charlie's eyes widened. She glanced at Naomi's hand. No ring yet. 'The sale for your mum's house is still going through, right? So at some point you'll need a place to live. That's all I mean.'

She was only making it worse.

Charlie seemed to relax a little. 'The sale should go through at the end of the month. I can stay with Max then.'

'Though if Hiccup can really improve,' Naomi said shyly, 'maybe you can stay with me.'

Charlie couldn't control his grin. 'Then let's definitely work on Hiccup.'

Naomi and Charlie stood well apart with bags full of toys. 'Throw them away from the other dog for now. We don't want fights over the toys, we just want the dogs to get used to each other being in the same space while they're relaxed and having fun.' In theory, Hiccup should be enjoying herself so much that she wouldn't mind Charlie's proximity to her mistress.

It didn't take long for Hiccup to forget her guard duties. She tore after the squeaky toy and when she got it in her mouth, she flung her head back and forth, shaking the life out of the plastic hamburger. But her high-pitched growls were playful.

Barkley still gave her a wide berth, chasing down his own plastic prey.

Naomi and Charlie got closer and closer. Tentatively, Naomi reached out for his hand. As their fingers clasped, both kept their eyes on Hiccup. There was a tense moment when the dog looked back at them joined together, and dropped her toy. But when Naomi threw another, she tore off after it.

Unfortunately, it bounced awkwardly. Barkley had been going for another toy when he spotted the new option. He went for it.

Hiccup went for him.

The bite was savage and fast and caught Barkley

right in the muzzle. He yelped in surprise and pain.

'Hiccup, no!' screamed Naomi as Charlie went to his dog.

Hiccup scooted away from Naomi's clutches with her ears back. 'Is Barkley hurt?'

Charlie was rubbing his hands over his dog's face. 'There's blood. I think she got his lip.'

Scarlett knelt down to see how serious the bite was. 'I don't think he'll need stitches, but he'll have to see the vet to have that cleaned out. Naomi, have you got control of Hiccup?'

Naomi nodded, wiping her eyes with one hand and holding the dog's collar with the other. 'I'm so sorry, Charlie.'

Charlie smiled at his girlfriend. 'It was an accident.'

'No, actually, it wasn't,' Scarlett said. 'I really don't like using restraints on dogs, but we can't have Barkley in danger while you work on changing Hiccup's habits. I think it's best to get her a muzzle. She'll need to wear it whenever she's around other dogs or people. Hopefully she won't need it forever, but just to be safe, I think she does now. I'm really sorry. I misjudged it. I thought we were past the biting stage.'

'I understand,' Naomi said. 'I don't want anyone to get hurt. I'm sorry!' She called to Charlie, who was still on the opposite side of the room.

Scarlett walked over to where Naomi was standing with Hiccup. 'I'll hold her.' She clipped on her lead. 'You and Charlie take Barkley outside for a few minutes. You'll all feel better.'

Hiccup whined as she watched them leave.

'You've got to give them a break, Hiccup, seriously.' She rubbed the dog's little ears. 'As if life isn't hard enough.'

Chapter 34

Shannon was sick of having her emotions buffeted by the winds of everyone else's drama. Too much of the last few months felt out of her control. Yet she couldn't just walk away and leave Rufus and Scarlett to sort themselves out, because the sad fact was: they were all she had. If she lost them, she'd lose everything.

Instead she had a plan to take control. Starting with Rufus. That utter knob.

'Let's meet,' she said when he answered his mobile.

'I was just about to go for a run,' he said.

'Fine. I'll come with you. We need to talk.'

'You? Run? You're joking, right?'

'Sod off,' she said. 'I'll meet you in your lobby in twenty minutes.'

'I didn't realise you were a serious runner,' he said when he saw her. 'Is that your official training gear?'

She glanced down at her pink Converse high-tops, purple tights and red velour romper. She had a baggy purple cardigan buttoned up over the romper so he couldn't see that it was strapless, but she had to admit she was no Mo Farah. 'I like to be colourful when I exercise.'

'Uh-huh. Let's go, and remember: you invited yourself along.'

She regretted that within about a hundred metres of the Travelodge.

'How are you feeling?' he asked as he jogged easily along the pavement.

'I'm fine... How far do you usually go?' She squeezed the last of the words out between breaths as she hoiked up her romper.

'Only around three miles.'

'Yeah, that's my usual distance too.' Her chest was catching fire.

'So you wanted to talk?' He couldn't keep the grin off his face. 'Go ahead, I'm listening.'

'You're trying to kill me.'

He slowed to a walk. 'I'd feel bad if you actually had a heart attack. Nice effort, though.' He checked his watch. 'Nearly four minutes.'

'That marathon is going to be a piece of cake,' she wheezed.

She shrugged off her embarrassment when he put his arm round her shoulder. Somehow, they'd have to get past his unfortunate Freudian slip. 'What's up? I'm guessing it's about me and Scarlett?'

'Cleverly deduced, Mr Watson.' Her pulse pounded in her ears. She really should try doing some exercise one day. 'You and Scarlett have got to start talking again. Don't shake your head at me. I've been thinking about this and… it's pissing me off, to be honest, because you know the answer, Rufus. You'd better get over your ego or you're going to lose the best thing in your life.'

He rubbed the back of his neck. 'I know. But it's not that easy, Shannon. Don't you think I'd have done it already if I could?'

'You can't keep Scarlett from being a mother. It isn't fair.'

He spun round to face her. 'Don't talk to me about fair! Jesus! What's not fair is that I can't give a child to the woman I love more than anything in the world. It's not fair that loads of guys knock up women they don't even like. That's what's not fucking fair.'

It was her turn to hug Rufus. He stood immobile with his hands at his sides, but she squeezed him anyway. 'I know. I know it all sucks and the answer's not easy. But you've got to try to get over this hurdle. There are other ways to be a parent.'

There was no humour in his laugh. 'You don't know what you're talking about. What you're asking me to do. I don't want someone else's child, Shannon. I want mine. Scarlett might be able to overlook that it's not mine. She'd still get what she wants. Especially if she used a sperm donor. It'd be hers. But it wouldn't be mine.'

Tears filled Shannon's eyes. 'You'll love that child as much as if they were your own. You have to trust me, Rufus, you will.'

'But what if I don't?'

'Honestly? Then you divorce Scarlett and leave the child.'

'Wow, that's brutal.'

'It's as brutal as you saying you won't love a child because it's not genetically yours. What about the fact that it could be Scarlett's genetically? Would that be enough for you to bestow your love? Maybe you could just give her half the love,' she sneered. 'Is that *fair*?'

'I'm not talking about bestowing or withholding

love, Shannon.'

'Aren't you? You seem ready to put conditions on what you're willing to give a child. You'll love it *if* it's biologically yours. That's shitty.'

'I can't help how I feel. Why are you attacking me?'

'Because I'm adopted, you fucking twat, so actually I do know what I'm talking about. And I also know that my parents love me more than anything in the world. You're the one talking in hypotheticals, not me. I've lived in an adopted family, but if you don't want to do it, then that's your choice. Just don't make it sound like it's unnatural to love a child if your sperm didn't create it. What's unnatural is your refusal to see that love isn't always about biology.'

He frowned at her. 'All this time we've been friends and you never told me you were adopted?'

'You're missing the point, Rufus! And why would I tell you? Have you ever told me that you're a biological son to your parents? No, because it's not relevant.'

'That's different. That's normal.' His hands went to his chest when he saw her expression. 'Don't punch me again.'

But his words leeched the strength from her. 'Being adopted is normal. What world do you live in?'

'Come on, you know I didn't mean it like that. It's just more unusual to be adopted than not. That seems like something you'd have talked about at some point, like maybe when you found out.'

He actually had the nerve to look hurt.

'I've always known, Rufus. My parents told me from the start. My adoption isn't a secret, but I also don't feel like I have to justify to anyone why my parents love me. They just do. I'm no different than any other kid whose parents love her.'

Her parents never used platitudes about her beginnings. They didn't call her chosen or special because she was adopted. She was simply their daughter. That's why she was special. The same way her brother was special because he was their son. They didn't sugar-coat her birth story either, and they didn't tell outsiders about it. It was hers, they said, to share or not as she wanted.

She'd been taken by Social Services at birth from a young woman who couldn't look after herself, let alone a baby. Shannon was the woman's third child. Her first two had already been adopted by other families and Shannon came to her parents straight from the maternity ward.

Of course she'd had questions over the years about her ancestry. She wondered if it was genetics making her so lanky (probably, since she ate like a pig) and who to blame for her ginger hair (that was a mystery). Once, she asked if her birth mother had loved her. Her parents were honest about that too. They guessed she did, since she had tried to keep her babies. Shannon could go on the adoption register when she was eighteen if she wanted, they'd said, and possibly meet her to ask. She didn't do it, though. She felt like her birth mother's circumstances were tragic enough without stirring things up for the poor woman eighteen years later. Besides, except for the ginger mystery she was satisfied with her parents' answers. She didn't long for blood-related parents or siblings, cousins or aunties. Her family had always been her family.

'I did look at my adoption records when I was at uni, but there were no big revelations in there. My parents had told me the whole story already. They never made me feel like it made any difference.'

'You never tracked down your real parents?'

Her fist found its strength again. She put her hand in her cardigan pocket. 'They are my real parents! Crikey, haven't you been listening? I'm banging my head against the wall for nothing if you can't at least see that. Seriously, Rufus, this isn't about me. It's about you. You need to get some perspective or you're going to lose the best thing that has ever happened to you.'

As she stalked off, leaving him standing alone on the pavement, she realised it might not only be Scarlett she meant.

Their friendship had always seemed unshakable. She was as sure of it as she'd ever been of anything. Yet his pig-headed stupidity *was* starting to taint her feelings for him. That was hard to admit. It was even harder to know how to deal with.

By the time she picked up the pugs in the afternoon she was walking like Frankenstein's monster. 'Four minutes,' she told Shaggy as she squatted down with a groan. 'I am so unfit!' Carefully she pulled his paw out of his pinstriped suit. 'That's better. Come here Velma.' She unhooked the dog's blue beaded flapper dress.

Their owner had gone through her usual faff, searching for Scooby's fedora this time, while Shannon waited in the hall. 'Don't forget, if anyone wants to post a photo…' she'd said as she pushed more business cards into Shannon's hand.

'Hashtag Supercalipugalicous, I know.'

She'd rung her mum on the way to the park. Partly she wanted to hear her voice. But she also had a question. 'Do you think you'd have loved me and Simon more if you'd given birth to us?'

'More? I can't imagine how I could,' she said in the high-pitched nasal tone that Shannon *was* glad she hadn't been in line to inherit. 'Differently, maybe, but I haven't got anything to compare it to since I've never given birth. I only know how much I love you. Why do you ask, honey? I mean, why are you asking now?'

'It just came up with Rufus. I told him I was adopted.'

'I guess I assumed you'd told him already. Are you upset? Do you want to come over?'

'No, no, I'm fine. I only told him because of some issues he's having. He doesn't think he could love an adopted child like he would his own.' It sounded like an accusation. She hoped hearing it wouldn't hurt her mum. 'He thinks biological love is different.'

Her mum was quiet for a moment. Thinking. She always thought a lot about everything. Shannon got that from her, genes or no genes. 'I guess, maybe, if there is a difference, it's that my love for you and your brother began the day I met you. It grew from there. I guess when you carry a baby it starts for the parents before the birth. But I think that love for your child is absolute once you feel it. At least it is for me. Besides, only the mother carries the child, so Rufus couldn't feel the same hormonal bond to a biological baby that Scarlett, for example, might. His love will have to grow from outside, as it were. And we know how devoted some fathers are to their children.'

Shannon smiled into the phone, thinking of her dad. She really couldn't have asked for better parents. 'Thanks, Mum. Love you.'

'I love you too, honey. Did you remember your brother's birthday on Monday?'

'… Yes.'

'I can tell when you're lying, Shannon.'

Parents were parents after all.

The pugs strained at their leads when they spotted

Mr Darcy's greyhounds in the park. *Josh, she reminded herself, he was Josh.* It was an unlikely friendship between the dogs – they didn't exactly match each other stride for stride when they played – but it worked.

Josh unclipped Stevie and Nick, who charged at the pugs to catch up on their bottom-sniffing. It was a stretch for the pugs.

He was wearing his Dark Side of the Moo T-shirt again. It seemed to be his favourite. It was becoming hers too.

They coordinated their walks now, meeting every day for a few minutes at least. And time had smoothed the sticky bits of their conversation as they got used to each other.

Shannon noticed a brunette teen pointing at the dogs. 'It's them, yeah? It is! It's like, Zoella but with dogs, yeah?' she said to her friend as she took out her phone. 'Supercalipugalicious.'

'Oh, no,' Shannon said. 'I'm really sorry, but could you wait just a minute?' She rushed to the dogs as fast as her seized-up legs would let her.

'What's up?' Josh asked as she shoved a dress into his hand.

'Put this one on Velma, please. No, wait, that's Daphne's, the black one with the wonky eye. Sorry!' She called to the teen, who had her head cocked sideways. 'I'll just be a minute. You want them in their outfits, right?'

Getting wriggling dogs into costumes wasn't nearly as easy as getting them out, but she couldn't let them be snapped au naturel. Anastasia would have a fit if she found out Shannon undressed them as soon as she got around the corner.

She arranged the dogs on the grass – in what Anastasia claimed was their homage to The Great Dogsby

– and let the teens Instagram to their hearts' content.

'Well, that was weird,' said Josh when they'd left. 'Supercalipugalicious?'

Shannon rolled her eyes. 'It's their owner's blog. She puts them in outfits and takes photos. It is weird, but it's a huge blog. Well, you saw. That girl recognised them even without their clothes on.'

'And you dressed them up because…?'

'Because I take the stupid outfits off as soon as I leave the house so they're not humiliated.'

Josh watched the dogs. 'Those costumes are cruel.'

'Tell me about it.'

'Really cruel. We'll need to make it up to them.'

We! 'What have you got in mind?' Suddenly her heart felt again like she was sprinting, even though she was standing perfectly still.

'Well,' he said with a glint in his beautiful green eyes. 'I'm not sure dogs are allowed in many restaurants, so I guess we'll have to have dinner together without them.'

She couldn't think of anything she'd like more. As they set off with the dogs, her phone started to vibrate in her pocket. ''Scuse me a sec.' It was Rufus. He probably wanted to apologise.

She turned off her phone. 'It's not important.'

It was about time it got to be her turn.

They met that night at a little Italian restaurant near the university. 'You look pretty,' Josh told her as he kissed her cheek and pulled out her chair.

She looked down at her floral dress and orange tights. 'Thanks, so do you,' she said. He was still in jeans, but he'd traded his T-shirt for a finely woven black jumper. Or maybe the tee was still under the jumper.

She tried not to imagine what was under his jumper. She'd never make it through the starters if she dwelled there.

The decor was pure Dolmio advert, complete with bunches of fake grapes nailed to the walls and Chianti bottles dripping with candle wax, but she liked the kitsch of it.

'Do you live far?' she asked. Did that sound like she was suggesting they go back to his?

His expression was sheepish. Maybe he was thinking the same thing. 'No, I'm back near the park, but I know the restaurant from uni days. My parents always took me here when they visited. That sounds sad! Just to be clear, I have been out to restaurants without my parents too. I am a big boy.' His blush deepened at the innuendo.

She was glad they had that in common. She'd hate to be the only one who always stuck her size sixes in her mouth.

The waft of garlic nearly overwhelmed her when the waiter brought their starters. 'Mm, this was a good suggestion,' she said, breathing in the tomatoey aroma of the minestrone she'd ordered.

But she didn't get to taste it. Instead of shifting her chair closer to the table and daintily dipping her spoon into the soup like a normal woman would do, she shifted the bowl closer.

It was a bit too fast for the laws of momentum not to have an effect. A tidal wave of hot soup sloshed over the wide lip around the edge of the bowl. She watched it pour over the edge of the table. Then she felt it pool in her lap.

Of course she hadn't put her napkin down first.

'Did you just...?' Josh asked.

She nodded. 'I did.'

'Isn't it hot?' When he trained his green eyes on her she nearly forgot to answer him.

'Mostly it's wet,' she said. 'Will you excuse me for a minute?'

She gathered as much dignity as she could with a lap full of minestrone soup, blotted up some of the mess with her napkin and went to the loo to rinse out her dress.

The two women who came in while she was in her bra and tights were surprised to find her feeding her dress into the Airblade hand dryer, but they were sympathetic.

As far as first dates went, nobody could say it wasn't eventful.

Their conversations tumbled over one another, carrying them through the first seating, then the second and finally to the point that the waiters were conspicuously cleaning the floor around them. 'I guess we'd better go,' Josh said about half an hour after he paid the bill.

He put his hand gently on her back as they walked together outside.

'This was—' she said.

'I'm really—'

'Sorry, go on.'

'No, you first, please.'

'I was just going to say that this was fun. Thank you.'

He moved closer. 'Thank *you*.'

She did everything in her power not to lean in with her lips puckered.

She didn't need to. His warm lips met hers in a tantalisingly slow, amazing kiss. She opened her eyes for the briefest of moments. His gaze was questioning.

She wasn't in the habit of snogging men on the pavement. But then, she reasoned, she wasn't in the habit of not doing it either.

She leaned in to make sure her answer was clear.

Chapter 35

Scarlett didn't need to look through the window to know who was banging on her front door. That wasn't Rufus's style. 'Good morning, Shannon.' She looked fevered, though she was so pale that even the mildest chill in the air raised the colour in her cheeks.

'Morning. Guess what? Mr Darcy took me out for dinner last night,' she said. 'We snogged each other's faces off. Can I come in?' She didn't wait for an answer.

At least someone had good news. Scarlett needed it.

'I had an epiphany,' she said.

'Are we talking about sex?'

Shannon laughed. 'No. I wish. I think he's really keen, though. We're going out again tomorrow, but that's not the point. I came to tell you about my epiphany.'

Scarlett waited.

'When I got home after our date, the one person I wanted to tell about it most in the world was you. I wanted to tell you all about it, maybe even more than I wanted to be on the date.' She shifted from one foot to the other. Her eyes darted to Scarlett's and away again.

That accounted for her message late last night. 'So... good. You're telling me now.'

Shannon made a frustrated noise in the back of her throat. 'No! I mean, yes, I know I am, but that's not the point.'

Scarlett crossed her arms. 'You keep saying that. What is the point?'

'Don't make this hard. I can't stop thinking about you and Rufus, about what's going on. That's normal, right, when your best friends are having trouble? But this goes beyond friendly concern for you. I care what happens to my friends, of course. I'd want to know if Rufus was having trouble, obviously. I care a lot about what happens to him, but with you it's like my own flesh and blood is hurting and I'm... I don't know, I'm desperate, I guess, to help you make things okay. What I'm saying is that you're the most important person in my life. Even when you're being a dick, it's you, Scarlett. You're my best friend. Without going all lesbian about it, I think you're my soulmate too. That's what I realised last night. So, I have something to say, about you and Rufus and me.'

'Let's sit down,' Scarlett said. They moved to the stools in the kitchen. 'Do you want coffee?'

'No. Let me get this out.' She took a deep breath. 'I don't want to lose you, Scarlett. I can't lose you. And you can't lose me. I know I've been friends with Rufus our whole lives, but you and I, we're connected by... something. I don't know what it is, but I know it might even be stronger than what Rufus and I have.' She raised her closed fist. 'Uteruses over duderuses. Yay. That's really what I want to say. Whatever you need to do, I'm here for you. It'll be devastating if you two break up, but if you decide that's what you need to do, then I'll be here to pick up the pieces for you both. And if you want to have a baby on your own, well, you won't have to be on your own. I'll help you. We'll do it together, you and me. Whatever you need, Scarlett, you'll have me here to lean on, no matter what.'

Scarlett didn't expect to cry. The tears just came, too full and fast to trace them back to every source. She knew that immense sadness was in there somewhere. Shannon was letting her know it would be okay to leave Rufus.

She didn't want to. She loved him. But she also knew herself. As intense as her love was, it would sour into even more intense resentment eventually. As months and years passed – knowing that Rufus wouldn't, or couldn't accept the alternatives that science gave them – it would wear away all the good that had been in their relationship. Then the whole thing would be left threadbare, even the part that had been so tightly woven that it seemed bulletproof.

But she could keep that part of their relationship in her life, if only in her memory, as long as she didn't give it the chance to turn.

It would mean raising a child on her own. It terrified her to do that, but she felt like she might have the strength.

'You really will do that for me, won't you?' she said through her tears.

'Of course I will! We'll be just like the two mummies from your book. Only without the living together part. Or the sex. Sorry about that. I'd rather get off with Mr Darcy.'

Scarlett laughed. That felt good. 'Thank you,

Shannon. I love you.'

'I love you too.' When she gathered Scarlett into her skinny arms, they felt as secure as steel.

'I've got to get to Margaret's,' she said when Shannon let her go. 'Today's Biscuit's last session.'

Shannon nodded. 'I'll take the dogs with me.'

And just like that they were back to normal. Only stronger, together.

She thought about Shannon's proposal all the way into London. Because that's what it was, right? It was a proposal, and a promise.

As good as it felt to have Shannon's support, she couldn't really be happy about it. It still meant losing Rufus.

She would not let herself think about that, though, not sitting on the train. She didn't want to be that crazy woman snivelling into her croissant on the London commute.

There were things that she'd have to say to Rufus, though, things that made her sick to think about. Even though he was the one making it an either/or situation, not her. No matter how she phrased it, she had to say that she wanted a nameless, faceless, possibly non-existent baby more than she wanted him.

She felt woozy just peeking over that precipice. Once she jumped and the words went out into the world for him to hear, she couldn't scramble back to safe ground. There was no undoing that conversation.

Her phone rang just as she came upstairs from the Tube station. 'Hi, Max.'

'Do you know anything about Neuticles? I've been reading about them on the 'net. They're prosthetic bollocks,' he explained. 'Murphy would never even know he's lost his. They're silicone. They'll feel like the real thing.'

'You cannot be serious, Max. A boob job for your dog's testicles?'

'Why not? The Kardashians got them for their boxer.'

'That's not a medical endorsement. You can't have implants put into Murphy.'

'But he might get depressed. That happens, you know, after surgery. I know I'd be depressed if I lost my balls.'

Scarlett thought of Rufus. 'From the research I've read, some dogs show signs of depression after surgery, Max, but it's not specific to the type of surgery. It can be from the trauma of the procedure or the pain of recovery, or the anaesthetic or drugs causing a chemical imbalance. Males aren't depressed because they miss their bollocks.'

'Well, then, what if he has self-esteem issues when he sees other dogs and realises he's different?'

Max just wasn't giving up. 'I wouldn't worry about Murphy's self-esteem. He's a secure dog.' She couldn't believe she was actually having this conversation. 'Besides, it's a moot point. I'm pretty sure giving a dog silicone implants would be banned here under the Animal Welfare Act. Why don't you try to relax?'

'Easy for you to say.'

'I'm just about to get to another client's, Max. Can I ring you later?'

'No, that's okay. I'll ring Charlie. Thanks, Scarlett.'

The trees in Margaret's front garden were dense with dark foliage now. She hadn't noticed before. What else had she missed these past few months while her marriage was crumbling?

She remembered the first time she saw Margaret's house. She'd thought the woman's life was perfection personified, straight out of *Better Homes and Gardens*. But perfection only existed from the outside, assumed by people who didn't know the whole story. It was such an illusion. Everyone was really just getting by as best they could, and wondering if they'd get found out.

Margaret answered the door with a smile and a steaming mug of tea. 'Mrs Deering, hello!'

'Margaret, won't you ever call me Scarlett? Really, I appreciate such high regard, but it's not necessary.'

'Come in, then, Scarlett.' She smiled shyly. 'Oh, that still feels odd to say, but I suppose I can get used to it.'

'Good, because I have a proposition for you and it's not work-related. Finish your tea and we'll take Biscuit for a walk on the Heath and make sure you won't have any difficulties when she's outside her comfort zone. Then I'd like to take you to lunch after, if you're free.'

Her face crinkled into a smile. 'You want to have lunch with me? I'd love that!'

'You'd love what, Mummy?' Her daughter came down the stairs.

'Scarlett, you remember my daughter, Cleo? We're going for lunch, darling.'

'But it's barely eleven,' said Cleo, her tone turning petulant. 'I thought you were making us quiche for lunch?'

Margaret downed her tea and grabbed Biscuit's lead. 'Everything's in the fridge and the recipe is in the Mary Berry cookbook.'

Cleo's hand flew to her hip. 'But why are you telling me this?'

'So you can make the quiche if you want, darling. It's not hard. You've seen me do it a million times.'

'Couldn't you make it before you go? It'd only take you a minute to put together.'

'Then it'll only take you about twenty.' Margaret kissed her daughter on the temple. 'If you don't want to…'

Cleo's expression was hopeful.

'… then you can order something from Deliveroo. We're going out to lunch.' She turned to Scarlett. 'There's a Japanese restaurant on the high street I've been wanting to try. But maybe you prefer French?'

'It's your lunch, Margaret, so we'll go wherever you want to. I'll love whatever you choose.'

Margaret didn't seem to know what to do with this information. She was obviously still not used to getting what she wanted.

But then she nodded. 'Japanese, I think. Maybe I'll change my mind on the way.' She chuckled with excitement over the very idea.

Biscuit trotted along the pavement beside Margaret as if that'd always been her place. Scarlett liked this new and improved Biscuit formula.

'She's really very obedient now, isn't she?'

'I don't suppose you train families too?'

'Sorry, no, just dogs.' A service like that would have a waiting list as long as her arm.

'That's all right,' said Margaret. 'They are learning. I suppose one day they'll start fighting me, but right now they're too shocked when I stand up to them. You should have seen Arthur after the party. It was like when we first went out. That man can't bend over far enough backwards these days.' She looked about a decade younger when she laughed.

Scarlett tried not to be jealous of Margaret's change of fortune. If an arrogant arse like Arthur could see how lucky he was to have someone like Margaret, then what was Rufus's problem?

'Are you happy that you married, Margaret, and had children?'

Margaret looked as surprised by the question as Scarlett was to have blurted it out. Totally unprofessional behaviour.

'Wow, that's a question for wine!' she said.

'Sorry, Margaret, I shouldn't have—'

'No, no, it's an interesting one. I would say that, on balance, I am, although it's not what I imagined. I wonder if the reality can ever live up to your ideals, though. It's been a lot more drudgery than I expected. Still, there are moments of utter joy, even now that the children are grown. As much as Cleo and Archie can be exasperating, sometimes I look at them and I love them so much that I get light-headed. And then they're rude and I want to kill them.'

She laughed, but she didn't ask why Scarlett was so curious. Maybe she guessed it would be a touchy subject.

They walked up the hill and on to the Heath. It was Scarlett's favourite park in London. She loved the paths zigzagging up- and downhill through tall waving wildflower-strewn grass and the surprising little woods where trees arched overhead in a dense green canopy.

The sun shone, giving the glade they wandered through a dappled light that reminded Scarlett of the church on her wedding day. That morning had been overcast, but as she'd peeked out through the vestibule, with tiny Fred and Ginger (as yet unnamed) at her feet, the sun suddenly beamed through the stained-glass window at the front. Then she walked up the aisle to Rufus.

And now she was thinking about leaving him.

'Isn't this lovely?' Margaret said. 'I live so close and I bet I've not been here more than a few times in a decade. We're going to come here more, aren't we, Biscuit? We're going to do a lot of things.'

The dog looked up when she heard her name. It was hard to recall the surly spaniel who bossed Margaret around just a few months ago. If Scarlett thought really hard, she could summon the feeling of exasperation she'd felt every time Biscuit had talked back. Maybe memories were like that. The feelings stayed sharp after the situation blurred. No, that couldn't be right. Otherwise people would be left with loads of feelings without context. It must be the other way around. Feelings faded.

Perhaps then one day she'd be able to look at the past year objectively. She'd be able to see how a couple who loved each other as much as she and Rufus did (had?) could go from trying for the baby they both wanted to separating and talking through their best friend.

Part of her wished she'd never asked him to go for tests in the first place. She'd been so sure it was her fault. They didn't have to get tested. She remembered that she hadn't wanted to. Hadn't she told herself it was better not knowing for sure? She wished she'd listened. Then they'd have been one of those couples for whom children just never happened. Heart-breaking, yes, but without blame. Maybe if Rufus didn't feel at fault he'd have wanted to adopt.

What did they call it in gambling? A busted flush.

Her flush was well and truly busted.

Biscuit's silky butterscotch ears whipped round as a commotion caught her attention. Then Scarlett and Margaret heard it too.

A little golden Chow Chow charged over the hill dragging his protesting human. 'Will you please?!' the girl cried. The puffball on legs stopped pulling long enough to bark savagely at the girl's reasonable question. 'Candy, no!'

Barkbarkbarkbarkbarkbarkbark. Candy was having none of it.

Biscuit sat to watch the spectacle. When Margaret's hand found her head, the dog gazed up at her. *Some dogs are* so *ill-mannered,* her look said.

'Remember those days?' Scarlett asked.

'I'll never bloomin' forget. Hopefully they're behind me now. You know something? I think it's going to be a good decade.'

'I'm so glad, Margaret.'

She only wished she was as confident about the prospects for her own future.

Chapter 36

Scarlett's phone rang just as she was brewing her coffee. She smiled. How wonderful not to have to ignore Shannon's calls anymore. It was hard enough ignoring Rufus. He still rang every day, but she found it even harder to talk to him now with the prospect of dismantling their marriage lodged in her mind. The precipice loomed.

'I've missed our weekly business updates,' Shannon said when Scarlett answered the call. 'Not that we ever talk much business.'

'Your love life is my business.' Scarlett stirred sugar into her coffee. The one time she'd tried going sugar-free had sucked every last drop of enjoyment from her morning.

'Puppy classes are finished, right, so you could see me today? I've got Sampson and the poodles this morning. How about at ten? There's someone I want you to meet.'

'Not Rufus.'

'Better than Rufus. Mr Darcy!' Shannon's voice hitched with excitement. 'Meet me at the gate at ten, okay? I've told him all about you. Remember to call him Josh, though. He doesn't know about his nickname.'

Scarlett couldn't keep the stupid smile off her face. And the dogs couldn't believe their luck to get extra walkies in. The warmth of summertime? Sunshine *and* fresh leavings to sniff on the way? Life was feeling just fine for them.

She should take a page from Fred and Ginger's book, she thought, as they made their way to the park. Not the page where they sniffed bottoms or the chapter on eating toilet roll, but the ones where they found joy in the tiniest places.

Her world did have pretty deep pockets of happiness, as she thought about it. Leaving her marriage aside, everything else was good. In a few months she'd be an auntie for the first time. Her mum and dad and Julia were all healthy and happy. Businesswise, she would soon have to start a waiting list for clients, and not many people got to play with dogs for a living.

Plus, there was Shannon. She was her biggest support in whatever was to come, and now Mr Darcy had finally realised what an amazing woman her best friend was.

She was better off counting the blessings she had, not the ones that were missing.

Fred and Ginger began straining at their leads long before they reached the park gates. 'You see Shannon, eh? All right, relax, we'll get there.'

The poodles sniffed half-heartedly at her dogs as she kissed Shannon's cheek. Sampson might have been ecstatic about the meeting, but who could tell with that permanently grumpy expression?

'So, does Mr Darcy know he's meeting me, or is this an ambush?'

'He knows. I texted him after we talked. And it's Josh, remember.'

'Josh, right. Nice mascara, by the way. You're making an effort for the dogs, obviously.'

'Obviously.' Shannon grinned, self-consciously adjusting her glasses. She'd been wearing them more lately. 'Crikey, Scarlett, this is fantastic. Why didn't you tell me how much fun it was to go out with someone you're mad about? If we're not with each other, we're on the phone planning when we'll see each other next. I could happily spend the rest of my life like this! I hope it lasts till we're old and grey, surrounded by grandchildren.'

Then she caught Scarlett's stricken look. 'Oh my god, I'm so sorry. Forget I said that, please. Romance really isn't all it's cracked up to be. All that emotion, it's so cringy. I don't know how people stand it. It sucks. I hate it.'

'Yeah, all that snogging and excitement,' Scarlett said, trying to recover. 'Just awful. I don't know how you put up with it.' She bumped Shannon's shoulder with hers. 'Don't worry about me. Just enjoy this. You deserve it, really. I would be seriously annoyed if my situation meant you weren't happy.'

'We can both be happy, though, don't you think?'

'You just worry about yourself,' Scarlett said. She'd love to tell Shannon that everything would work out for them both, but whichever route to happiness she took meant giving up something important.

She just wished she could be sure which she wanted more. If only it was as clear-cut as choosing Victoria sponge over chocolate cake, or ballet flats over stilettos. But no, those were silly comparisons. If she snubbed chocolate cake, it wouldn't then refuse to have anything to do with her for the rest of her life. Choosing comfortable shoes didn't mean she could never wear heels again.

Ginger began to whine.

'There's Ginger's boyfriend,' Shannon said through a megawatt smile. 'And Josh.'

Scarlett squinted to get a good look at him. Her eyes must be playing tricks on her.

'That's Josh?'

Shannon nodded, waving to him.

Shannon had described him so many times that Scarlett figured she could pick him out of a crowd. Who was the tall, lanky ginger guy walking the greyhounds?

His rock band T-shirt hung from bony shoulders and his legs looked skinnier than Scarlett's. Up close, he was ever-so-slightly more auburn than ginger. His eyes squeezed nearly shut as he smiled and his wide mouth was at odds with his slim face. It did help to balance out his caterpillar-thick eyebrows, though.

Josh was proof that beauty was in the eye of the beholder, and Shannon couldn't stop beholding him. 'Josh, this is Scarlett.'

Josh stuck his hand out. 'I'm really glad to meet you. Shannon talks about you all the time.'

'She talks about *you* all the time!' Scarlett replied. 'You and the dogs, I mean. Which one is Stevie and which is Nick?' Ginger's furry back end wriggled with excitement at being reunited with her twin loves. 'They've got a devoted fan.'

Josh threw himself down on the path to stroke Scarlett's dogs. As he toppled he reminded her of Shannon. She wondered if her friend noticed the resemblance. 'They're great dogs,' he said. 'I had a Westie growing up. They might be little, but they've got huge personalities. Though quiet personalities are nice too.'

When he got to his feet he reached for Shannon's hand. He missed the oh-my-god-can-you-believe-this face she pulled.

'Shannon tells me you're a programmer when you're not walking in parks and picking up poo?' She unclipped the dogs' leads so they could play with the greyhounds.

He laughed. 'I'd rather pick up poo, to be honest, but it doesn't pay the bills. Not like Shannon's dog-walking business.'

There was so much pride in his voice for Shannon that Scarlett thought she might love him already. Anyone who was so obviously devoted to her best friend won a lot of points with her. 'She's built it from scratch too.' Scarlett sounded like she was comparing her child's science project with the other mums. 'And she ran it the whole time she was in art college.' *Little Shannon did all the papier mâché herself.*

Josh's eyes flicked first to Shannon, then behind Scarlett, back towards the way they'd come. 'Well, it was very nice to meet you, and I'm sure I'll see you again.'

The Westies bolted in the direction of Shannon's gaze.

Scarlett gasped when she saw why they were in such a hurry. She glared at Shannon. 'Josh was just a decoy? That's really low. You're both sneaky.'

Josh looked abashed, but Shannon said, 'I know, but just listen to him. Please.'

Scarlett kept herself from turning back around to face Rufus. He could probably hear her heart thudding. She listened to him approach with their dogs. *Don't be fooled by the jingly collars,* she thought. *That's actually the sound of your future cracking and crumbling under your feet.*

She wasn't ready to start the avalanche yet. As long as she stayed far back from the dangerous edge, she could go on hoping she'd find an alternative that didn't involve losing either Rufus or her someday dream of holding her baby. If she made her choice out loud, it would set a series of events into motion that, even if she changed her mind, or he did, the scars of the words would remain.

'Scarlett, can we please talk?'

'No, thanks, I don't want to.'

'Please,' Rufus said, 'we've got to talk.'

'We'll leave you to it,' Shannon said, kissing Scarlett on the cheek.

Judas kiss.

'Please, Scarlett. Nothing's going to change by putting it off any longer.'

He was intent on making her do this now. He was right too. She was being naïve. There wasn't some elusive third answer waiting to be discovered. The real world didn't work that way.

She watched Shannon and Josh hurry away. The sight of them holding hands brought her tears close to the surface. 'Can I talk first, please?' she asked, rushing on before he could answer. 'Since you're making me do this now, at least let me start. I haven't been honest with you for months. After the first three or four times I didn't get pregnant I guess you figured we were taking it easy, taking things as they came.'

'Because you told me that.' His forehead was furrowed.

'I know.' She sighed. 'I got scared when you said it was a lot of pressure. I didn't want you to think it was too much and decide it wasn't worth trying to have a baby. I told you not to think about it, even though it was all I could think about. I still took the pregnancy tests each month and tried to figure out which days were best for having sex. Only I didn't want you to know I was doing it.' She shrugged. 'But it didn't matter. It still changed us. You think the problems started when we went to the GP, but it was long before that.'

'I know.'

'I felt like you didn't want to be around me as much.'

'That's not true, Scarlett, I swear it's not. I just didn't want to keep disappointing you.'

They were both talking in the past tense now.

'I'm not sure where we go from here, Rufus. No, that's not true. I think I do know. I just don't want to admit it, but there's nothing else to do. My feelings about wanting a family haven't changed. If anything, I'm more sure. I'm also sure that I love you.' She took a deep breath. 'But maybe I love myself more, to even be thinking what I'm thinking. If I'm not honest with myself now about what I want, I'll only be unhappy later. And I'd make you miserable, because then I would resent you. I have to be true to myself.'

There were tears in his eyes. 'I'm so sorry I've put you through this, Scarlett. I know it's been hard for you, but I didn't know how to make it better. I couldn't give you what you wanted and the more I couldn't, the harder it got. I never imagined it could come to this. Not between you and me.' He wiped his eyes. 'I thought we were so solid, you know? I was so positive about that. Tsch. And here I am living in a hotel having to stalk my wife in the park to get her to talk to me.' He took a slim manila envelope from his bag. 'This is for you.'

She didn't take the envelope he offered. 'What the hell, Rufus, are you handing me divorce papers? You didn't waste any time. And you're not the only one who's not crazy about this whole situation, you know. Welcome to the real world.'

'Just open it, please.'

She slid the pages out.

They weren't divorce papers.

'What does this mean?' she whispered.

He dared to close the gap between them, but he didn't touch her. 'It means that I'm a total arsehole and I'll spend the rest of my life regretting the past few months. I've been so wrapped up in my own shit that I couldn't see… no, I *didn't* see what it was doing to you.' He sighed. 'Ego is such a bastard. And this has been all about my ego. I couldn't just see my infertility for what it is – a really shitty reality that loads of people deal with every day. No, I had to make it a challenge to my manhood. Me: man. Sperm no work. Jesus Christ, what a twat I've been. And there you were, all those months when you thought it was your fault you weren't getting pregnant. You went through all that on your own.' His voice became thick. 'And you didn't make it all about you. It was about having a baby. But not me, no. One sperm test and I act like it means the end of mankind that I can't father a child.' He rubbed the stubble on his chin. 'My behaviour's been appalling, and I'm not even talking about my views on adoption yet. It takes a whole other apology to cover that.'

Scarlett struggled to take in what Rufus was saying. She was stuck on the apology. And coupled with the contents of that envelope… 'What other apology?' Greedy Scarlett.

'I've got Shannon to thank for that,' he said. 'Not my arseholery, I mean my rethink. Did you know she's adopted?'

'No.' She thought for a moment. 'But why would I? I mean, it's not really something that would come up in normal conversation, is it?'

Rufus sighed. 'Apparently I'm the only person who didn't get that memo. Once again…' He put up his hand. 'Arsehole for making assumptions when I didn't know what the hell I was talking about. This is starting to be a trend with me.'

Scarlett shook her head. 'You've always talked out of your arse a bit.' She risked a smile.

'At least the fertility tests made me see how much I really do want a child,' he said. 'Otherwise I wouldn't have acted like the world fell apart. I thought it was because I wanted my own flesh and blood. But Shannon reminded me that love is love. How stupid that I didn't realise it already when I know how much Felicia loves you. Love is love. I want a child with you. I want to have a family together, and raise a little girl or boy with all the love that you and I were raised with. God, I want that so badly. What I'm asking is whether you'll let me have a family with you?' He pointed to the envelope. 'We could look into adoption or sperm donors or whatever we need to do to have our child.'

She thumbed through the printouts and leaflets that Rufus had collected, reams of them, all about their options for having a family. 'You're willing to do this for me?'

'No,' said Rufus. 'Not just for you. I'm doing it for me too, for us and for our family, because I want the same thing you do. I love you, Scarlett, and I'll love our child just as much because he or she will be part of us. We'll be parents.'

She didn't say anything. She stepped into his arms and put her lips to his. As his arms closed around her she felt the warmth and love she'd been so afraid of losing. They were a family again. Maybe they'd end up a family of two. Who knew what the future would bring? But perhaps, just perhaps, one day they'd have a child of their own to love.

Rufus broke off their kiss. 'Eavesdroppers.' He tipped his chin at the other side of the green where Shannon and Josh were whooping and flailing their arms.

'I don't mind the audience,' she said, waving at her best friend before puckering up again for her husband.

Chapter 37

There was no fanfare when Rufus moved back in. It didn't seem right given the reason he left. It wasn't like he was coming back from holidays or an extended business trip with chocolates from duty-free. He was coming back in from the cold.

The dogs acted like he'd been there all along. 'You've got goldfish memories,' she chastised them as they jumped straight on to the sofa when Rufus sat down. 'Off the sofa.'

They ignored her. So nothing had changed.

But things had changed, hadn't they? They'd been through the toughest trial of their relationship and, after an agony that Scarlett never wanted to feel again, had come out the other side. They were both so grateful for a second chance at their marriage that they'd forgive a lot.

Finally, they were a united front. That had really been their main problem all along, hadn't it? Even before the tests, Scarlett wanted a baby more than Rufus did. It wasn't till he found out he couldn't have one that his want turned to need. Now they were on the same page again. Shannon wouldn't have to be the other mummy, but she could still make a fantastic godmother. Besides, thought Scarlett, she'd probably be quite busy with her own relationship and maybe, one day, her own family.

The late afternoon traffic getting out of London after her dog classes made for a long drive to Max's vet. Charlie was already there when she walked into reception.

He checked his watch. 'Are you sure he's coming?'

'The traffic was bad. Maybe he's stuck.'

But they both knew Max might not turn up. He and Murphy could have run away together to let their balls enjoy the freedom they deserved. She'd been on the phone with Max quite a bit in the last week, finding a way around each of his objections. In the circumstances, she didn't mind. She could be magnanimous about sterility now that she and Rufus had another plan.

Even though Rufus had said he'd do anything necessary for them to have a family, she still felt the need to double-, triple- and quadruple-check that he meant it. It was all well and good saying so when you're afraid your marriage is ending. She needed to be sure he felt the same way with the pressure off.

He did. He wanted to have a family with her, he'd patiently repeated, whether that meant adoption or donor sperm. She was finally starting to believe he meant it, though they still had a long road to travel. She knew she'd repeat herself.

Scarlett and Charlie both jumped up from the plastic seats that ringed the vet's waiting room when Max and Murphy came through the door.

'Alright, Scarlett? Sorry we're late. Murphy was

nervous.'

They looked at Murphy's drooping ears and tucked-under tail and both rushed to pet him.

'How are *you* doing?' Scarlett asked. Max's bloodshot eyes and unshaven face told her the answer.

'About the same as Murphy, I guess,' Max said. 'I know he feels my nerves, but I can't help it.' He ran his hand through his hair, which already stood on end, and went to the desk to sign the consent forms.

The vet looked too friendly to be a serial castrator. 'How is everyone today?' she asked, reaching down to fondle Murphy's ears. His tail wagged tentatively from between his legs. 'It's a big day, eh, Murphy? We're ready for you.'

'Can I come in too?' Max blurted out. 'I think he'd be more comfortable if I was there.'

She appraised him with kind eyes. 'Of course, you can be there while we get him settled. We'll give him something to make him nice and calm and to help with the pain after. Then the general anaesthesia that we talked about, and you're welcome to stay for that. You'll need to come out here, though, after that's administered, since it's a sterile procedure. It shouldn't take more than thirty minutes or so.' She turned to Charlie and Scarlett. 'It's nice that you're here for him.'

Scarlett knew that the vet meant Max rather than Murphy. Max had been on the phone with the vet quite a bit too.

'Are we ready?'

Max looked anything but ready, but he followed the vet into the back with Murphy. If he had a tail, it would have been between his legs.

'Poor Max,' Charlie said.

'I know. Shouldn't it be Murphy we're worried

about?'

'Honestly, I think Max needs our sympathy more,' he said. 'The vet said thirty minutes for the op. That's not too bad. Maybe Max will want to go for a quick coffee when he comes out?' He frowned. 'No, probably not.'

She remembered feeling panicky when her dogs had been fixed. It didn't matter that there was little risk with the procedure. Her mind tortured her with the worst outcomes anyway. Max would do well not to break down blubbering on the floor.

He looked shaken when he emerged from the back. 'They're putting him under now. He's taking it pretty well, all things considered. He licked my hand when they gave him the shot.' His eyes welled up. 'He will be okay, won't he?'

'Of course he will! He'll be finished in thirty minutes and it doesn't take long for dogs to wake up from the anaesthesia. You'll have him home in a few hours.'

They sat together on the plastic chairs staring at the exotic bird wall clock as owners and their pets came and went. It was a busy office, and a noisy one, which was some distraction from the ticking minutes.

'How're you doing?' Charlie finally asked.

'I'm going nuts here, mate. How much longer?'

Three and a half minutes since the last time he asked, Scarlett thought.

'I can't stop thinking that something's wrong,' he said. 'What if he's allergic to the drugs? Or he chokes or wakes up in the middle of the surgery, jumps off the table and hurts himself?'

'What if a plane crashes into the building while the vet has the scalpel in her hand?' she said.

Max's eyes widened.

'I'm joking, Max. What are the chances of any of that happening? Really, I know Murphy's going to be fine.' She looked pleadingly at Charlie for help.

He smiled. 'I know something that might take your mind off things.' He pulled a box from his pocket. 'I just picked it up.'

'Naomi's engagement ring?' Max practically clapped with glee. 'Can I see it?'

The sparkling little diamond was set in yellow gold. 'Now I just have to find the right time. Preferably when Hiccup isn't around.'

'She's a lucky girl,' Max said.

Scarlett smiled to herself, remembering when she was a lucky girl. She and Rufus had gone to the London Aquarium on a bank holiday. She did notice that he seemed quiet, but they'd been out the night before, so she assumed a hangover. 'Come this way,' he'd said, taking her hand into the underwater ocean tunnel.

Rays, sharks and shoals of fish swam above and around them as they made their way deeper into the tunnel. 'It's just like our first dive,' she said. 'Only dry.'

He smiled. 'Exactly. Remember that turtle?'

Remember it?! That was when she realised that crying in a dive mask totally steamed it up. She'd stared into the turtle's gentle brown eye and wished she could hold on to that feeling forever.

Rufus pointed overhead as a turtle glided past. 'I wanted to come here—' His eyes darted behind her as the raised voices of a large group of children got closer. 'I wanted to come here because that was one of the most amazing experiences of my life. And most of what made it incredible was being with you.'

The children flooded into the tunnel. Their voices ricocheted off the thick glass all around them. 'Scarlett, that trip changed my life because I met you.' He raised his voice further. 'I can't imagine being happier these past two years.'

She was having a hard time hearing him.

'Aw, fuck it,' he shouted above the din as he dropped to one knee. 'Will you marry me?'

The kids made woooo noises and kissy faces at them as they stood frozen in that moment. Scarlett was aware of one boy nudging the other and saying, 'He's proposin', innit?'

'Sucker,' said the other.

'Yes,' Scarlett said.

The kids chorused their taunts. Scarlett couldn't have cared less as she kissed her fiancé.

They all looked up when a ponytailed young woman wearing royal purple scrubs appeared at the vet's door. 'Murphy's dad? You can go in now if you'd like. Murphy's groggy, but he's awake.'

Max bolted from the chair. 'My friends can come too?'

The nurse nodded. She was clearly used to nervous pet owners and despite probably being elbow-deep in Murphy's genitals a few minutes earlier, she might just as easily have been relaxing in a coffee shop as dealing with ailing pets. Her freckled face and clear grey eyes exuded calm efficiency and her smile made Scarlett warm to her right away.

She led them into a large back room that smelled of antiseptic. Stainless steel cages lined one wall, where dogs of all sizes were in various stages of recovery.

Murphy sat in one of the floor-level compartments with his head down. His curly-haired ears flopped forward as he stared at his nether region as if trying to work out what had just happened there. He gave a hoarse whine when he spotted Max.

'He sounds terrible!'

'That's just from the anaesthesia,' the nurse explained. 'It's normal. We use a tube down his throat to administer the drug during surgery. He'll be disorientated too, so try to keep him as calm as you can. He should be fine to go home in an hour or two.'

'Hi, buddy,' Max whispered. 'Are you okay?' He sat in front of his beloved pet.

Murphy couldn't look sorrier for himself. His ears drooped as he squinted at Max, though the end of his tail thumped against the cage's metal floor.

'Is he in much pain?' Max asked the nurse.

'He might be starting to feel achy now that the anaesthetic is wearing off, but we've given him some pain relief. You'll have tablets to give him at home.' She reached over Max's shoulder into the cage to stroke Murphy's head as Max seemed to notice for the first time that quite a pretty woman was standing inches behind him.

'As long as he'll be all right,' said Max. 'If I have any questions, should I ring?'

'Of course. The phone numbers are on Murphy's paperwork. You can ring any time.'

His eyes flicked away from her face to glance at her name badge. 'I hope you're on hand, if we call. It'd be nice to talk to someone we know already, Rebecca.'

'Well, I'm off tomorrow, actually.'

'That's a shame. He's really comfortable with you, isn't he?' Murphy had indeed perked up a bit under Rebecca's attention. They made a brazen double act. 'I wonder if... No, never mind... It's just that I'd feel uncomfortable talking to someone who doesn't know Murphy.'

Rebecca smiled. 'I know how you feel. I have two dogs of my own. I could give you my mobile number? That way you could ring if anything comes up.'

'That'd be great, Rebecca, thanks.' He put her number into his phone as Charlie and Scarlett tried not to make faces. Scarlett had seen less transparent window panes.

'I'm sure he'll be fine,' Rebecca continued. 'The procedure went well. Murphy's been a very brave dog. And you,' she said to Max, practically ruffling his hair, 'have been a very brave owner. Well done to you both.'

She caught Scarlett's eye as she turned. *Men, eh?* her look said. *They think they're so clever.*

Chapter 38

Murphy couldn't come to another session till he was healed enough to run around without popping his stitches, so by the time he returned to the community centre Scarlett was really excited to see him.

Not as excited as Murphy was for the reunion, though. He bounded towards Scarlett with Max close behind.

She braced herself for the hump. Just because Murphy couldn't act on his intention didn't mean he'd instantly stop trying. Sometimes it took a while to unlearn old habits.

But Murphy skidded to a stop on the lino as he approached.

'Well done, Murphy! He's learning.' Scarlett beamed at Max.

Murphy led with his nose, straight for Scarlett's crotch. 'Oh. We'll work some more on this,' she said as she tried to deflect his exploration of her jeans.

'I'm really sorry about that,' Max said. 'It's his new

thing.'

'It's not a problem. Just get him in the habit of sitting when he approaches someone new. It's natural for dogs to sniff other dogs or people. That's how they identify them. But they've got a good sense of smell, so they can do it from a few feet away without invading someone's space quite so much.'

They both did a double take when Charlie and Naomi came in. They weren't holding hands or anything reckless like that. They wouldn't dare with the wiry-coated chaperone keeping her beady eye on them. In fact, they walked arm's-length apart from each other, but they had Hiccup and Barkley sandwiched between them. And Hiccup didn't look like she wanted to tear strips off him. She was muzzled, though, so even with bad intentions she couldn't do any damage. It was still better to be safe than sorry.

Charlie couldn't keep the smile from his face. 'Welcome back!' he said to Max. 'How's Murphy?'

Murphy made a run for his four-footed chum, but pulled himself up when he heard Hiccup's warning. She might accept Barkley, but she wanted nothing to do with an over-exuberant Irish setter.

Muzzle or no muzzle, Murphy backed up at the same time that Naomi moved Hiccup back a few steps. As she turned the dog, Scarlett caught a flash on her hand.

'You popped the question?' Scarlett whispered to Charlie.

'I did. Naomi and I are getting married!'

They did very little training and a lot of wedding planning over the next hour. Hiccup still had some work to do, and they'd meet a few more times, but Murphy and Barkley were changed dogs.

She watched them play and saw the happiness, and the relief, on everyone's faces. She loved this part of her job.

But then, she also hated this part. 'You know something? I'm really going to miss you guys,' Scarlett said as they all got ready to go.

There'd been a few dozen dogs over the years that she'd become really fond of. She liked to think that if she ran into them again, they'd remember her. They probably wouldn't, but she liked to think that.

Barkley and Murphy were definitely dogs she was fond of.

Max and Charlie traded glances. 'We were going to ask you something, actually,' Charlie said. 'I hope it's not weird, but we wondered if you might want to meet up sometimes, with the dogs? I mean, somewhere in London, maybe when you've got another class here anyway. We could meet you.'

'I don't really want to say goodbye,' Max added.

'I'd love to meet up again.' She thought about Margaret. 'Sometimes my clients do become my friends. I'd like that a lot.'

She felt ridiculous that tears were welling up in her eyes. They'd only asked her to meet up, not adopt their dogs.

She noticed a movement in the doorway just as Murphy ran to greet the newcomer. 'Can I help you?' she asked.

The woman looked really familiar. Maybe one of Krishna's yoga devotees? 'Yoga was before us, I'm afraid, but Krishna's cards are on the noticeboard outside if you want to get in touch. Her schedule is there too.'

'No, sorry, I'm only here for Max.' She reached down to pet Murphy, whose tail thumped her calf.

Scarlett peered at the woman again.

'Actually, I think we've met,' said the woman. 'I'm Rebecca?' She walked towards Max. 'Sorry, babe, I think I'm early.' She had to stand on tiptoes to reach his lips. His arms snaked round her waist.

Of course! She was the nurse from the vet's office.

Max beamed at them over Rebecca's shoulder.

'No,' said Scarlett. 'I'd say you came along at just the right time.'

They were late for dinner at Dad and Felicia's the next night. 'Do me a favour,' said Rufus. 'Don't blame me for being late. I don't want to give your parents any more reason to hate me.'

'They don't hate you,' she said as they turned off the motorway. 'Are you really worried about that?'

'Hmm, let's see. I caused months of anxiety and unhappiness for their daughter, denied them grandchildren and then said your best friend's name in bed. Yes, I'd say I'm a little worried.'

'Well, don't be. My parents love you. Even with everything that's gone on, that hasn't changed.'

He glanced at her from the driver's seat. 'Though they did tell you to leave me.'

'Well, yes, but your parents would have done the same thing if the situation was reversed. Parents are supposed to be protective. Besides, they didn't tell me to leave you. They told me to figure out what I most wanted and then make my own decision. That's different. Really, I wouldn't worry about them. It's Gemma you shouldn't be alone with if she's got a sharp instrument.'

She felt awful when she caught the look on his face. 'God, I'm kidding! Rufus, my family loves you. I love you.

Stop worrying.'

But it was the first time he was seeing them since she'd chucked him out of the house. She might be exaggerating about Gemma and knives, but she wasn't completely sure how her family *would* react to Rufus.

They'd loved him when they first met him, and Gemma knew him already so they'd already cleared that hurdle. But Mum didn't suffer fools, and Rufus had definitely been one lately. Maybe this dinner wasn't such a good idea.

By the time she gave Dad's door a cursory knock, she was as nervous as Rufus.

Nobody answered. 'That's weird. Maybe they're in the garden.' She dug around in her handbag. 'I've got my key here.'

'Your parents have never been in the garden as long as I've known them.'

She didn't tell him that she'd never seen them out there either. 'Barbecue? Maybe Dad's got a grill.'

They let themselves into the quiet hall. 'Hello?'

'We're all back here,' Felicia called from the living room.

She and Rufus traded worried glances.

Dad was in his chair with Felicia, Gemma and Julia sitting primly on the sofa.

'What's going on?' Scarlett asked. But she had a sinking feeling she knew.

Rufus couldn't have looked more uncomfortable if he'd had a cactus down his pants.

'We'd like to talk to Rufus, please,' said Gemma.

'Gem, no. You know we've worked through—'

'Scarlett,' her dad warned. 'Let your sister talk.'

'Sit down, Rufus.'

They both looked at the kitchen chair that faced the

sofa and Dad's chair. This was to be an inquisition. Scarlett stood behind the chair as Rufus sat.

Gemma cleared her throat. 'Rufus, you are aware that we know all about what's gone on between you and Scarlett. And I assume you can imagine how we feel about it all.'

'I do, and—'

Julia cut him off with her raised hand. 'You'll get your chance. You know how much we love our daughter – me, William and Felicia – so you know that we are not about to let someone take away her happiness. I would die rather than do that, Rufus, do you understand me?'

'Yes, ma'am.'

'Scarlett is a smart, beautiful, loyal and amazing woman and she picked you to spend the rest of her life with,' Felicia carried on from Julia's train of thought. 'And more than that, she wanted to have a family with you.'

'I know,' Rufus said. 'She is amazing—'

Julia cut him off. 'Stop interrupting.'

'So when we say that you are her happiness,' Felicia went on, 'you'll understand that we are not about to interfere with that.'

It took Scarlett a split second to understand what they were saying. It took Rufus a bit longer, though. His blanched face was shocked into stillness.

'Scarlett chose you because you've got the same qualities that she has,' said Scarlett's dad. 'And I suppose you're good-looking too.' He smiled. 'So what we're trying to say is… welcome back, son.' With that he got up and put his arms around Rufus. Within seconds, Scarlett's husband was enveloped in a Fothergill love scrum.

She could hear his muffled thanks, and laughter, as they all hugged.

She caught her mum's eye over her family's shoulders. 'Thank you,' she mouthed.

Her mum nodded once and hugged her son-in-law again.

The End

Well, Not Quite…

'Happy birthday to you, happy birthday to you, happy birthday dear Flynn, happy birthday to you!' The Fothergills weren't known for their musicality, but what they lacked in pitch, tone and diction they made up for in volume. Except Scarlett's dad. He only ever mouthed the words.

Scarlett snivelled at the sight of her nephew in front of his jungle animal birthday cake. He was so beautiful that he took her breath away every time she looked at him. He'd inherited the Fothergill freckles (sorry, Flynn), but had Jacob's dark hair, with Gemma's curls and caramel skin.

He'd probably grow up wondering why his auntie stared at him all the time.

Because I love you so fiercely, she'd tell him.

Nothing could have prepared her for the feelings she had for that child. She thought she loved Rufus as intensely as it was possible to love, but what she felt for Flynn was different. From the moment she held him, hours after his birth, she knew she'd lay her life down without question to protect him. It was overwhelming and wonderful.

'Oh no, Scarlett,' Gemma said. 'You promised! You're such an ugly crier. Now all the photos are going to have you looking like you've had an allergic reaction. Jacob, get a photo of Mum, Julia and Dad with the baby. Scarlett, sort yourself out, seriously.'

'I'm sorry,' she said. 'I thought I could hold it together. I've been warning myself to man up since we got here. Blame the hormones.'

Gemma cuddled Flynn, who was much more interested in his sippy cup than the cake in his honour. 'You're even worse than I was, but that's probably because it's a girl.'

A girl! Scarlett scrunched up her shoulders like she did whenever she thought about their baby. She grinned at Rufus, who was busy sending Flynn into fits of giggles with his fish-faces. But when she caught his eye, something passed between them. That happened a lot now.

'Though I'm sorry you'll miss the experience of getting wee in your face when you change the baby,' Gemma continued.

'I've had the pleasure with Flynn, don't forget,' she said. 'And, who knows? Maybe the next one will be a boy.'

'Or the one after that,' said Rufus, moving to Scarlett's side to rub her big tummy gently as he kissed her temple.

'She likes that,' Scarlett whispered as their baby kicked Rufus's hand.

'She's got a good boot,' he said. 'Maybe she'll play football. We can practise together in the park like I did with my dad. He taught me to play, did I ever tell you that? It's a family tradition.'

ABOUT THE AUTHOR

Michele Gorman writes comedies packed with lots of heart, best friends and girl power. She is both a Sunday Times and a USA Today bestselling author, raised in the US and living in London.

Michele also writes cozy romcoms under the pen-name Lilly Bartlett. Lilly's books are full of warmth, romance, quirky characters and guaranteed happily-ever-afters.

www.michelegorman.co.uk

@michelegormanuk
@MicheleGormanUK
Michele Gorman Books